Praise f

He's a powerful new writer you may not have heard of, but one I think you'll know better in the coming years. Without having any wish to start a new moment or movement, I'd call him kind of "Next Weird." His work is transgressive and hard-edged and yet sometimes also experimental, while the influences seem to be everything from, well, authors typified as New Weird to mainstream literary to graphic novels.

Jeff VanderMeer,
Nebula award winning author of the Southern Reach trilogy

With characters like Head Wrecker, Smart Brutality, and The Piper Who Calls the Tune, Alistair Rennie's *BleakWarrior* is so full of hooks, it is probably illegal. If this isn't the first highly collectible book of a craved-after series, may every steel blade in the world be turned into cotton candy.

Anna Tambour,
author of *Crandolin*

BleakWarrior is a hell of an impressive feat of imagination. I've not read a book dedicated to conjuring death, violence, and inappropriate sex in such spectacularly gory variety, and it's all done with consummate, if maniacal, precision by a skilled wordsmith.

Neil Williamson,
author of *The Moon King*

How do I describe *BleakWarrior* when there is nothing else like *BleakWarrior?* What is BleakWarrior, and why? I can always resort to the common critical shorthand of listing authors in the same general ballpark . . . China Miéville, Molly Tanzer, Jack Vance, Ed Dorn, Jeffrey Thomas, Alan

Moore, Jesse Bullington, K.J. Bishop, Anna Tambour, Gilles Deleuze, Fritz Leiber. I can offer a tagline and say it's as if Clark Ashton Smith and Michel Foucault had first told the story of the X-Men as a philosophical/transgressive secondary world epic awash from one end to the other in pussy juice and gore. I can say truthfully that reading "The Gutter Sees the Light That Never Shines," the portion of this novel published eight years ago in the VanderMeers' anthology *The New Weird* was a turning point in my own decision to have a serious go at fiction. Rennie's writing is that fresh and powerful. It will make you think strange thoughts. It will make you do weird things. It makes me think Alistair Rennie might just be the Cuisinart Hat Rack come to unite the Weird and lead us all through clouds of orange spice to the Uncompromised Land in a single giant Leap of Cynosure. What else can I say? Follow him and experience Bleakwarrior in all its true mad glory.

Scott Nicolay,
World Fantasy Award winning author of *Ana Kai Tangata: Tales of the Outer the Other the Damned and the Doomed*

BleakWarrior is flabbergasting Black Metal New Weird that opens on thundering Wagnerian strokes that quickly mirror GWAR in scope, tone, and bass. Manichaean, Nag Hammadi level mythology going on here. I wish my old pal Phil Farmer was still alive to read this. It's totally his bag. It is Science Fantasy in power-chords, and you will be too busy trying not to snarf whatever you were inhaling, imbibing, or swallowing to put it down. Rennie delivers.

Edward Morris,
author of the Blackguard series

With this seething tour-de-force, Alistair Rennie rightfully comes and sits with today's most notable storytellers by the campfire of The Weird, offering uncompromising readers his magnificent visions and memorable language.

Joseph S. Pulver, Sr.,
author of *A House of Hollow Wounds*

BleakWarrior

Alistair Rennie

ISBN 978-1-940250-23-6

Artwork by Maxwell John Hudetz
maxconcept.tumblr.com

Interior Layout by Lori Michelle
www.theauthorsalley.com

Printed in the United States of America

First Edition

Visit us on the web at:
www.bloodboundbooks.net

Also from Blood Bound Books

400 Days of Oppression by Wrath James White
Habeas Corpse by Nikki Hopeman
Mother's Boys by Daniel I. Russell
Fallow Ground by Michael James McFarland
Cradle of the Dead by Roger Jackson
Dark Waves by Simon Kearns
Loveless by Dev Jarrett
The Sinner by K. Trap Jones
The Return by David A. Riley
Knuckle Supper by Drew Stepek
Sons of the Pope by Daniel O'Connor
Dolls by KJ Moore
At the End of All Things by Stony Graves
The Black Land by MJ Wesolowski
Yeitso by Scott M. Baker
The River Through the Trees by David Peak
They Don't Check Out by Aaron Thomas Milstead

Contents

Book 1: Random Feuds and Family Missions

1. BleakWarrior Meets the Sons of Brawl

The Folly of Brawl is a tower of disproportionate girth, besmirched at the base with festering lichens and nettled clumps. Venomous ivies scale its roughshod masonry. Dripping vines encircle its mildewed heights. The bloated misalignments of its elapsing stiffness represent an ominous departure from the orthodoxies of architectural form. Below its corroded lintel a single door of blanched iron offers sole access to its interior.

Lord Brawl himself can be heard proclaiming aloud from the un-turreted heights of his Folly in the arboreal wastes. The various species that flock to his abode, feeding on the discarded body parts of victims, will cease their scavenging and stare up at him, blankly, as if to listen.

"My fifty Bastard Sons!" he cries, with a voice that carries through the veins of his offspring. "Bring me the living body of a chief rival. I tire of these sops of linear flesh. They are sources of amusement only—but I need the pain of one after my own kind."

It is a regular summons which the fifty Bastard Sons of Brawl will readily obey, as they travel the world on various missions, in subdivisions of two or three, hearkening to their Father's grim requests, though they are easily distracted by the allure of havoc.

"My Bastard Brood," says Lord Brawl, willing his words

through the blood of his spawn. "Daily I toil in the midst of my wretchedness, but seldom am I gratified by common atrocity. I have administered every torture ever conceived, and devised many others that no ordinary cruelty could sustain. Yet I receive nothing more than the mild satisfaction of the visible terror on a maiden's face, which, at best, hardly arouses my fancy.

"Bring me, then, the living body of a rival whose capacity to endure is proof of an unbearable suffering. Do not mock me with the linear kind, but delight your Father with the most infected specimen of our stock. Bring me the living body of Mother of Peril, Head Wrecker, BleakWarrior, Hecticon or the Nailer of Souls, and I will show them woes that are mine and theirs in unison."

Sons 21, 24 and 39 have proved particularly adept at adhering to their missions and, presently, have aligned themselves to a linear dignitary by the name of Layman Sohk. Layman Sohk has many spies who have brought reports of a stranger taking residence in the City of Indulgences, whose demand for excessive pleasures exceeds even that of the indigenous people. The stranger shuns the attentions of Free Traders of Interest who wish to sensationalise his achievements which are, to him, the *ennui* of his removal from ordinary life. Privacy, however, often proves the mother of infamy; and soon word spreads of his exploits which, by the time they have reached the collective ear of the masses, are almost legendary.

He has debauched for several weeks and his appetite for more is like the tide that never wanes, pleasuring himself with harlots of all sexes and types; assaulting his senses with lurid concoctions; and fighting to the death with hired ruffians in the combat clubs. But he lives: and, as he pleasures himself, he feels no pleasure. These pastimes, instead, are a kind of erasure of the need to serve causes which he hates because he does not understand them.

In the private salon of a leisurely bordello, a prostitute, who does not hire her body but hires her mind, was bathing with him in the juice of stipple berries, which are full of toxins said to relax the muscles and skin. She said to him:

"Seeing as you will remain nameless—"

"I have no name worth knowing," he said.

"Why?" she asked.

"Because I might never be seen here again."

"So my memory of you will be a nameless one?"

"Do memories have names?"

"Memories have people. People have names."

"Better to forget, then."

She scooped up some stipple berry juice in cupped hands and told him to drink. "The stipple juice is full of chemicals that have the same effect on the brain as endorphins. It will make you feel better."

He drank.

"You *do* have a name, don't you?" She wouldn't let it go. It was, after all, what she was paid for.

"What use is a name," he said, now scooping up the juice and drinking for himself, "when you don't know who or what you are?"

"A name will begin to make you someone."

"But not some*thing*."

She began to massage his emaciated shoulders.

"To most people," she said, "I am some*thing* before being some*one*. Most of them never even think of me as some*one* at all. I'd say you were lucky."

He laughed with little amusement and they were silent for a while. Then she said, "Why do you wear those lenses?"

The Warped Lenses. She had to ask. He said nothing.

"Can I take them off?" She raised her hands.

"No." He span his head away from her. "I have a problem with my eyes."

The head-whore, who was a professional, quickly changed the subject:

"You think it's possible?"

"What?" He frowned.

"To forget."

"There are ways and means."

She sank beside him, leaning an arm on the edge of the bath. "You really have that kind of control over your own mind?"

He looked at her.

"No," he said. "Why else would I be here?"

His head was shaven almost to complete baldness, revealing a longitude and latitude of scars over his cranium that seemed like the map of a ruined and ravaged world of another dimension. His features were refined and remotely feminine, yet reflective of a chiselled hardness which signalled a true veteran of bloody campaigns. Further wayward escapades of violence had knocked several prominent features out of joint. His body combined its inlying rawness of strength with a sparseness of form that indicated long periods of undernourishment—hence, also, the pulsating veins that pushed against his skin like the roots of trees. A prevailing haggardness likewise suggested sustained episodes of debauchery and a habitual lack of sleep. Insurrections of wildness dominated his aura; but it was the Lenses, above all, that stood out among his chief attributes—like the eyes of a mythical beast which, through him alone, had resisted the downfall of its evolution.

His attire, meanwhile, was of exceptional quality yet worn beyond the appearance of its actual worth. He wore baggy black pantaloons made of the under-hides of turtles tucked into *knee-high leathern boots with kick-studs on their heels and toes. His three quarter length sealskin coat overlay a black jerkin with a lining of protective resins to deter the attentions of sharp instruments. The sealskin coat itself was of a mottled black hue, with assorted pigments and blood stains covering its watertight and slightly hairy veneer. He was dressed for the darkness and for the night, for fleeing from scenes of slaughter without a trace. But, most of all, he was dressed for killing his victims whilst instilling in them the terror of their coming death.*

This was how he looked; and this was how he would be remembered by those who beheld him—casting an impression too vivid for them to forget so easily.

—The Private Testimony of Achlana Promff,
Priestess of the Church of Nechmeniah

21, 24 and 39 were already intent on investigating the stranger's presence. It was, for them, a routine measure. But when they heard of the extent of the stranger's capacity for physical and mental stimulation, they began to get suspicious and, on discovering his identity, were aroused by the prospect of violent action.

It had been a while since they'd received their Father's edict and, dutifully, they had turned their attentions to the City of Indulgences, which was often a favourite hideaway for Meta-Warriors capable of controlling their Random Leaps. BleakWarrior had no control over his; and the Sons of Brawl had no control over theirs either. They could, however, depend on their Father's guidance, whereas BleakWarrior was bereft of any mastery of self-navigation and, to this extent, was likely to find himself in the wrong place at the wrong time.

Which is where he was now; and 21, 24 and 39 were about to make him pay for his shortcomings.

Outside the door of BleakWarrior's room (where he was shacked up with some psycho-slut parasite getting kicks out of some heart-to-heart hoo-ha), the Sons of Brawl were preparing themselves for an abduction, regrettably with some restraint. 21 was jittery with eagerness, his cleaver in his hand wavering with as much excitement as he was. 24, wielding a hatchet, was very calm, which only emphasised his talent for hate. 39 was rubbing the tip of his poniard like it was some kind of phallic totem destined to bring him additional vitality.

But when they burst into the room, they saw nothing of the girl; and BleakWarrior was now poised at the window, ready for a Random Leap. The stipple bath stood between them and steamed; and, as 21, 24 and 39 made their move (which they knew was in vain), BleakWarrior, not looking at *them,* said, "Better to forget."

And he threw himself through the window, which exploded in a mass of splintered muntins and shivered glass, and flung himself free from the grip of his would-be captors.

21, 24 and 39 stood still and gaped, too angry even to move. Then a bubbling noise arrested their attentions and, looking down at the bath, they saw a head, gasping for air, emerge from the steaming ooze of stipple juice.

The whore who does not hire her body but hires her mind gazed up at them. The Sons of Brawl rounded on her and, with their weapons raised, vented their fury on her delicate flesh, afterwards pausing to savour the brew of stipple juice mixed with female blood, which, they agreed, was a highly satisfying remedy for failure.

While vulnerable to starvation, Meta-Warriors can only die through acts of violence (including death by drowning, poison and fire) and are physically immune to the linear disorders of disease and aging. They are also immune to death in cases of violent impacts sustained through Random Leaps, when the fall, from a linear point of view, has to be high enough to be fatal. In which case, Meta-Warriors simply fall through, rather than onto, whatever they hit, whereby the effect is like jumping into water, except that it is the body that becomes like a liquid, sifting quickly through the hard matter of the targeted surface and reforming itself as an organic whole on the other side of the transition.

There are some who have learnt (by Leaps of Cynosure) to navigate their way through what they refer to as the Intersecting Differentials of the matter through which they are capable of travelling (often called IDs, which state that the chaos contained by the material order of the universe also contains inversions of that principle). But, generally, the destination (or node) is entirely random—hence, the name: Random Leap.

The process of a Random Leap comes at an excruciating cost of mental trauma in the form of a presentiment that, when they go "in," they might never come out again, to the effect of remaining confined within the inverted molecular framework of the planet's interior—to wit, the metaphysical abatement of linearity is considered vulnerable to an everlasting static movement (the so-called Random Loop), to the extent that Random Leaps are mostly avoided, except in cases of extreme danger or irresistible tactical gains.

This is not, however, the way it stands for Meta-Warriors engaged in Leaps of Cynosure, whereupon the randomness of the Leap is rectified by a measure of control that induces a sense of calm that, in turn, reduces the sizable fear of the Random Loop to a vague sense of trepidation. Whether or not a Leap of Cynosure actually offers a full protection from a Random Loop, or whether it simply provides an illusion of security, is unknown; but it is clear that Meta-Warriors capable of controlling their Leaps are far more likely to use them.

—The Private Testimony of Achlana Promff, Priestess of the Church of Nechmeniah

BleakWarrior shot up through terrain that felt like a pavement. A few moments of disorientation, then . . . Nemeden: the City of Riches. He was beside the River Tho and could see the High Street squirming with dandified tourists, merchants, soothsayers, acrobatic troupes, fortune tellers and affluent street vendors. Last time he was here, he'd stayed in a luxurious tavern that was famous for its wine selection and extravagant orgies. This time, it might be better to get out of the city altogether and seek refuge in some anonymous ancient village in the hills.

Money, however, was a major problem; and this is where the tourists came in.

BleakWarrior slid unseen into a labyrinth of decaying streets where idling visitors wandered aimlessly—just right for being dragged into some deserted alley and beaten up for every sovereign they had in their possession.

In a private salon at the Palace of Layman Sohk, 21, 24 and 39 conspired.

"What shall we tell Father?" asked 21, wringing his hands like some kind of aristocratic ponce with too many gambling debts.

"The truth," said 24, ever the pragmatist.

39 agreed: "Our failure to catch the rat is only temporary. The sooner we tell Father, the more chance he'll have of tracing the location."

"Let's do it now," said 21.

"*Consider it done!*"

The voice came shafting through their veins like liquid ice and into their ears like a sudden hoarfrost.

"Father!" they cried, falling to their knees with fear and awe in equal measure.

"Little worthy fragments of myself, your various murdered mothers would be proud. Fear not my wrath when accomplishments are forthcoming. Though they be done by half, they are half-way to being whole; and, for this, I am pleased. Go you, then, to the highest point of your current place of habitation and cast yourself from its prodigious height. Empty your minds of all things and let a Father's guidance direct you to your goal. In the aftermath of your good work, all has been accounted for: sons 8 and 47 await your arrival with the obedience of good brothers. Go, now, and bring me the rival whose roasted bones will enthuse my grief."

They did as they were told and, within a matter of hours, had rendezvoused with 8 and 47 who, in the meantime, had been tracking BleakWarrior who, in the meantime, too, had been well aware that he was being tracked.

Nailer of Souls was face to face with a Meta-Warrior of growing renown called Be My Enemy. Be My Enemy was taunting him with verbal abuse that had about as much effect on him as flecks of dust against the void.

"Your ugliness resembles the facial contortions of a hog at the slaughterhouse," she spat. "You have the elegance of a bat with its ears removed. If I were forced to love you I would cut out my heart and feed it to the dogs to please me better. Tell me, Nailer, do you sleep in the sewers of the linear folk? Why else would your robes stink so forcibly? I would likely vomit if it weren't for the fact that you disgust me so much."

Finally, she leapt, spider-like, towards him, her flails raised, one in each hand, ready to slam with precision into his temples. It was her favourite move against Meta-Warriors with big reputations. She liked symbolism, which was the basis of the reputation she was trying to build now.

But Nailer of Souls responded as if he was made of air rather than flesh. His club, spiked with a single nail, swung up in an arc and impaled itself in the underside of her chin.

It was the best piece of symbolism Be My Enemy had ever seen.

She had failed, having counted on speed. Nailer of Souls had counted on the will to be faster. Her tongue had been pinned to the roof of her mouth; her teeth had been shattered; and, more to the point, her mouth had been shut. When the Nailer removed his weapon, she fell limply to the ground, too stunned even to whimper.

Nailer of Souls bent over her and, reaching *into* her body, dragged her soul from its containment of flesh, proceeding to devour it in a series of gulps that resembled a gannet scoffing a speared fish. Be My Enemy's belated scream was of utter desperation compared to the physical pain she'd received from the force of the blow.

As Nailer of Souls stood enjoying the moment of resuscitation, he suddenly caught a whiff of some ghastly concentration of bitter and twisted life essences, against which the soul of Be My Enemy had smelt positively sweet. He raised his head at an angle and sniffed, filling his lungs with definite traces of putrescent anima. And there was one among them, too, full of agonies too deep to conceive, even more infested with rot than the others.

Drooling at the mouth, Nailer of Souls walked to the cliff edge of the hill upon which he had slain Be My Enemy, and leapt. He followed the stench through a maze of IDs, which led him, in the end, to a place he disliked more than most.

The City of Riches.

But he had emerged on the outskirts of the place, and the smell was coming from well within its intricate clusters of marble domes and minarets.

But it wouldn't take him long to get there, not even by the inconvenience of linear means.

The Free Traders of Interest spoke of a highly unusual spree of violence which had resulted in the deaths of two visitors to the city and the serious injury of six others. Nemeden had never known anything like it. Among the victims were men and women of all ages, beaten and robbed within a space of four hours during an average market-day afternoon.

The killings were to some extent regrettable because they tended to attract attention in linear societies where law enforcement was more advanced, but they were necessary due to the dangers of being recognised (two of his targets had caught a glimpse of the Lenses, while the others had been more efficiently dealt with). They had served their purpose, however; and BleakWarrior now had the means for financing his stay in a private residence of considerable luxury.

One useful effect of the killings was—precisely—to ensure that the City Arbiters were especially vigilant, which meant that the Sons of Brawl, much against their habitual tendency, would be forced to tread carefully in mounting their attack. It was in the interests of Meta-Warriors to keep a low profile in places like this—places where they'd be regarded and pursued as freaks rather than embodiments of Nature. There were already one or two linear humans or groups who'd made certain discoveries about the presence of "unusual visitants," but who were luckily too wary of the repercussions (the accusations of craziness or eccentricity) to be profligate about voicing opinions of the facts. Because of that, they (some of them known personally to Meta-Warriors) had determined to take a more secretive course in widening their investigations, tending to form clandestine academic factions or mysterious sects reportedly engaged in queer religious or cultish practices.

BleakWarrior knew one of them himself—a priestess from the Church of Nechmeniah—who had gained his confidence and, on one occasion, had even helped him. But Achlana Promff couldn't help him now; not now that there were five of the Bastard Brood on his tail. There was nothing for it but to knuckle down and face up to the fight. The Sons of Brawl were hardly versed in the arts of diplomacy: but, then again, neither was he.

In the preliminary stage of his existence, BleakWarrior wanders over a vast and vacant territory of desolate hills and staggered peaks, where granite cresses overhang the marshy fens and discoloured summits elapse into long ridges of twisted rock. Storms rage and abate over a dreary terrain where rain ravages the foremost heights and sinks to a heavy pelt in the lower braes. No living creature, warm- or cold-blooded, could withstand the conflagration of raw conditions, that to the mind and body bring dreadful hardships, without resorting to a savagery that rivals the hostilities born against it. And, for this reason, BleakWarrior is wild; and wilder still because of the all-too-seeing sight—the penetrating gaze of the Lightning Vision—that enables him to see the supernatural aspect of the natural world, where the metaphysical hues of physical reality are as clear to him as corporeal objects.

It is the world outside of linear time, where an eternal stupor of elemental forces manifest themselves as distorted beasts that war without pause or as feasting deities too beautiful or strange to gaze upon. Ghosts and denizens populate his vision with terrors and splendours; celestial figures dance naked over the glowing heaths: and, for all his sense of fear and wonder, BleakWarrior cannot conceive of them without going mad.

Eons have passed, and BleakWarrior is drawn from the world of excessive marvels by the ululations of a harp that trails on the wind like the residue of sorrow. It is the music of The Bard who, when approached, does not open his lips to speak, but on his harp invokes the utterance of words:

"One who wanders, from your madness now afforded some relief, the timbre of my strings has reduced your visionary convulsions to a material calm. My bardic offerings have delivered you from your impressions of lunacy. Come sit by the blaze of my hearth and slake your thirst on the draughts my naiads bring."

BleakWarrior sits and drinks. The Bard takes up his harp and sings:

"Your restricted madness compels you to a mastery of your senses, which is all the more ferocious for its underlying dereliction. This, your weakness, now your strength, to enemies will convey their bodily ruin; and to you will bring your dedication to their doom."

It was time. The freshness of the morning before sunrise would keep his instincts keen. The streets, by and large, were deserted. East of the market square lay a clutter of alleys and arcades that would provide a sufficient territory for secluded combat.

He didn't have to search the shadowed nooks to know that the Sons of Brawl were following his progress through the maze of ancient conurbation. And as he rounded the bend of a long and empty street, crammed to the heights with intersecting layers of Fiddithian and Mharothic architecture, they were there, five of them, waiting for him with weapons poised.

BleakWarrior approached and made a ritualistic motion that was his personal prelude to battle. Finally, he drew his Weapon of Choice, which flew from its sheath with an ominous ring of honed steel.

The Dirk.

And holding it clasped in both hands, with his legs apart and arms outstretched before him, BleakWarrior bade the Bastard offspring do their worst.

"Nay, BleakWarrior," declared 24. "You will receive a good beating at our hands, but you will live to suffer much greater torments at the hands of our illustrious patron."

"Best lay down the Dirk," added 39, "which will soon be ours by virtue of our victory. Lord Brawl awaits your company with anguishes contrived at your expense."

BleakWarrior's frown only deepened and the ripple of his brow increased.

"Waste not your words on speculative discourses," he said, "which have no root in the decisive consequences of action. The Dirk and I have other plans concerning the distribution of pain between us."

But as BleakWarrior prepared himself for an onslaught, he saw behind the Sons of Brawl a figure glide with ethereal swiftness out of the gloom. Sensing an untoward presence, the Sons of Brawl turned to look; and their faces, suddenly, bore the expression of their shattered bravado.

"*Nailer of Souls!*" gasped 21.

And a long silence passed between them; and Nailer of Souls was almost within striking distance when 24 took courage and said, "There stands a confluence of miseries no duty to our Father can allow us to deny. Good brothers, take heart. We have pursued a rat and discovered a Mastodon. Think of our Father's joy when such a prize falls wrapped in blood into his lap. Cripple him but do not kill!"

The instruction given, the Sons of Brawl pounced on their prey, but the match was one of saplings to a hurricane. Nailer of Souls went about his business with chilling elegance, stealing among them with ease and with an exactness in every parry and stroke that struck asunder the Bastard host.

Yet the Bastards were no novices. Their adroit ferocity allowed them to avoid the more precipitous blows of their adversary. Desperation, too, played its part. Empowered to bravery through the reflexive impetus of sheer panic, 21 embarked on a rolling manoeuvre that enabled him to clip the calf of Nailer of Souls with his jagged-edged cleaver. The Nailer lost his balance by an inch or two—not much. But it was enough to rouse the Bastards to a less evasive approach in coping with the Nailer's deftness.

BleakWarrior, meanwhile, saw that the time was ripe for his discreet withdrawal from the melee. There was no adherence to codes of honour in the world of universal strife. Far better to let Nailer of Souls indulge his hunger for souls composed of cosmic filth, for he was not to be challenged when newly revived by their nutritious boons.

But a rational acceptance of the risks involved was not a thing to motivate BleakWarrior; nor was it courage that determined his actions: it was madness that defined him and laid his course, and it ran in his veins with unstoppable motion like a river in spate.

21 was the first to fall. BleakWarrior slit open the back of his neck and felled him like a sacrificial ox. 39 came next. BleakWarrior planted the Dirk in the small of his back, causing him to crumple like a burning leaf.

The confusion caused by his appearance played into the hands of Nailer of Souls, who promptly smacked the jaw of 47 with the butt of his club and sent him spinning. Number 8 made the mistake of seeing this as an opportunity to make a move. He swung his studded cosh towards the Nailer's upper body with all the force he could muster. But the Nailer dropped himself to his knees and lowered his head—the cosh passed over him—then sprang to his feet and delivered an almighty thwack into number 8's groin.

8 went down and didn't rise. The Bastard's candle had been snuffed.

BleakWarrior, meanwhile, was busying himself with 47, whose jawbone had been unhinged like a piece of machinery. It seemed appropriate to BleakWarrior that he should tear it off completely from the Bastard's face. So he took a grip of 47's chin and wrenched it sideways with all his strength. A few vicious twists accomplished the deed, and it was good to hear the Bastard squeal like a puppy roasting on a spit.

And now the Nailer was closing in on 24, and there was nothing 24 could do about it except die.

Accordingly, the Nailer leapt into the air and turned like a bird on a swirling eddy. The club, spiked with a single nail, impacted almost with delicacy into 24's forehead. 24's body wilted with an instantaneous limpness like a piece of string.

BleakWarrior wasted no time as the Nailer endeavoured to prise his weapon from the perforated skull of 24. He charged full on, ready to slam the Dirk into whatever part of the Nailer's body presented itself first. But Nailer of Souls turned to meet him with an unpredictable rippling of his form. He caught BleakWarrior's arm and stayed the Dirk, then span low and buried his head in BleakWarrior's abdomen. BleakWarrior felt himself being hoisted and twirled; and the Nailer dumped him onto the ground like a man offloading a heavy sack.

BleakWarrior wanted to struggle to his knees, but a foot on his back pinned him to the cobblestones.

He knew it, then, that he was going to die.

Badly.

It is written in *The First Book of Absolutes* that the soul is a derivation of the Fundamental Awe of Nechmeniah when first she developed an awareness of herself as the Over-Notion of Existence and Time.

As practitioners of the Church of Nechmeniah, it is our belief that we are able to receive the same extreme of realisation whenever we encounter new things or experiences that appeal to the Fundamental Awe in all of us. Crucially, however, the arousing freshness of these encounters is brief because of their obfuscation by the degrading animal distractions that characterise our physical condition. Needless to say, a sustainable Awe is recoverable through death, whereupon our souls are re-absorbed by the primacy of the Life Before the Body.

But my visitor tells me that this is wrong.

Instead, he says, we are strictly bound to a material existence that has no root outside of itself. Anything that exists beyond the reach of our senses is but a part of the expansive interaction of all things operating as a contingent body of differential states. What cannot be seen can be felt, he says, which makes all things, mental or physical, equally real. Some substances are less palpable than others—that is all. And, to this extent, the body and soul are a single unit consisting of extremes of materiality which cannot exist in dualistic separation.

The soul, he says, is a metaphysical extension of the physical order of the body which, in turn, is a physical extension of the metaphysical chaos of the soul: to segregate one from the other is to obliterate both, and to extinguish the flame of Life.

Forever.

—The Private Testimony of Achlana Promff,
Priestess of the Church of Nechmeniah

The hand of the Nailer slipped into BleakWarrior's flesh as if through liquid. BleakWarrior's sense of selfhood seemed to fold in upon itself, to implode upon an internal core of gravity so strong that it must shrink to a material density.

It did.

And the Nailer wrapped his fingers around it and began to manipulate it from its home of flesh; the feeling—not of pain—was akin to having the viscera removed through some powerful means of vacuum suction.

BleakWarrior squirmed like a maggot on the end of a stick. He tried to scream, but his power of utterance was beyond him. His eyes, too, were beginning to fail. The last thing he saw was the Nailer leaning over him with his mouth ajar and slavers dangling from his lips.

BleakWarrior was being drawn out of himself, and the sensations were awful, like being sucked through a miniscule abyss, but in reverse, as if the abyss were being sucked through him.

With an unusual lack of suddenness, however, the Nailer began to recoil from BleakWarrior's degenerated physique, as if someone or something were pulling him away. All at once, he released his supernal grip on the soul of BleakWarrior and, more suddenly now, keeled over as if struck on the face by a blunt object.

BleakWarrior felt his inner vitality return to the entire compass of his being with renewed vigour. He had sampled aphrodisiacs that had given him a similar injection of desperate urgency.

But not like this.

The smoothness and speed of his movements were such that he didn't fumble for the Dirk where it had spilled from his hand during the course of his fall. He whipped it up nimbly and rolled to his feet. Nailer of Souls was sprawling before him, coughing and spewing like a man brought back from the brink of drowning. BleakWarrior grabbed the Nailer by the hair and drew his head back so that his throat was exposed to the ruminations of the Dirk.

"Nailer of Souls," he said, "how came you to abandon your efforts to devour me? It makes no sense in the eyes of the Dirk and me."

The Nailer's eyes rolled as he unloosed his tongue to speak:

"Your soul to me is poison, BleakWarrior. It has reduced my thirst to a sickening repulsion. I am desolate, yes, and I feed on the desolation of others. But your madness is a toxin in the blood of my being I cannot endure.

"You have me within range of the Dirk, BleakWarrior. I have a mind that the Dirk and you will satisfy my drooth, forever."

"Then since you are about to die," said BleakWarrior, "tell me what you know of our uncommon purpose. What are we, Nailer? What are we and *why?*"

"We are what we are, BleakWarrior—no more, no less. I am the manifestation of the desolate mood that underpins me. You are the embodiment of the madness that empowers you to your probable doom. We are the physical expression of natural states that serve no purpose beyond their immediate function."

"But surely a strain of consequence must bind our absent purpose to some singular aim."

"Must the wind blow for a specific reason?"

"I am stirred too much by wafts of madness to swallow this."

"The wind is free to swallow anything."

"None of this conveys an answer," said BleakWarrior. He pressed the Dirk against the Nailer's throat.

"It is all the answer I can give."

"Then the Dirk compels me to erase your life in bitter haste."

BleakWarrior drew the Dirk across the Nailer's throat with a swift incision that splashed blood across the cobbles freely as wine. He let go of the head and watched it fall to the stones with a delicate smack. He gazed upon the face of the Nailer. The expression he saw was more of relief than pain.

Tears were seeping under the Warped Lenses of BleakWarrior when he sheathed the Dirk and stepped from the bloody pool that welled around his feet. The trail of gore he left behind him subsided by degrees as he departed from the scene of the melee. A sudden urge to rip the Lenses from his eyes—to immerse himself in the thralls of madness—rose up in his gorge like a volcanic spume. But it was quickly dispersed by the exultant thought that, by not knowing who he was, not knowing what he was, he would kill to find out.

Or die trying.

2.
The Gutter Sees the Light That Never Shines

The Gutter moves among men like the waft of a deadly chemical that has assembled itself in human form. He stinks primarily of brine. But there are other smells that fortify his breath; and his body, too, reeks powerfully of dreadful odours.

There is no telling the liquids with which he has soiled himself, but the oddity of their collective hue on the front of his smock is as ominous as it is filthy. Yet it is more than repulsion that causes people to maintain their distance. His face is a living image of nastiness, with a perpetual scowl that could easily be mistaken for a deformity. And there is a hunger in his eyes—more feral than human—that betrays an insatiable need for satisfactions that lie far beyond the tastes of ordinary men.

The Gutter walks the streets of the City of Thrills, the second city of the Republic of Noth. On his back he wears some kind of apparatus: a leathern harness holding what looks like a milk churn. A thick, heavy slosh accompanies his steps, the sound of something fleshy and fetid. On more than one occasion a City Arbiter, tapping a studded cosh on the side of his leg, has thought about stopping The Gutter and investigating the contents of the churn. But the stench of The Gutter has convinced him otherwise.

The Gutter is aware of this, which is one of the reasons

why he allows himself to smell so badly. The violence of his aroma is an excellent deterrent against the curiosities of linear men.

The City of Thrills is an aborted geometry of narrow streets, decaying arcades and dim-lit porticos. A shambles of buildings lean simultaneously in all directions. The mangled brickwork and shoddy masonry interact as if by accident rather than design. Depictions of naked revellers, cosmic symbols and chimerical beasts adorn the lower portions of each edifice, adding an unexpected life and colour to the amplitude of disrepair. It is the custom of artists that inhabit the city to embellish its walls with expressions of beauty over uttermost states of dereliction.

The walkways under the porticos are abuzz with wineries and debating chambers, artists' missions and fetish clubs, drinking studios and pleasure galleries. There are few establishments equipped for catering for practical needs. Artisans and ironmongers are outnumbered by craftsmen working with soft metals and precious stones. Butchers and bakers are diminished by gastronomic deviants capable of producing absurdly delicate pastries and marinated meats. An illustrious drapery of precious cloths hangs ragged over the entrances of the numerous guilds.

And The Gutter fucking despises the place.

He passes through one district to another, of which there are three: the Carnal District, the Cymbeline District, and the Cerebral District. The Gutter is on the edge of the Carnal District. He passes several girls attired in reptilian sex-suits whose hair is braided with live snakes. When he passes them, even the snakes recoil at the sudden blast of the stench he bears.

It makes him smile: and, when he smiles, you can see how he has removed his teeth with a set of tongs for the purposes of sucking up his foodstuffs with greater efficiency.

But now The Gutter is growing restless, his glances darting like sparks from his eyes, and his gums chaffing with slavers smarting from his lips. He is looking for a particular door with a particular sign carved upon its lintel, but not so visibly as anyone might see.

Within two or three hours of conducting his search, he discovers the sign—a cleft circle—over a heavy door made of parched oak. It is the sign of the Information Syndicate. The Information Syndicate have offices throughout the entire continent, but finding them isn't so easy. It is often said that the whereabouts of the Information Syndicate is their most precious commodity. But, if and when you find them, they will sell you information at a price that is equal to the value of whatever it is you wish to know.

But The Gutter doesn't think he'll have to pay, because The Gutter doesn't have any money. He does, however, have a currency that serves him better.

The Gutting Knife.

The Sisters of No Mercy were up against a dangerous adversary.

Whorefrost.

Whorefrost was utterly reviled by female Meta-Warriors because of the extreme nature of his preferred method of killing them.

He had a pale, bloodless physique that looked like gelatine rather than flesh. His skin was smooth and greasy and largely hairless. His arms and belly seemed to consist more of muscle than fat by the slightest of margins. He was big but not ungainly, with a huge mouth, thick-set lips and heavy jowls that swung pendulously as he walked.

Whorefrost's movements were deliberate and glacial. His preferred method of killing was exactly the same. First, he would try to disable his enemies by shattering their kneecaps, breaking their arms or stunning them with a carefully measured blow to the head. His Weapon of Choice was suitably designed for this approach: a heavy metallic baton forged in the shape of a gigantic penis. His aim was to keep his enemies alive for as long as it took to satisfy the requirements of his bodily ritual.

And this was the part that female Meta-Warriors reviled the most.

Death comes in many guises, some of which are more desirable than others. Death by Whorefrost is perhaps the most undesirable of all.

Should all things go according to plan, Whorefrost's enemy will be lying in a stupor of helplessness before him. It may be necessary to make them even more helpless than they already are, but this is a formality. As long as they're not *too* helpless, Whorefrost is happy.

And happier, still, when he begins to remove their clothing, which he does with a ponderous delicacy that ensures the maximum arousal of his vital parts, which are by no means a source of arousal for his victims.

Whorefrost's cock is long and thin with a remarkably bulbous head that makes it look like a bauble on the end of a stick. His testicles are disproportionately huge and, like the rest of his body, hairless. More to the point, his egg-sac is teeming with semen that has an unusual potency: it is deadly cold and, to this extent, is biologically devastating.

Whorefrost's sperm is as thick as pus. It is also capable of causing the spread of frostbite within seconds which, when it spreads, causes a slow and insidious destruction of the body, from the inside out, that lasts a matter of minutes or even hours.

Extreme cold burns like fire.

When he has dumped his seed in his enemy's nook, she feels a sudden numbness that, by gradual stages, begins to burn. The numbness is like a chill of ice which rapidly diffuses with the forcefulness and feel of acid. The acid sensation quickly grips the womb and begins to spread throughout the internal organs—the bowels, the guts, the spleen, the stomach, the kidneys and so on. The insides begin to boil, then become gangrenous and begin to rot. A further stage of numbness may occur, but only after a lengthy period of emphatic suffering that no other pain in the world can equal.

Which is why Whorefrost is especially reviled by female Meta-Warriors. But which is also why he is *more* reviled by their male counterparts.

An anal ravaging is bad enough at the best of times. But when Whorefrost is doing the buggering, the degeneration of the anal cavity, followed by the deterioration of everything else, is not a thing to be taken lightly.

It is apparent, then, that The Sisters of No Mercy were up against a dangerous adversary.

And the only comforting thought about it was . . .

So was he.

The stairwell was in darkness. It smelt of damp plaster, mildew and dry rot. The stairs curled upwards in a crooked spiral. Sometimes they sagged. Sometimes they stiffened. Sometimes they increased their steepness. Sometimes they almost flattened out. Sometimes they seemed so brittle that they would break. But they didn't. There were no landings, no doors, except at the top.

The room at the top of the stairs was a room of shadows. Two men lay on either side of the door posts, their limbs twisted, their bodies soaked in blood around the chest, midriff and thighs.

They had died quickly. Too quickly. Their cries had been silenced before they could summon the breath to make them. Two broad cuts across their throats had silenced them forever.

These men had been assistants to the Information Master. Their true purpose in life, however, was to act as his protectors.

Clearly, they had failed.

The Gutter had the Information Master by the throat, the Gutting Knife poised against his belly.

"Rest assured," he said, "that you *will* speak." He cocked his head. "Unless, of course, you prefer to be gutted."

The Information Master wheezed because The Gutter was gripping his throat too tight. The Gutter slackened his grip.

"Speak," he said. "Or . . ." He applied a miniscule amount of pressure on the Gutting Knife.

It was enough.

This time, the Information Master didn't refuse to tell The Gutter everything he needed to know—about the Psychomatics, about where he must go to find them, and about where he might go to finish them off.

"So this is the fucker who likes to fuck all the other fuckers," said Little Sister.

"Looks like he's fucked himself with a fucking claw hammer." Big Sister scowled like her mouth was full of sour milk. "His face shows years of experience of being ugly."

Whorefrost smiled, and it was, as Big Sister had said, a truly awful sight.

"I will take great pleasure in dipping my oar in your waters," he said, rubbing his baton against his groin to emphasise the point.

"The only thing that'll be getting dipped is our blades in your blood."

Little Sister drew her Long Sword. Big Sister drew her Short Sword. Whorefrost unstrung his greatcoat made of wild heifer and threw it behind him. He was bare-chested, his torso glistening like a chunk of lard. His tight pantaloons showed the full measure of his excitement. It was big.

"Pretty soon," snarled Little Sister, "we'll be ramming that cock of yours down your own fucking throat."

"Oh," said Whorefrost, "I think that me and my cock'll be doing the ramming." His huge mouth formed a broad, lascivious sneer. He raised the baton, rubbing it between his forefinger and thumb, and took a step forward.

Little Sister spat an unintelligible curse. Big Sister

slapped the flat of her blade against her palm and positioned herself in a super-intensive crouch.

No wonder Whorefrost was aroused. The Sisters of No Mercy were an impressive pair who did little, clothes-wise, to conceal the fact. Little Sister was short and extremely curvaceous, her thick arms and solid thighs betraying an immensely powerful strength in one so small. Big Sister was sinuous and agile, her flat breasts taught and masculine alongside Little Sister's sumptuous orbs. But anyone with any pretensions of fucking them was asking for trouble. The only people The Sisters had sex with was each other, and anyone who tried to prove otherwise would pay a very heavy and painful price.

Except for Whorefrost.

As far as he was concerned, their cunts were his.

Once, they had been three, clutching each other as they slept. In the recollections of their dreams, they would walk again in the Forest of Sores, hand in hand through trees as thick and closely knit as they were.

But these trees were of no ordinary caste; nor were they the product of the functions of Nature as they are normally perceived through linear means of scientific inquiry.

The trees of the Forest of Sores were a corruption of the basic elements of form—with whips and flails instead of branches, razor-wire instead of leaves, and shards of glass instead of blossoms.

Corruption, however, is of itself a consequence of Nature.

And so it was with The Sisters. With every step they took, their naked bodies were shorn of skin or cut to the bone or flayed of flesh; and their blood would turn to pus instead of scabs because of the constant rawness of their wounds.

At night, they wept together in the darkness, shivering on beds of wet moss, soothing each other's wounds with tears. In the morning, when they woke, they would begin again their aimless migration through the abysmal vastness.

There was no sense of the world's passing in the Forest of Sores, no fleeting indication of the motions of time. The momentary provocations of agony were equal to a prolonged suffering that defined them forever.

Random violations of innocence are liable to induce a reaction of ferocity. The wild beast that suffers the taunts of the baiter responds with a superior malice in its defence. There is an abiding equality between chasteness and cruelty—just as a diamond is an intensification of the mineral compositions of coal.

The Sisters of No Mercy were in a very bad way when the Mother of Sores called them to her roost. But the Mother soothed them with her balms and tended them with a loving hand they had known only for each other. Then the Mother told them of what they must do to purge themselves of their eternal suffering in the Forest of Sores.

And then the Mother gave them Weapons.

Once, they had been three, searching together for enemies in the world of linear men.

But not anymore.

Middle Sister was dead.

And The Sisters of No Mercy would honour her with a measure of cruelty that was equal to her prodigious chasteness.

The Light That Never Shines was accustomed to shadows. Or maybe the shadows were accustomed to her.

Either way, she slipped from the gloom like she was casting a cloak off her back, and blended in with a shaft of light that filled the street like liquid metal fills a mould.

The Light That Never Shines was hungry for a skin to wear. She dressed herself in skins and could reproduce one for every occasion. That was the secret of blending in. Her body had absorbed them and she could muster them at will—a skin for all seasons—and right now was the season for harvesting.

She smiled to herself like a girl who had lost her virginity, but it was nothing to do with feeling happy. She smiled because it was *always* the season for harvesting.

And tonight she was planning a good yield.

The Salon of Catastrophists lay on the border between the Cerebral and Cymbeline districts. It was a guild frequented by an exclusive coterie of artists, poets and theoreticians renowned for their speculations on the various ways in which Life as they knew it would come to an end.

The Salon of Catastrophists was a square-shaped, spacious auditorium with a high ceiling and no upper floors but, it was said, plenty of lower ones. On the whole, it was grim. It was also one of the few buildings in the city whose walls were divested of the pictorial extravagance that was common to others. This was in keeping, however, with the principle that buildings should be decorated according to what they were used for; and, given that the Salon of Catastrophists was used for discussions about catastrophe, it is only right that its walls remained bare.

Members of the guild generally assembled to practice rituals of attainment and loss, consisting of recitals, readings, performances and exhibitions, followed by uproarious drinking sessions (lasting for days) that were intended to convey the passage of Life through various stages of degeneration. Yet, in spite of the seeming absence of formality, the Salon of Catastrophists was organised into two distinct intellectual groups.

Overall, it is agreed by the Catastrophists that the Universe is encoded with contradictory conditions of order and chaos which necessitate its failure as a sustainable entity. To this extent, all things are destined to perish: but the question remains as to the nature of *how?*

In their attempts to resolve this issue, the Salon of Catastrophists has become divided into the Continuity and Discontinuity Schisms.

The Discontinuity Schism believe that the destruction of the Universe will come as a result of a catastrophic deterioration or collapse—a Cataclysm—while the Continuity Schism is firmly opposed to the "idolisation of single events," and prefers to concern itself with theories such as the "Permanence of Disorientation." The Permanence of Disorientation states that the Universe consists of a continual extinction of its contingent parts, which are simultaneously replenished by their re-emergence as universal forces (life, light, precipitation, and so on) which, in turn, begin to decay at the very moment of their re-emergence as existing phenomena.

There are, of course, various interpretations that apply to Continuity Theory, but the Continuity Schism can be roughly summarised as a belief that the world exists in a state of perpetual calamity, which also implies that Existence and Time are essentially meaningless.

As such, the Continuity Schism tended to appeal to thinkers who were not inclined towards divine interpretations of catastrophe, while the opposite was true of the Discontinuity Schism. But the Continuity Schism did have its share of total fanatics.

The Psychomatics, for example, were prepared to take extreme measures in order to emphasise the legitimacy of their position. They were the militant wing of the Continuity Schism who sought an active involvement in the way of the world as they defined it. In other words, they liked destroying things—or, more to the point, they liked destroying people. Which is why they had developed a formidable range of expertise in various means of sabotage and assassination.

It had taken The Gutter a lot of effort to find this out—and a lot of gutting. He had first been alerted to the Psychomatics when he was doing some reconnaissance work on a Meta-Warrior called Hecticon who was posing as a linear usurper in the disputed northern province of Uìn. As luck would *not* have it, the Psychomatics had tried to assassinate Hecticon while The Gutter was trying to figure out a way to do the same. When their attempt had failed, Hecticon stepped up his security measures which made him temporarily unavailable for an appointment with the Gutting Knife. So The Gutter decided to do some reconnaissance work on the Psychomatics instead. The fact that they'd targeted a Meta-Warrior like Hecticon had led him to suspect that they might have been acting under the influence of a non-linear element.

Which, as it happens, is exactly how it really was.

There was a bee wrestling with a bud on the ground that had fallen off the broken stalk of a wilting flower that was growing from a crack in the ruptured brickwork.

The Light That Never Shines reflected on the fact that she had seen linear men and women work with the same mindless vigour, and with the same failure to comprehend the underlying motivations of their most rudimentary tasks.

"*Are you any different?*"

"Of course," she replied. "My automatic functions are distinguishable for their emphasis on the wilful elimination, rather than preservation, of my species. To this extent, it is not a question of performing rudimentary tasks in order to survive, but a question of killing or being killed."

"*Is there a difference?*"

"Yes, there is. It depends on the amount of risk you are exposed to. I am exposed to an extreme measure of danger in performing my routine tasks; a common bee is exposed to much less; while a linear human (except in cases of disease, famine or war) is exposed to almost none at all."

At the same time, The Light That Never Shines had been careful to take advantage of occasional individuals who surfaced from the linear tide with an almost Meta-Warrioristic compulsion to commit themselves to *a cause.*

"*But who's to say they're right to do so?*"

That's obvious, thought The Light That Never Shines.

She was.

The Light That Never Shines arose from her basic element wearing a singularity of dark matter that had no basis in—was a precursor of—the totality of form.

Emerging from her non-awareness, and having only been able to register her existence through emotions, she was formulaically integrated into a linear means of physicality.

The Light That Never Shines had known the primordial absence of herself without ever knowing that she had existed.

Until that time.

"Existence can only be measured by the fact that it must come to an end," she told herself. "Is this what it means to say, *I live?* Which is only another way of saying that *I must die?*"

The Light That Never Shines had harvested a multitude of skins in order to saturate herself in the depths of personality that she was lacking until, finally, she consisted of more expressions of herself than she could account for. The intellectual capacities of her various aspects are boundless to the point that, mathematically, she is devastating and, poetically, she is the purveyor of many fine examples of genius.

"*But are you afraid?*" she asked an emerging version of herself.

"No," she replied—but, in actual fact, she was.

There was a bad rain blowing in the faces of The Sisters of No Mercy. Their vision was blurred. Their long hair swept dark and lank across their faces. The Wilden Howe was a dismal place. But The Sisters didn't mind. It was an ideal place for killing an enemy, which is why they were there.

The Wilden Howe was a broad piece of intermediate headland that swung into the Sea of Absences off the westerlands of Noth. It was a barren waste of scraggy sward and rough massifs that degenerated into cliffs along its coasts, with occasional lagoons and shingle beaches offering treacherous points of access from the broiling sea.

The currents around the Wilden Howe were a distortion of the Laws of Nature. On the north-east side, a gigantic maelstrom presented a terrifying hazard to ships and skiffs, many of which had been swallowed up in its liquid maw.

The Howe itself was a harsh domain of haggard grasses and windswept moss, with stagnant pools and peat-bogs in the lower reaches, and broad summits of granite that rose like warped skulls through skins of vegetation.

It was a perfect place for smuggling cartels to ply their trade, which is why Whorefrost was there. Whorefrost was posing as a Harbour Lord from the Isle of Balloch who specialised in trafficking sex slaves to the mainland from a wide variety of island groups. It was a position that afforded him a reasonable degree of power and influence, which he was able to use for the more pressing business of destroying his foes.

"Not a bad racket," admitted Little Sister, as if being forced to swallow a live insect.

"No," said Big Sister, "not bad at all."

"But not," said Little Sister, watching the lone figure of Whorefrost approaching through the mist, "*that* good."

"No," agreed Big Sister, "not fucking good at all."

Whorefrost was up against a dangerous adversary. Perhaps it was the extent of their erotic appeal that was making him lose his concentration. But Whorefrost knew that he didn't require any concentration when it came to a fight.

The smooth strokes of his baton were deftly applied but, oddly enough for a weapon forged in the shape of a penis, lacking penetration. His every move was curtly blocked, his every subtlety anticipated, his every parry brushed aside by unexpected countermeasures.

The Sisters were good—*too fucking good.*

As his frustration increased, he began to lose his balance; and, finally, he overreached with a blow that was aimed at the little one's head. She whirled her body out of his range while the other, the big one, swung her sword upwards in a gentle arc.

In a sense, he was lucky that it struck him directly on the point of his elbow, or else it might have lopped off the lower portion of his arm. The pain, however, was outrageous. But what alarmed him most was the sight of his baton flying out of his hand and landing well beyond his immediate reach.

In the meantime, the little one had recovered her poise. She smacked him across the back of his head with the flat of her blade and sent him sprawling forward onto the wet grass, face-first.

And vulnerable.

"Well, fuck me," said the little one behind him. "I bet you were thinking you were lucky you didn't lose the lower portion of your arm."

Fuck her, she was right.

The next thing he knew there was a muffled thud that sounded like a spade being driven into wet soil. It wasn't. It was Little Sister's Long Sword hacking into his lower arm which, this time, was removed within two or three fleeting strokes.

Everything after that was a blur.

First: the big one started to hack off his other arm so that he was left completely helpless. But alive.

Second: the little one was doing something he couldn't work out, untying his pantaloons and dragging them down around his ankles, but leaving them there so his legs were tied.

Third: the big one turned him over and sat on his chest, pinning him to the ground (as if he was capable of doing anything anyway).

And that's when the real pain started.

Little Sister liked to keep her blade raw and jagged so that, when she cut somebody, it was going to hurt, which is exactly what she was intending now. She took a grip of Whorefrost's penis and started sawing through it with a lazy vigour, and the screams of Whorefrost confirmed the fact that her intentions were being well met.

Whorefrost may have been bleeding to death already, due to the gushing stumps of his missing arms, but he was going to die by choking on his own cock. Little Sister made sure of that when she rammed it down his throat; and, to this extent, no one could fault her for not remaining true to her word.

The removal of Whorefrost's cock had been a piece of butcher's work, deliberately undertaken with a fastidious lack of care. The removal of his testicles, however, was a different affair, whereby Little Sister demonstrated an expertise and sleight of hand that was worthy of a master surgeon. She sliced open his egg-sac and eased the testicles into an alchemical container that would keep them nice and fresh for whatever purposes they had in mind.

Which is why The Sisters of No Mercy were already making their way south, to the City of Thrills, to rendezvous with their linear informers—the Covenant of Ichor.

Things were happening in the City of Thrills. Things were always happening in the City of Thrills.

But not like today.

Up until now, the City of Thrills was a vacuum of architectures avoiding collapse. Now, however, it seemed like the collapse was inevitable.

But it wouldn't be the buildings. No. The feeling of collapse was wholly concentrated on the people—not the people-people, but the *other* people.

Some of them were here.

The Light That Never Shines could feel it, as surely as she would feel a knife in the guts.

Guts? Why was she thinking *Guts?*

In spite of the prodigious range of her mathematical genius, The Light That Never Shines had only a vague presentiment of why she was feeling the way she was now. But she was seldom wrong, so it seemed right that she should expose her feeling to the failsafe scrutiny of a few calculations.

She stopped to take a seat outside a winery where some poets and philosophers were sitting on stools arranged around half a dozen massive barrels. She bought herself a skin of wine and proceeded to knock it back like there was no tomorrow.

Maybe there wouldn't be.

When she had reduced herself to a suitable level of artificial calm, she wrangled through the various permutations and, within an hour or so, had come to a conclusion.

Some of them were here. But the odds, she reckoned, were in her favour.

She gazed into her tumbler and began to brood. Then one of the poets from an adjacent barrel took notice of her (you could tell he was a poet because of his wide-brimmed hat). He rose and took a seat beside her, the way that linear people sometimes do.

"Are you lonely, friend?" he asked, setting a fresh-filled skin of wine on the barrel before them. "Are you a poetess? Is that what ails you? I can well understand the burden of fashioning words into things of beauty. It is my trade, too."

She looked at him as placidly as her anxious mood would allow.

"No, she said. "I'm . . ."

The poet frowned. "What, my friend?"

"A mathematician."

"I see," said the poet.

But The Light That Never Shines could see he couldn't see anything.

"And what can your mathematics tell us of our world?" asked the poet, smiling as if to an adorably stupid child. "Can it tell us as much as poetry?"

"It can tell us that we're doomed," said The Light That Never Shines, looking into the poet's eyes as if willing them to burst.

"Well," he laughed, "if that's the case, then so can poetry."

"But mathematics can tell us *when*."

The poet stared.

"Lady Mathematician," he said, "I wonder if you are not a poetess, after all."

"No," she said. "But if you come with me I'll show you what I am." She adjusted her skin to make herself more alluring. The poet gasped. *Even if I cannot show you why.*

The Light That Never Shines walked anonymously through the dimming streets. It was nearing twilight, her favourite time of day. She had adjusted her skin-tone to suit the occasion. People passing by her may have registered her presence in some subliminal way that their awareness, however, couldn't account for. She was seen and, yet, she remained unnoticed.

She had taken the poet into a backstreet with promises of sexual gratification, but the pleasure had been entirely hers. She had peeled him like a piece of fruit, absorbing his skin with an orgasmic thrill that had restored her to her uttermost vitality.

And now it was time for her to act.

Time for her to summon the Psychomatics.

The Gutter stood out like a moth among butterflies. He didn't try to hide the fact. Instead, he was a gaunt-looking fucker with sleepy eyelids that hooded his eyes and made him look like he was capable of doing very bad things.

He was.

He eyeballed people as he walked passed them: they didn't hold his gaze. They looked away like he'd sent an electric shock through their line of vision. This was typical of The Gutter, who was careful to exert his influence over people.

He had found the Salon of Catastrophists on a street called Patron's Way. Patron's Way divided the Cymbeline and Cerebral Districts and was one of the city's liveliest thoroughfares. This explained the heavy presence of City Arbiters idling among the gregarious hordes, with studded coshes dangling from their wrists.

Which, of course, presented certain difficulties when it came to organising an open confrontation with the Psychomatics.

Which is why The Gutter had developed a plan.

The Covenant of Ichor led them to the door of the stairwell for the office of the Information Syndicate.

"I warn you, Sisters, it's an ugly sight." The leader of the local order smiled faintly. "Men are rarely beautiful, especially when they're mutilated. The sight of them may please you nevertheless."

"No," said Little Sister. "It will. Let's go."

The smell of the corpses grew stronger as they ascended the stairs. When they reached them, The Sisters were indeed pleased, but not for the reasons the Ichorites were thinking.

The Sisters of No Mercy quickly assessed the situation—two corpses with their throats cut; the other sliced open along the underside of the belly, with bits of him still hanging out.

"Interesting," said Little Sister.

"Very," Big Sister agreed.

"The two goons at the door were taken out with minimum fuss, leaving plenty of time for interrogating the Information Master."

"In more ways than one," said Big Sister.

"Quite. These goons can count themselves lucky."

"Very lucky."

"But not *that* lucky."

"Not fucking lucky at all."

Little Sister sat on her haunches and examined the Information Master. "Looks like he had one of his eyes removed first."

"Looks like he did."

"I guess it was a case of 'Tell me, bitch, or I'll skewer the fucking other one.'"

"Guess it was."

"Well—" Little Sister stood up—"this Information Master looks fat enough to have eaten his own mother. The Gutter must have had himself a rare old treat."

"A very rare treat."

"But not as rare as we'll be having."

"No," said Big Sister, "not so fucking rare as that at all."

The Gutter entered the foyer of the Salon and was immediately accosted by two receptionists who asked him brusquely to declare his business.

"Catastrophe," he said, and proceeded to knock them unconscious with the butt of the Gutting Knife.

He hastened into the auditorium, where a debate involving about fifty attendants was fully underway.

Gradually, the feverish exchange between rival factions began to subside as the whiff of The Gutter spread among them like a toxic fume. Heads were turned. A mixture of bewilderment and disgust washed over their faces like a vapour.

"What is the meaning of this?" declared one wizened old scroat with a coiffed mustachio.

The Gutter fixed a stare on him. The mustachio drooped, perhaps for the first time ever.

"I have a message for the Psychomatics," he said.

The faces of the Catastrophists turned pale in unison.

"Tell them," said The Gutter, "I'll be waiting outside."

Which is where he was now, on the opposite side of Patron's Way, making no attempt to hide himself. He wanted to be seen. Or maybe they would smell him first.

Either way, he didn't have to wait long. And it was interesting. Because when the Psychomatics stepped out of the Salon they arranged themselves in a line and stared straight at him through the crowd—four of them, all fit looking fucks with headscarves wrapped around their—No, there were five—a lithe little bitch who looked like a wastrel, hardly noticeable at all.

The Gutter caught her eye and grinned. She was the one. And all the time she stared straight at him.

Clearly, she had recognised him for what he was.

The Light That Never Shines had dressed herself in a skin that made her look as ordinary as possible. As she led the Psychomatics out of the Salon, she quickly assessed the crowd. Within seconds, she saw him.

"There," she said. "Across the street."

"The filthy one?"

She gave a single nod.

"Stop here," she said. "Stare at him. I want to get a measure of his reactions, see if I can work out a weakness."

She couldn't. He didn't give her time.

Instead, he grinned and vanished up a lane that led into the Cerebral District—an interesting choice.

"The dog wants for us to follow him," said one of her companions.

"All right," said The Light That Never Shines. "Let's do what the dog says."

The Covenant of Ichor were an underground sect of religious fanatics who adhered to the belief that it was the role of women to moderate the predominance of their masculine counterparts with whatever ruthless or violent measures were necessary.

The Sisters of No Mercy had, on occasions, aligned themselves to the Ichorites on the pretext of being volunteer assassins who were sympathetic to the Ichorite cause. The Ichorites were in awe of The Sisters, and saw them, perhaps, as a physical embodiment of an ethereal female influence that permeated the world in its entirety.

"And who's to say they're not fucking right?" Little Sister had said.

"*Fucking* right," Big Sister agreed. "Even though they're fucking wrong."

But they weren't wrong about other things. They weren't wrong, for example, about where The Gutter had taken up his temporary residence in the City of Thrills.

"Interesting choice," remarked Little Sister when the leader of the local order told them.

"Very interesting," said Big Sister.

"But not a good one."

"No," said Big Sister, "not fucking good at all."

Little Sister turned to face the leader of the local order. "So, he killed the servitors and spilled their guts in the basement, right?"

"Right," said the leader of the local order. "The place is his."

"And now he's playing some game of cat and mouse with these fuckers from the Salon."

"Yes. It appears he's leading them to the Museum itself."

Little Sister looked at Big Sister.

"What do you think, Sister?" she said.

"I think he's fucking leading them into a fucking trap."

"Why?" said Little Sister.

"Because he's after someone."

"Who?" said Little Sister.

"Someone he wants to lead into a fucking trap."

"But," said Little Sister, "who the fuck would be dumb enough to fall for that?"

Big Sister smiled. "Someone who thinks they can trap him back."

"Someone like us?"

Big Sister nodded. "Someone *very* like us."

"But not as good."

Big Sister frowned. "You've got to be fucking kidding me."

The Museum of Darkest Arts was one of the most forgotten buildings in the entire city. To call it a Museum, in fact, was something of a misnomer. In truth, it was more a repository of disastrous failures accumulated over eons of artistic endeavour which had resulted, naturally, in its fair share of flops. Many of these flops had come to rest in the Museum of Darkest Arts, which had acquired its name more in jest than objective literal accuracy.

The building itself was largely obscured by the buildings around it, which was no bad thing. Inside, it consisted of innumerable corridors, stairways and halls, all of which were bent out of shape and designed as if by an architect bordering on insanity. The near darkness of its interior was also patrolled by two decrepit servitors who were now lying dead in one of its many basements—their throats cut, their bellies razed.

The Light That Never Shines could sense the aura of death when she entered, but couldn't be sure if this was the result of a mathematical or sensory deduction. She was sure, however, about her plan.

"We split up," she said, ignoring the uneasy looks of her companions.

She was reckoning on implementing an increased number of distractions by instructing the Psychomatics to wander separately through The Gutter's hunting ground. If they remained as a group, The Gutter would monitor them and trap them too easily. By multiplying the targets, she would improve the ratio of possibilities as regards turning the hunter into the hunted.

It was all about odds; and, from the point of view of saving her skins, her plan was not so much a plan as an absolute necessity.

Toran Finniff was a specialist in pyrotechnics who had joined the Psychomatics over a year ago. He wasn't adept at stealth missions like this one. He was usually a behind-the-scenes man who preferred operating from afar.

Which made him easy meat for The Gutter, who leapt out from behind a garish figurine fashioned in the likeness of fuck knows what.

The Gutter plunged the Gutting Knife into the man's abdomen and dragged it sidewise with a vicious twist that tore a gash across his belly. The Gutter felt the warmth of entrails spilling over his hand, and it was good.

Toran Finniff didn't scream when he was eviscerated, but merely exhaled like a punctured bladder. When he hit the ground, he groaned in despair at his sudden demise. The groan wafted like one of The Gutter's smells through the gloomy halls and corridors of the Museum.

The Gutter was pleased by this effect.

It would scare the living shit out of them.

The Jiggler was an assassin who specialised in the use of a blow pipe loaded with poison darts. The environmental drawbacks of the Museum of Darkest Arts displeased him.

He had found himself emerging from a staircase onto a causeway suspended over a space of darkness which he took to be some kind of architectural feature.

He leaned over the railing and peered.

Nothing.

He leaned back and flinched when he heard the lingering groan of someone dying. He froze and listened.

The noise of the groan was coming from everywhere.

The Jiggler hastened across the causeway and entered a meandering corridor where The Gutter was waiting for him with a grin on his lips that writhed like worms.

A blow pipe was useless under such circumstances.

Even as the Jiggler backed off from his attacker, the blows were reigning down on his chest, splitting his ribs like bits of kindling and bursting the organs underneath.

The Jiggler neither screamed nor groaned. He spluttered.

And the splutters resonated like an underground stream across the awkward vaults of the Museum.

And, once again, The Gutter was pleased.

Mattosis was drawn by the sound of the splutter—first one way, then the next.

He didn't like it. Not one bit at all. He was a big man who carried a war hammer under his cloak. But there was no room to swing his mighty weapon in this musty confusion of thwarted pits and warped passages.

He drifted into a stairwell that took him deeper into the murk of a lower level of display chambers. A single torch-light blazed in one of them. Like a moth to the flame, Mattosis was drawn.

The restricted illuminations revealed a multitude of obscure paintings screwed to the walls; and, for a moment, Mattosis lost himself in the fantastical array of artistic fiascos of bygone epochs.

He smiled when he recognised a post-Apocalyptic landscape created by Meral of Skitten, a pioneer of the Catastrophist Movement whose works were later diminished by the greater accomplishments of his successor, Potriech of Skow. While Potriech's masterpieces took pride of place in the City's galleries, Meral, it seems, had been demoted to the Museum of Darkest Arts, which appeared to Mattosis to be an injustice of the highest order.

He fixed his eyes on the canvas splattered with motley shades the colour of gangrene. "The Wrath of Ages," it was called. And, if truth be told, it was an appalling work that conveyed little beyond a congregation of blurs.

Mattosis reflected on the fact that perhaps the work of Meral of Skitten had found an appropriate place of exhibition, after all. He took a step backwards so he could consider the painting in its entirety.

And walked directly onto the point of the Gutting Knife, which pierced his lower back, then slid up at an angle and severed his spinal cord.

Mattosis fell like a piece of timber. His scream was loud but quickly hushed when his vocal chords succumbed to his paralysis. Nevertheless, it tumbled through the gloom of the Museum like a boulder through a gorge.

And The Gutter's lips twitched, which was the nearest thing he would ever come to forming a smile.

Sweet Dena'han was described by many as the most beautiful woman they had ever seen. Her form was near perfect—her face a living image of grace—and, inside, she was as twisted and gnarled as a withered root.

The curve of her blade matched the curve of her body: they were equally deadly. Sweet Dena'han was an expert at finding her way into the beds of lovers who were actually her victims. They didn't know this until they woke up in the small hours of the night, choking on their own blood. But it was all part of her delicious charm, which was remarkably false for one so beautiful.

Sweet Dena'han was a Catastrophist fundamentalist who was prepared to allow the violation of her body for the sake of achieving her philosophical aims. It was not that she was cold-blooded in some mentally detached or subjectively callous way. She did what she did with a selfless dedication to the task, and with an admirable disregard for her personal ambition (prior to joining the Psychomatics, Sweet Dena'han had been one of the most promising scholars of her generation).

She searched the precincts of a muddled anteroom that was over-furnished with figures and busts that vied with each other for the absurdity of their composition. Comically hideous faces stared at her from rough-hewn pedestals.

Contorted plaster-cast carcasses stooped and lurched as she wove her way between them.

And, suddenly, one of them moved.

It was fortunate for Sweet Dena'han that she had been on her guard. When The Gutter swung the Gutting Knife at her, she raised an arm in her defence, her torcs deflecting the blow successfully.

She span on her feet with her dagger whistling, expecting to land a slash across The Gutter's chest.

But he was gone.

No. He had ducked under the trajectory of the swinging blade and was leering up at her out of a pool of shadows. When he thrust the Gutting Knife up at her, it slammed like a shaft of ice between her legs. Sweet Dena'han produced a scream that filled the entire Museum with a declaration of agony few others could rival.

And there were many would say that her manner of death was perfectly fitting for one so mindful of her charms.

After the Psychomatics had followed The Gutter into the Museum of Darkest Arts, The Sisters of No Mercy had followed after them.

But nobody knew that they were there.

Now they were in the basement examining the corpses of the elderly servitors who, after a long life of easy living, had died in monstrous pain at the behest of the Gutting Knife.

"Serves the fuckers right, really," observed Little Sister.

"Damn right it does," said Big Sister.

"Still," said Little Sister, "it's a crime."

"It's an absolute fucking atrocity," said Big Sister.

Little Sister stood up from the body she'd been bending over.

"But this," she said, now walking over to the corner of the cluttered holding, "is the biggest fucking crime of all."

Big Sister followed her. She was speechless.

"We couldn't have wished it any other way," said Little

Sister. She took hold of the lid of The Gutter's churn and began to twist.

Big Sister said nothing. The tear in her eye surely said it all.

The Gutter was pleased he had found the linear stragglers, but disappointed he hadn't found *her*.

But not surprised.

He *was* surprised, however, when she found him.

He was in the Room of Charmless Faces, where you could find some of the most abysmal portraits of leading figures ever seen. Anyone else might have been unnerved by the dozens of sightless eyes staring down at them, but The Gutter was oblivious. He stepped lightly across the floorboards—paused and sniffed—then cocked his head to one side and listened, sure of the fact that his quarry was within range.

She was.

The attack not only came from the shadows—it *was* the shadows. The Gutter reeled away from the clawing hands of The Light That Never Shines, unable to see them. The hands, he knew at once, were her Weapons. The fingers of The Light That Never Shines had been fitted with barbs designed to get under the skin, quite literally, of her adversaries. But The Gutter's attire was giving her problems.

The Gutter's smock was thick and greasy with the collective slime of his activities over the years. Unbeknown to him, it had provided him with an impenetrable defence mechanism against the kind of assault he was facing now.

The smock was layered in the bodily juices of a thousand victims whose guts he'd eaten with a messy voracity that had soaked the thing repeatedly in liquid filth. The result was the formation of a reptilian integument that was both slippery and tough as lead. When The Light That Never Shines tore at the smock, her fingers slid harmlessly off its surface without purchase; and her desperation, with each failed attempt, was beginning to show.

The Gutter span away from her frantic grasps until it dawned on him their effect was minimal. He immediately increased the frequency of his counter-attacks, while cautiously avoiding her swipes at his exposed head. Patience, he decided, was the key to his success. He would bleed her dry—bleed her to death, if necessary.

The Gutter teased her rather than retaliated; but the effect was the same. Within minutes, The Light That Never Shines began to show signs of wilting. The Gutting Knife drew fresh wounds across her arms and legs and upper-body, diminishing her strength to a point where she didn't have any. Finally, exhaustion overcame her, and she slumped to the ground with a breathless acceptance of her doom.

The Gutter leaned over her with a mind to savouring her distress. But the look of melancholy on her face (The Gutter had expected terror, rage, contempt or incredulity) unbalanced him.

"Gutter," she panted, her eyes like distant moons. "Tell me," she gasped, "what are we, Gutter? What are we and *why?*"

The Gutter's lips tightened. There was a gleam in his eye that might have been sorrow.

"I eat guts," he said at last. "How the fuck would I know?"

And the Gutting Knife fell with a hideous glimmer.

And finished her off.

The Gutter entered the basement dragging the wasted frame of The Light That Never Shines behind him. He dumped her corpse amid a heap of broken effigies that had lain there for years.

The churn was in the corner, where he had left it during his encounter with the Psychomatics. He hastened towards it and drew it over to the still-warm body of The Light That Never Shines. He unscrewed the lid, set it aside, and proceeded to slice open her belly and shovel her guts into the churn with cupped hands that were used to this manoeuvre.

The guts of the Information Master were already in there, and the remnants of others from previous weeks. The brine had kept them reasonably fresh or, at least, succulent. The stench that erupted from the churn was making The Gutter drool like a cur.

When he'd emptied the belly of The Light That Never Shines, he squatted over the churn and began to scoop large portions of innards into his eager mouth. He sucked on wet strands of disgorged viscera that slithered between his gums like snakes, and thrust his palms into his face to lick up the remainder. He must have been about half way through his feast when he ladled one of Whorefrost's testicles into his mouth and swallowed it whole. As far as The Gutter was concerned, it was just another piece of deliciously stinking meat.

But The Sisters of No Mercy knew otherwise.

It only took a matter of minutes for the testicle to succumb to the initial stages of the digestive process.

It was enough.

The Gutter's body suddenly stiffened without his effort. He groaned weirdly, like a fish on a hook might do if it could make one.

The Sisters stepped out from their place of hiding. The Gutter fell to one side, his head at an angle staring up at them in disbelief. His confusion, however, was secondary to the sensations that were rifting through the internal parts of his physique. The crippling immanence of Whorefrost's sperm was doing its worst, feeling its way through the labyrinth of his anatomy. The Gutter squirmed like a maggot on a pinhead. Guttural sounds came from his throat. It appeared that he no longer possessed the vocal capacities to issue a scream.

"Well, well, well," said Little Sister. "What have we here?"

Big Sister rested an arm on her Sister's shoulder and said, "Well, blow me hard if it's not the little fucker who killed our Middle Sister, Sister."

Little Sister said: “You don’t fucking say.”

“Oh yes,” said Big Sister, “I fucking do.”

“In that case,” said Little Sister, “maybe we shouldn’t bother to explain what the fuck he’s eaten.”

“You mean the demon semen of that motherless fuck whose balls we clipped the other day?”

“That’s the one.”

“Naw,” said Big Sister, “I wouldn’t want to know if I was in his fucking position.”

“Right,” said Little Sister. “So let’s shut the fuck up and watch the fucker die like the fucker he is.”

Which is exactly what they did. And The Gutter didn’t disappoint them. He lasted for about three hours, as long as someone of his constitution would be expected to.

After it was done, Little Sister sighed and said, “So that’s that.”

Big Sister bowed her head and said, “So it was.”

“It was good to watch the bastard die so fucking horribly,” said Little Sister.

“Damn right,” said Big Sister. “It was the fucking best.”

“But,” sighed Little Sister, “I kind of feel it could’ve been better.”

Big Sister took her Little Sister in her arms, her eyes full of tears.

“I know,” she said, her voice no more than a whisper. “I know.”

3.
BleakWarrior Has Sex at a Price He Didn't Bargain For

The appeal of beauty was not the same as the appeal of wrinkled lips around a bloated cock or swollen nipple. The lips might have the look worms until they tightened into leeches when the mouth began to gnaw and suck on a rampant member. The cheeks grew gaunt. The face retracted into its skull in imitation of decay. It was a signal of submission to a symbolic death—but vaguely real for its emphasis on the transience of human form.

It is to be supposed that this is what forms part of the attraction of this particular species of sexual encounter: the simulation of death as ecstasy, where a sense of harm gives way to an orgasmic rancour that is somehow pleasing.

BleakWarrior was thinking about this as he slid his cock into the mouth of the Night Bitch whose beauty was negligible but whose face and body were faintly grotesque and, therefore, perfectly arousing. Beside her lay her parlour boy. He was naked except for the snakeskin shanks that rose to his thighs. He was slick with oil like some hominid fish, smearing his cock with a lubricant as if preparing himself to be served on a platter with lemon and herbs. His body was deliberately underweight in order to convey his selfless dedication to his erotic charges. His ribs stood out against his chest, thrown into relief by the alternating light that bloomed from the fire.

The purpose of the parlour boy was to assist the Night Bitch in providing additional pleasures to those included in her routine service. But it wasn't the kind of service that people had to pay for. The Night Bitch was an adept in a religious order whose major form of worship was sex. For her, sex was a religious rite in which she was able to establish a fleeting contact with the Godhead through the portal of the orgasm. BleakWarrior's cock was instrumental in invoking the passions required for gaining access to the portal and, to this extent, was a phallic symbol of literal worth—both sacred (as an object of reverence) and secular (for the significance of its biological function).

Portalitarianism was a delusion, of course, but BleakWarrior had to admit that it was a good one. It was viable in the sense that the experience of ecstasy was genuine instead of imagined, which is more than can be said for most examples of religious euphoria. Likewise, the combination of dogmatic fervour with sexual profligacy was extremely satisfying, which had nothing to do with its theological implications and more to do with the attention to detail it required of its practitioners.

The Night Bitch, certainly, knew how to use her deficiencies to her advantage, while the parlour boy knew how to eroticise his physique by making himself appear more feminine. He pouted his painted lips like a seasoned whore and immersed himself in an aura of submissiveness as if presenting himself on a platter to be fucked, which he was. BleakWarrior was keen to have them both. He withdrew his cock from the wormy lips of the Night Bitch. His mighty erection was rigid and fierce, like a hungry creature in need of succour. The parlour boy stared up at it with parting lips. The Night Bitch prepared to sit back and enjoy the spectacle.

And this is when the door smashed open and two of the Sons of Brawl barged in—numbers 44 and 36—with sneers on their faces that looked as if they would never be removed—and weapons in their hands that looked as if they would never be removed either—and a voice in their heads (that was not their own) that exhorted them to:

"Kill! Kill! Kill! Kill! Kill! Kill! Kill! Kill! Kill!"

And it was at that moment that Lord Brawl realised that he didn't want BleakWarrior to die. He wanted him to live—under his supervision, tied to a rack, or stretched across a bed of hot razors, or dangling from a set of hooks attached by long chains to the dripping roof of his most lurid dungeon.

"My Sons!" he cried, his words like blasts of lightning in the brain. "Show immediate restraint! For in my second thoughts I have ordained that the fiend who trashed your siblings now must live to endure my vengeance over gradual stages of decay."

The Sons of Brawl, who had begun their rush against their foe, were abruptly confused by their Father's order. They dithered in their motions to attack, whereupon BleakWarrior, naked and exposed to their onslaught, perceived himself without the Dirk.

All eyes, meanwhile, had been diverted from the parlour boy, who had deftly slid from his place on the divan towards the blazing hearth. From there, he plucked a poker from the grate and, honing every muscle of his fine young body, launched himself at 36. 36 received a heavy smack across the face and fell to the floor like an ornament falling off a table. The parlour boy rolled away and sprang to his feet to confront the second Bastard—

44 disarmed the parlour boy, grabbed him by his long dark hair, which had been conditioned to a brilliant sheen. He forced the parlour boy to his knees and said—

"It's time for this dripping maggot-featured fuck to come round to my way of thinking."

—and he drove his weapon, a one-handed pick, into the crown of the parlour boy's head.

Blood flowed from the wound like an overturned inkwell.

But the good thing was, BleakWarrior had been able to make a decisive lunge for the Dirk, which lay ensconced among his personal effects in a distant corner of the room. The remaining Bastard let the boy drop and readied himself for what was to come.

Number 44 was handy with his one-handed pick. He twirled it over his wrist like a circus performer, then tripped across the floor with a lightness of foot that was both elegant and threatening. Without warning, he whirled on his feet and staved the point of the one-handed pick into the eye of the Night Bitch. She had been sitting unnoticed on the divan, with her hands drawn up around her face, but not unnoticed enough to avoid the mindless fury of a Bastard Son of Brawl. The Night Bitch gave a solitary whimper and slipped to one side like a lowering flame.

44 removed the pick from her blasted eye and turned to face BleakWarrior. BleakWarrior had stationed himself like a wading bird. He was planning some kind of complex manoeuvre. The Bastard took the stance of a stalking cat. The two of them stood and stared at each other in silence.

And remained that way for at least an hour.

In the fire-lit dimness of the room, there was a distraction.

The stare of BleakWarrior met with the stare of the remaining Bastard like a fusion of particles. There was a sense in which, if the stare was broken, it would cause an explosion that would destroy the entire town.

In the meantime, the distraction was becoming increasingly noticeable, like a shadow cast by the light of the fire that was slowly acquiring the distinction of life.

But it wasn't a shadow. It was number 36 who, having been struck on the face by the parlour boy, was now regaining consciousness.

A flicker of triumph flashed across the face of number 44.

It was a signal for BleakWarrior to give up or take (depending on how you looked at it) the initiative.

Breaking the stare, BleakWarrior flipped his body at an angle that reduced the distance between himself and 44. 44 was wise enough to maintain his stance. BleakWarrior rushed him, then feinted. 44 swung his weapon in anticipation of deflecting or scoring a hit.

BleakWarrior wasn't there.

Instead, he had somersaulted over the resurgent form of 36 and landed near the dimming hearth. 36 made a noise like he was coughing up blood.

He was.

BleakWarrior had allowed the Dirk to puncture 36's chest as he passed over him; and, this time, the Bastard moved like a shadow cast from the light of the fire that was slowly acquiring the distinction of its violent death.

44 wheeled on his feet, still holding to his position of cautious readiness. It was clear that 44 was untypical of the hothead Sons of Brawl, who were ferocious fighters but vulnerable to the rashness of their temper.

BleakWarrior couldn't care less about the rashness of their temper. He scooped up a handful of embers from the fire and threw them at the remaining Bastard's face. 44 reeled, then righted himself quickly.

But not quick enough to prevent the Dirk from glancing the back of his thigh and severing his hamstring.

44 shrieked: his leg gave way.

And he was down.

Lord Brawl felt a screed of panic run through him from the veins of 44 like a fish before an ancient predator. He uttered a sob and fell to his knees on the battlements of his Folly. The slithering, crawling, hopping things that came to his abode looked up at him in insignificant wonder of his consummate distress.

Lord Brawl blundered like a loon, his eyes wide with

distant fury. His mind remained embedded in the mind of his Son through torrents of shock that threatened to break their neural intimacy. Terror and rage came to him in dizzying abundance. The presence of the Dirk hung over him as if he were there in person. Through the ears of 44, a voice came to him. He recognised it immediately as the foremost murderer of his Bastard offspring.

"Bastard Son of Brawl, prepare yourself for the blackness of your extinction. The Dirk lays waste to those who oppose our mission; and, though our mission is unknown to us, we have replaced its absent purpose with decisive aspirations of our own."

44 recoiled from the Dirk. His breath grew sour in anticipation of its blade across his throat. He opened his mouth to articulate a curse against his tormentor. But his will to speak was overturned by the will of his Father who spoke in his place (even in death, a Son of Brawl was disallowed the birth right of his self-determined action).

"Speak not to me of purposes, BleakWarrior. To tolerate suffering is our burden: yet we make of it our aim in life, which makes the aim of life worth living."

BleakWarrior marvelled at the Bastard's intellect, so much so that his suspicions were aroused.

"It is not for a Bastard Son of Brawl to speak like this," he said.

"You think us dull in the head because of our love of slaughter. And yet our intellect is steered by our Father's mental rein."

BleakWarrior narrowed his eyes.

"I know you to be dull in the head," he said, "because I have spilled your brains upon the streets and seen the lack of colour in them."

"Aye," said the Bastard, "and for this you will be disbanded—sinew by sinew, nerve by nerve."

"Your Father is bent on vengeance, then?"

"With all his heart."

"Then he furnishes himself with false purposes that are the basis of your ruin beneath the Dirk."

"His Sons are many to the point that your days are few."

"And all of this to satisfy a Father's vengeance?" BleakWarrior shook his head in disbelief. "We are Meta-Warriors, Bastard. Our emotional gratifications are extraordinary for their emptiness. Like mariners drinking cups of brine to quench our thirst, they make us mad."

"Madness, BleakWarrior, is what you are renowned for. For myself, I am inspired by the futility of my independent sufferings, which I mean to make your own."

"For yourself?" BleakWarrior gripped 44's throat and squeezed. "You are a mere Bastard," he snarled, "yet you speak with the authority of a Bastard's Father."

44 grinned through his obvious pain.

"Stay your hand," he rasped, "or yet again you risk the multiplication of my wrath."

BleakWarrior bore a look of indifference that was breathtaking for its lack of poignancy.

"If it is a contest of wrath you want, Lord Brawl, behold in me a more than willing foe."

Lord Brawl felt a sudden thrill of horror rising in the gorge of 44 as the Dirk expressed its opinion of him. He felt a blank expression of spent consciousness—a sense of nothingness more terrible than an awareness of the foulest pain.

44 was dead. BleakWarrior was no longer within range of his communication. Lord Brawl collapsed upon his battlements and gasped:

"BleakWarrior, my every thought is an avenue to my further pain. In the furtherance of myself I ask: is it for this that I was born—to go against the grain of my purposes in order to have none?

"The light in me diminishes. My sorrow burns. I increase my darkness to a blacker pitch of wondering, What am I, BleakWarrior? What am I, and *why?*"

My appraisal of my visitor has led me to conclude that he lives a sad and disorientated life and that his state of mind appears incapable of accommodating the philosophical subtleties that characterise our race.

In the meantime, I am led to believe that there are some among their number who are driven by certain addictions which they must feed in order to function properly (one, for example, who is required to feast on the guts of his victims in order to appease a nefarious hunger which, when satisfied, only perpetuates in him a need to eat more). This suggests that the basis for their cruelty is not wickedness, but that it is driven by a range of chronic appetites which are as natural to them as a common thirst, a hunger, sleep or sexuality.

All in all, I am led to suspect that Meta-Warriors are nothing less than a physical manifestation of inanimate states of Nature which have somehow acquired the efficacy of self-awareness which, in us, represents the essence of our difference from Nature.

And yet, there is something about them—which I have failed to grasp—which stands in contradistinction to whatever it is that we call Natural.

And, so, I am forced to consider that, in the end, our philosophical subtleties are incapable of accommodating them.

—The Private testimony of Achlana Promff,
Priestess of the Church of Nechmeniah

4. The Soliloquy of Lord Brawl

Lord Brawl is reeking of stupendous odours, which are his inheritance from the mire of his birth. Remembering little of those preconscious moments, they appear sporadically in dreams—*never* at will—and, when he wakes, he is even more disturbed by them than he already is.

By now, he is more than mad with the need to inflict suffering; but the need comes by degrees, depending on the importance of the victim.

Today, the need is magnified beyond its infinite number: the victim is Lord Brawl himself; and the importance rests, not with himself, but with the unthinkable loss of:

"*Seven dead sons!*"

The voice of Lord Brawl carries over the mirthful chattering of the many beasts that come from the leafy vastness of the woods, eager to explore the assorted scraps of carrion on offer. He stumbles, strides and reels upon the abortive battlements of his Folly. He flings his arms against the phantoms of his accumulating grief. It's as if he is undergoing the removal of stitches from mental wounds; but, slowly, his paroxysms subside into a dismal calm. He gazes over the many beasts who gather to eat.

And bids them listen.

"Come, my little friends, come hearken to your feast. No

dainty spoils are these, but the nutritious pulp of ages in the making—no truant scraps, but the microscopic parts of the unbreakable whole.

"Creation has wrought these properties and wrung them forth upon its table of wonders. Time has fashioned them from the industry of chance. Random variations of biochemical growth are from a single principle drawn disparately to the fore. Yet the illusion persists—and is the basis of our relations with Nature—that the material separateness of solid forms is the mark of an absolute difference between them.

"You, my little friends, harbour no such recreant thoughts: for well you know, in your unknowing, that when the body falls the clay resorts to a general matter. You, my little friends, are actors in this statement of finality; I, in turn, am its orator.

"Alas, these scattered fragments that ornament the lawns of my abode are not the rich pickings of Nature's estate; nor do they represent the enormity of our total measure. The distinctive parts of carcasses are mere abstractions of the whole, for which these linear examples are too abruptly shorn from the limbs of time. The undoing of their physique is easier, then, than the undoing of the spatial kind, whose *doing* is the result of more impressive confluences.

"Aye, those wastrels, cannoning loose through the unloved silences of space, whose effects are the objects of greater causes, and who are immune to the predetermined courses of decrepitude you nibble on now. Their insuperable resistance to the passive strokes of annihilation must be met with the aim of active plots—to wit, the application of my will is a pronouncement on their doom.

"That it was weaned, my will, on the fleshy saps of the pit, enriched with carnal infestations, so that Lord Brawl arose from the molten life-stuffs, his current mood the product of the strife he did endure with gladdened agony. The tolerable limits of desire were breached and the amorphous thrill of wretchedness absorbed to points of literal clarity.

"Clearly, then, the effects of an almighty suffering inundate the passage of my being, defining my very ideas on life. My intemperance pays homage to my pain and my pain pays homage to my passion for pain. Manifold pain, therefore, divides me from a standard core of emotions that are to my torrential sorrow a slight convergence of smaller streams.

"But my gluttony, as such, is no mere greed, jealously guarded with an indifference towards the plight of others. I make it my aim to share the torments that I hold so well, and to distribute the pain that is my pleasure in life.

"There is no atonement for the torments I have suffered, no unravelling the strings of my humiliation, no restraints upon the resources of my protracted grief, no solace but for the pressing need to murder the murderer of my seven dead sons."

Lord Brawl scrawled a signature of odium on the air itself, and sighed.

"BleakWarrior, most despised, you will adhere to new extremes of bleakness. The map of your significance will be redrawn to the level of dirt. Realise now the spoiling of your marrows, hapless Metaphobe. The House of Brawl prepares itself in order to prevail.

"The replacement of our loss requires the erasure of its causes. Strength does not make vows but merely gains. Our collective grief must bleed itself to a drier consequence of sorrow. BleakWarrior must perish by the foulest means at my disposal; and you, my little friends, will find him strewn in little bits across your lawn."

5.
Conversations with a Physician

Middle Sister was being kept in cold storage in the City of Praxis under the supervision of a physician who specialised in reanimation techniques and cryogenic preservation.

Most of what he had to say (even The Sisters knew this) was total bullshit.

However:

"You get the picture," Little Sister had told him. "Now tell us what we have to do or else you die."

"That's right," said Big Sister, craning an arm around his neck. "And, if you don't, you're going to end up in one of your own cryogenic vats."

"And no one—and I mean *no one*—is going to fucking reanimate *you*," said Little Sister.

"That's right," said Big Sister, "cause you're the reanimation expert, and if *you* die, consider yourself truly fucked beyond recovery."

The physician's eyes flashed from one Sister to the other. His terror was impressive for someone so used to dealing in death.

"I can't say for sure," he gibbered. "I'm sorry."

"No need to apologise," said Little Sister.

"No," said Big Sister, "no need to apologise at all."

"All we want to know is, how the fuck do we get our Middle Sister back?"

"And, if we don't get her back," said Big Sister, "you're going to end up in one of your own cryogenic vats. I mean, how many times do I have to say that before it becomes fucking true?"

"She needs—" Began the physician, who could hardly speak for fear—"She needs to be restored with something much more powerful than anything I've tried. The human feeds have proven useless."

"So tell me, Doctor, what the fuck *haven't* you tried?"

"Well," he stammered, his lips quivering like the wings of moths. "I haven't tried you."

The Sisters of No Mercy embarked on a programme of donating various parts of their body until there was very little left to donate that wouldn't kill them.

"It's not enough," said the physician, marvelling over his gauges with eyes like moons through giant spectacles. "There has been a response—yes—a definite response." He nodded with too-much enthusiasm. "Her body temperature has increased, but . . ."

"But what?"

"The reactions are slight. She needs more of you than you can give—much more."

"Well," said Big Sister, "she can't get much more of me. I mean, I don't even have a fucking spleen left."

"Me neither," said Little Sister.

"So what the fuck are we going to do?"

"Doctor," said Little Sister, tightening up her face and thinking hard. "Given what you know of us—given what I told you—and given the fact that you won't tell anyone else—*ever*—" The physician nodded frantically—"I would like to ask you if you are really fucking sure about what you told me yesterday."

"It stands to reason," said the physician.

"What does?" said Big Sister.

"That the administration of hazardous chemicals produces contradictory conditions of regenerative influx. That which kills you gives you life." The physician smiled.

"What the fuck are you talking about?" said Big Sister, who was both disgusted and bewildered by her lack of knowing what the fuck they were talking about.

"Hair of the Dog," declared the physician.

"Fucking what?"

"The action of applying something in order to gain the opposite effect," explained the physician. Badly.

Big Sister stared at him with an implacable face and said, "Fucking what?"

"Negative Biological Stimulus," he said. "It's how I reanimate the, uh, ordinary humans when the normal methods of regeneration fail to take effect. The risks are great, or would be in the case of live specimens. But, in the case of the dead, the risks are negligible." He gave a nervous laugh and stared up at Big Sister with the face of a boy expecting a slap. "It's the only thing I can think of," he said, swallowing hard.

"I think I haven't the first idea what you're fucking talking about," said Big Sister, turning to Little Sister and saying: "I haven't the first idea what this little fucker is talking about."

"Tell her better," said Little Sister, staring at the physician with eyes like death knells.

"Well," stammered the physician, "it's a matter of applying a cogent set of scientific principles but in reverse—such as enriching the wombs of barren women by feeding them with rotten eggs, or swallowing a scorpion to cure a stomach ulcer—such as they do on the Isle of Smir."

"Forgive me, Doctor," said Big Sister, "but if you don't get to the fucking point, I'm going to fucking stick you on one."

"What the good Doctor is trying to say," said Little Sister, "is that it's possible to create a cure out of something that ordinarily does you damage."

"Right!" said the physician, hurriedly. "The venom of

snakes will kill you when you're bitten, yes? But to mix a placebo from the venom of snakes will make you well."

"Or so the theory goes," said Little Sister.

"Yes," said the physician. "But, in your case, and from what I have learned from our in depth conversations of yesterday night, I believe it's possible to restore your Sister with bodily extracts taken from other members of your species which, under normal circumstances, would certainly be the death of you."

"Fucking what?" said Big Sister.

"He means that we need to get as much of the most destructive bodily parts of our fucking enemies as possible so we can bring them here to be used as feeds for our Middle Sister, Sister."

Big Sister scowled.

"This is one crazy fucker of a theory," she said.

"It stands to reason," said the physician.

"Yeah," said Big Sister, "but how does it stand in practice?"

"Uh . . ." The physician was caught off-guard.

"In practice," said Little Sister, "it's never been tried on people like us. But in linear terms, the failures outweigh the successes by a significant margin."

"How significant?"

"The principle is sound!" cried the physician.

The Sisters of No Mercy stared at him in some surprise. Little Sister nodded and said, "Good for you, Doctor."

"Fucking good," said Big Sister.

The physician mewled and backed off, wisely.

"Right, Sister," said Little Sister, now looking her Sister in the eye and adding: "So what do you think?"

"About what?"

"Our plan."

"What plan?"

"This plan."

"I haven't the first idea what you're talking about."

"I'm talking about a mission, Sister."

"What mission?"

"To get the bodily parts of more like us."

"More like us?"

"Yes."

"But we're unique, Sister. There are no more like us."

"I don't mean more like *us*. I mean more like us but worse."

"Worse?"

"Much worse."

"How much worse?"

"The worst of the worst."

"But we're the worst, Sister. We're worse than fucking all of them."

"That's not what I mean, Sister."

"What do you mean?"

"I mean a mission."

"What mission?"

"A mission in life to give our Middle Sister some."

"But I thought we were bent on getting revenge."

"We are, Sister, don't you worry."

"OK, then," said Big Sister, folding her arms, "so where do we start."

"We start by paying a little visit to the Covenant of Ichor. And then we're going to make a list. And then we're going to plot a course of all-out fucking mayhem, Sister, with us as navigators."

"You mean like a ship?"

"A death ship, yes."

"OK," said Big Sister, not really sure if she'd caught the drift. "Then what?"

"And then we're going to take our revenge," said Little Sister.

And Big Sister was silent for a moment, and said, "OK."

This all happened over a year ago and The Sisters of No

Mercy had only a single testicle to show for their pains, having used the other to dissolve The Gutter's innards from the inside out as a means of securing their vengeance against him.

"It's a really fucking powerful testicle, though," suggested Big Sister.

"Be that as it may," said Little Sister, "it's not enough. We need more."

"Let's go get it, then, Sister, because there's the fucker over there."

Big Sister raised a hand. Little Sister followed it.

They saw a figure dressed in a grey robe who looked like a pilgrim slipping through the door of a stairwell that was half-ajar and, for the City of Honours, strangely lacking in fresh paintwork. The figure glanced behind it, took a quick sniff and pulled the door shut.

"Fuck," said Little Sister.

"Fuck what?"

"That fucking door," said Little Sister. "Let's go."

The Sisters of No Mercy crossed the busy avenue of Grim Street, zigzagging between a pandemonium of carriages and horse drawn gigs that rattled like sticks in a box being dropped from a great height. When they got to the door of the building the figure had entered, they found it shut, and locked, which prompted Little Sister to say:

"I fucking knew it."

But Big Sister was already looking up and down the street with an eye as keen as a nocturnal predator.

"Up there," she said, pointing towards a gap—a lane—in the giant wall of facades. "Let's see where it takes us, Sister. Come on."

Little Sister gritted her teeth and, following her Sister, went to see where the lane would take them.

6. BleakWarrior Takes the Toll

He came to me with blood on his hands and said, "This is the way it happens sometimes—as if everything is drawn by a magnetic impulse of desires and needs that culminate at some ultimate point of devastation. Forces are at work that exceed the physical boundaries of the bodies that produce them—forces that expand through a metaphysical or electrostatic physical route. In a sense, it's like a reversal of the trans-organic properties created by neural networks or brain cells, which supersede the limitations of their organic containment and are able to convey their emergence through an external, rather than internal, source of generated energy. Or maybe it's something else—perhaps the force of desire taking root as a volcanic pressure that resolves itself through an outward manifestation of ultra-violence that concludes itself on a massive scale of singular eruption."

—From The Private Testimony of Achlana Promff, Priestess of the Church of Nechmeniah.

The acid was jettisoned in twin trails from Burn Freak's

breasts. Breasts that were not round or globular but aggressively formed, with nipples stiff as teeth that would chew them.

Teeth that had.

Teeth that had ground her nipples to a rawer stiffness, with a rapacious indelicacy and superabundance of carnal lust that made her . . .

So angry she was ecstatic.

They lapped her saps—men, women, animals, anything—the preparatory excretions of gluttonous sweetness that swathed her nipples in a thin veneer of protective resins.

Then, with deliberate muscular applications, she would launch her underlying solutions into their yearning mouths, with a projectile inevitability that sent them sprawling, first, in a stupor of shock and, second, into a ridiculous fit of serious agony.

"Some agonies are more serious than others," she would giggle like the girl who'd never grown up.

"Whaaa! Waaaah!" is all they'd reply.

"That's *exactly* what I mean!" cried Burn Freak, clasping her hands together like she'd received some tawdry gift from a secret admirer.

Mouths and teeth and tongues fizzled like fried organs—the gullet awash with bloody foams and the emulsifications of oral features. Faces collapsed like inadequate morphologies, withdrawing into the redundant posture of their skulls, like water receding in the aftermath of widespread flooding. It was an aesthetic spectacle to be studied closely: the thawing tissue—the eventual sag of the jawbone—the evacuation of organic materials from their residences of bone.

Seductions like this were lifestyle choices—frivolous encounters with the arts and sciences. Combat, however, was a more exacting pastime, where choice gave way to the requirements of necessity.

And, because of that, it was more exhilarating—watching

enemies dance to the tune of avoidance, as she propelled her streams of acid at them.

Like BleakWarrior was doing now.

The City of Honours was among the dullest in the whole of the continental mainland.

Its streets were aligned in a grid work of square-shaped buildings that intersected with an architectural exactness that was over-symmetrical and stunningly bland. The streets were also clean and spacious, like rivers that flowed with a flat veneer of marble slabs, polished to an insipid pitch of whiteness and wholly lacking the natural beauty of their mineral roughness. And the buildings, too, were clean and spacious, with brickwork dressed to an excessive sheen of mottled sterility—blending in with the pavements, steps, arched and pillared entrances, the lacklustre monuments, the architraves and austere doors, and the shapeless decor of stilted rows of costumiers, ladies' boutiques and pretentious eateries.

The populace of linear humans were equally measured to a point of stifling neatness that was almost obscene. Their garb was restrained but luxurious, skilfully tailored to fit their over-abundant physiques with uncomfortable precision. Their uniform manners were blatantly false and barely concealed their mutual awareness of each other's dubiety and thinly-veiled conceits. The clamour of respectability was founded on paper-thin promises and business agreements that were effectuated through cunning or naivety rather than trust. It was all handshakes and bows and superficial facial expressions—the public face of political and social power-mongering which, for all its unethical gratuity, was accomplished with unshakable politeness.

Even the air itself, pristine to a point of unhealthy clarity, was laden with perfumery and the aromatic evidences of prodigal repasts—the soiled breath, insufficiently freshened with dental ointments, of the overly rich.

What chance of detecting an invigorating potency of bodily odours in this?

And yet, there were definite wafts of an animal flavour—an innumerable cache of glandular essences that pervaded the chemical contagion of manufactured scents like a pollen.

And like a pollen, each essence contained a glut of information that could be separated into general categories of men and women hungering after sex and wealth and positions of influence—the damp knickers of scheming dowagers; the seedy arrogance of the politically ordained; the wet cocks of bosses withdrawn from the mouths of secretaries; the smear of tongues on the genitalia of young careerists; the fresh ejaculations of social aspirants over the hairy buttocks of their peers.

The Gland Master let the air flow into his nostrils like a demonic possession and began to decipher each individual signature with a scrupulous take on every detail.

He was looking for something.

And as he angled his nose to acquire a more abundant rush of outstanding smells, he found it: the bitter tang of violence underpinned by powerful secretions of rage and sexual misadventure.

Strange, however, how it didn't appear to issue from the streets.

Stranger still, how it seemed to issue from . . .

The rooftops were tiled with deep grey slates that allowed for a decent foothold, in spite of the troublesome tilt of their surface inclination.

BleakWarrior struggled to acquire a sense of balance as Burn Freak rounded on him like a laughing animal enjoying the delimited actions of its prey.

"Come sup at the springs of my deadly paps—my womanly volcanoes—whose chemical stuffs are the basis of your abysmal ruin."

BleakWarrior spat a reply and, finally, drew his Weapon of Choice—the Dirk. It sang with an appeal to the need for its immediate use. But Burn Freak was restricting him to a precarious evasion of her concentrated rancour.

She let fly her shafts of vitriol, her bodice torn aside to reveal the acrimonious mouldings of her Weapons—her Breasts—which were not large, but anatomically consonant with their use as instruments of liquid assault. Her ribs formed struts upon her skin as if to support their strategic posture. Her skin itself was flush with a multitude of excitements, which apparently consisted of sexual as well as violent arousal.

BleakWarrior eluded her inconstant powerful blasts, attentive to the splashes and streaks of their lethal trajectory. He coerced his body with spasmodic movements that required a sustained mental alertness to the ejaculations of each draught.

Obligatory defensive measures are often a precursor for withdrawal. But BleakWarrior's underlying madness compelled him to seek a means for his retaliation which, for all his unending repositioning of himself, was beyond the circumstances of the encounter. Escape (he allowed himself to recognise the fact) was necessary as a matter of course.

He manoeuvred himself towards the edge of the roof in preparation for a Random Leap, the progress of which was coincident with the sudden appearance of a figure dressed in rustic garments that marked him out as some kind of pilgrim.

He wasn't.

The newcomer was armed with metallic utensils which he slammed with impressive force into either side of Burn Freak's head (she was too busy with BleakWarrior to have noticed his arrival).

"Ah for the joy of your excrescences!" he cried, letting Burn Freak's body wilt like an elapsing stalk of grass under an oncoming gale.

The Gland Master withdrew his utensils—two spoons

forged around their edges to the sharpness of razors. His smile, when offered, was far from cordial. It was the smile of a desire for retributions which were as natural to Meta-Warriors as the impulse to breathe among their linear counterparts.

"Next, please!"

The Gland Master turned to confront BleakWarrior, who had already abandoned his footing on the inclination of the rooftop.

And by the time The Gland Master was anywhere near him, BleakWarrior was falling onto the monotonous solidity of the marble slabs on the streets below.

The Gland Master wore a look on his face like he'd received a slap.

"And yet," he remarked, "why dwell upon failure when the pleasures of my success are forthcoming?"

The Gland Master turned his attentions to the sprawling body of Burn Freak, which was interesting. There was substantial leakage from her nipples, which would have to be avoided; and, naturally, The Gland Master would be wise to leave her mammary glands well alone (more's the pity). Those of the neck, the armpits and the regions of the groin, however, could be explored with an habitual thoroughness for their fine array of exotic flavours.

The Gland Master went to work on them using his Razor Spoons, ousting them skilfully from their fleshy enclosures. He fondled them for their succulent warmth and prepared to suck them dry of their nutritious juices. His lips and teeth were well-adapted to the task of gripping them with a leech-like firmness that allowed him to extract their fluids without accruing waste.

Before long, The Gland Master had littered the roof with about half of Burn Freak's withered organs. The remaining glands would suffice for later in the day. In the meantime, he stretched himself on the angle of the roof and, with his belly as full as a pothole after a heavy downpour, inclined himself to rest.

But as he basked in the heat of the afternoon sun, he became aware of a significant whiff of organic corruption which he immediately identified as a lingering trace of roasted flesh.

"Of course!" he cried, and sprang to his feet in a fit of urgency. "I'll be back for you later—" He pointed a finger at the remains of Burn Freak. "Don't go away!"

Having secured the Spoons in their specially adapted sheaths, The Gland Master hastened to the edge of the roof and, with due consideration, flung himself off in the direction of the cauterized particles.

As he collided with the marble slabs, the atomic composition of his body realigned itself to the transition. He located the Intersecting Differentials of inverted matter where the roasted flesh had secreted its chemical profusion.

And followed it like a spark through darkness, in thrall to the source of the flame itself.

The Gland Master would have counted himself lucky if he'd known; or unlucky, depending on whether or not he'd have fancied his chances.

One thing's for sure—he'd have fancied them.

Within moments of his Leap, two rogue females—one tall and thin, the other robust and small of stature—climbed out of a skylight onto the roof, where they were initially disappointed by what they discovered.

"So where the fuck is the gland thief?" said the tall one.

"Fucked if I know," the small one said.

"And just who the fuck is this?" The tall one prodded the body of Burn Freak with an outstretched toe.

"That," said the small one, "is Burn Freak."

"Hmmm," said the tall one, "not anymore."

"Absolutely fucking not," said the small one, now bending over the slaughtered body to take a good look. "Hmmm," she said, nodding cryptically, "looks like her glands have been ripped from her body like peas from a pod."

"That's right, Sister. And I do so like your use of metaphors."

"Thanks. Still, though, all is not lost."

Big Sister frowned. "It's not?"

"No. Observe, for example, the plundered portions of her womanly form—"

"OK."

"—and note how the most outstanding parts of her womanly form have been left untouched."

"I think I'm having trouble following you, Sister."

"Watch."

Little Sister delved into a leather bag she carried over her shoulder on a leather strap and produced an alchemical container like the one they'd used to transport Whorefrost's testicles.

"Sister," said Big Sister. "I've got to say I'm fucking intrigued."

Little Sister smiled and, bending over the mutilated corpse of Burn Freak, began siphoning the remaining contents of her Breasts into the alchemical container.

"Acid," she explained.

"Fuck!" said Big Sister. "What the fuck am I thinking? There are times, Sister, when my brain should be removed from my head and injected with an intelligence solution, then put back into my head, folded up inside my skull, and told to pay the biggest fuck of attention to everything."

"Hmmm . . . ," said Little Sister.

"But hey, Sister," said Big Sister, "this is a really great unexpected fucking boon, is it not, finding this blood-addled whore like this?"

"Not *that* unexpected, Sister."

"No?"

"Absolutely not."

"How come?"

"Because I knew she was here or here abouts."

"You did?"

"Yes."

"How come?"

"Well, you remember two days ago when you were drunk and I had to carry you home?"

"Not really, no."

"Well, I was carrying you home and I heard a Free Trader of Interest talking about a couple of corpses they'd found of people with their faces burnt off. So I figured that somebody of a unique disposition had to be responsible for shit like that one. So I checked the hit list and, lo and behold, there's a reasonably accurate description of this fucking bitch right here on the Log of Ultimate Death."

"She's on the Log of Ultimate Death?"

"Yup."

"Excellent," said Big Sister; and then added: "But hey, I wish you'd keep me fully informed of what the fuck is going on around here, Sister."

"Are you kidding? You've got a mouth on you like a fucking fog horn. I'll tell you when I want the world to know, Sister of mine."

Big Sister folded her arms and tapped her foot, shaking her head in little bursts of incredulity. Finally, she sighed and said, "I'm hungry."

Little Sister shrugged and carefully manipulated the nipples of Burn Freak so as to avoid getting her fingers doused in the devastating hyperplasms.

"Nice tits," she said, angling her head so she could take a good look.

"Very nice," Big Sister agreed. "But fucking lethal when it comes to sex."

"Yeah, well, that's kind of the whole point, Sister."

"Yeah, well, they're not so fucking nice, then, are they?"

"Not as nice as ours."

"Not as nice as ours at all."

"I mean, not that you really have any."
"I don't have any tits worth a fuck, Sister."
"I wouldn't say that. I think they're really worth fucking."
"That's because you fucking have."
"And with pleasure."
"Not with as much pleasure as I get from fucking yours."
"Maybe. But I like it like that."
"And I fucking like it that you like it like that."
"Later, Sister, I'll remind you of just how much I like it like that."
"And I'll remind you of just how much I like it that you like it like that."
"You will?"
"Yup."
"Where?"
"Here."
"On the fucking roof?"
"Why the fuck not?"
"Then we're agreed."
"Damn fucking right we're agreed. When the fuck have we never agreed on anything?"
Little Sister squeezed Burn Freak's nipples to the very last drop, filling the alchemical container to about half its total capacity.
"We're getting good at this kind of thing," remarked Little Sister when the task was done.
"Fucking right we are."
"But not good enough."
"Not fucking good enough at all."
"Nothing can ever be *that* good."
"No," said Big Sister. "We can only dream."
"And make our dreams a reality."
"Reality, Sister, is what we were fucking born for."

The Skitten Heights of Fiddith Fa consisted of a broad range of flat-topped hillocks divided by stark ravines where vegetation was sparse and the geology arid. Rainfall was untypical but not uncommon. But when it happened, the rain was soaked up with a scant regard for the extent of its downpour: and the Skitten Heights were equally voracious when soaked with blood.

The overall aspect of the Skitten Heights was of an orange duskiness that formed a half-luminous hue that invested the barrenness of the terrain with a soothing radiance that was entirely deceptive.

The Skitten Heights were dangerous.

But the dangers pertained less to the environmental hardships of the landscape than to a nomadic order of linear banditry who called themselves The Toll.

There were five of The Toll riding now over the brow of a long escarpment, dressed in lizard-skin helmets and multi-coloured robes, with thick, wiry beards bouncing over their chests like small monkeys.

"There," said one. "Towards the Hill of Banes."

The others pulled their muskins to a standstill and looked.

"Strange," remarked another. "He appears to be travelling alone and on foot."

"That'll make it all the easier for us to extract our dues."

"But if he is without transport, he will surely be without means."

"Then our dues will be received in blood, as is our custom."

And the five members of The Toll guided their muskins towards the Hill of Banes, where a lone figure stood in calm defiance of their approach, which was something The Toll were decidedly unused to in the attitude of strangers.

During the timeless immersions of a Random Leap—dissolving with atomic ease through vaster portions of material compactness—BleakWarrior was prone to having visions, none of which coincided with any rational degree of making sense.

They did, however, coincide with madness.

These visions alerted BleakWarrior to the secondary condition of his exposure to the chaos contained by the material order of linear physicality, which may or may not have been more real than his presence within the linear constraints of space and time. The feeling was one of an existential inside-outness, where neither condition was "in" nor "out" but juxtaposed to extremes of incompleteness which were not, however, wholly detached from one another.

Sometimes, during these moments of vision, BleakWarrior engaged in conversations with his mentor, The Bard, who had lured him from the origins of madness and settled his mind with cups of wine and the liberal use of his youthful cupbearers.

" . . . a class of being converted, much as you have been, to the physical orientations of the mind and body."

"And for what purposes other than to suffer the indignities of their confusion?"

"Why attend to matters of confusion when the activity of battle beckons?

"What battles are these?"

"Battles requiring the abolition of yourself from the universal tableaux."

"You lose me in the embroidery of your speech, old man."

"Speech is for speakers. I require of you the controlled release of your madness from its illimitable torpor."

"I will work foremostly as you ordain—and to a better understanding of who and what I am."

"You are the refinement of your component parts, redrawn to the rawer gradations of your psychological trauma."

"But this is not enough for me to say *I know*."

"Knowledge runs counter-wise to the thrill of life, BleakWarrior. Remember that, as you go upon your weary way."

"Then I will go along my way and *see*."

"Seeing is for seers. I request of you your blind adherence to furious undertakings."

"Then I will see to it with a blind adherence to your will, which is the basis of my recovery from the thralls of madness."

"I believe you will," intoned The Bard, "and, with equal measure, believe that you will not."

BleakWarrior emerged in spools of dust from the parched earth of the Skitten Heights and adjusted himself to a linear plenum. It was then that he felt the pain of the wounds he'd received on his arm and thigh—the corrosive dashes aimed at him of Burn Freak's nihilistic milks.

But it was nothing of any concern to a veteran of bloody struggles such as he.

What was, however, was the approach of five men riding muskins over the brow of a long escarpment, who BleakWarrior recognised immediately as graduate members of The Toll.

The five members of The Toll rounded on BleakWarrior with caution and without haste. It was possible that BleakWarrior's impassive reaction to their arrival had unnerved them. And, to this extent, they showed their experience as men accustomed to extending a hostile rather than hearty welcome.

"Well, then," ventured one, as they drew their muskins to a stumbling halt. "Who crosses the Skitten Heights pays The Toll. What items do you bring to honour our custom?"

BleakWarrior made no answer. He stared, not at them, but into the distance as if they were trees, merely, obscuring his vision.

"Ho, traveller. Are you new to these parts? Have you not heard of The Toll and the rites of passage attending to their domain?"

"Look at his eyes," said one, who now perceived the Warped Lenses glinting in the dimming light of day. "Ho, stranger. Are those jewels you wear for eyes? They will suffice for dues if you lack the means to pay your levy."

"I have nothing to give," said BleakWarrior, and drew the Dirk. "But much to offer."

The Toll allowed themselves a moment to consider the stranger's audacity. Then one of them said, "The man is mad. I say we take him alive and bury him up to the neck for the crows to pick at his eyes when we have divested them of their ornamentation."

"Agreed," declared another.

The five members of The Toll dismounted from their muskins and drew their weapons—not swords, but heavy wooden batons appropriate for the live capture of a custom-breaker.

In unison, they fell upon BleakWarrior with a perfunctory malice.

BleakWarrior stood his ground.

The Dirk stood firmer.

The Gland Master didn't engage in Random Leaps but in Leaps of Cynosure. In other words, he possessed an uncommon ability to navigate the maze of IDs in ways that other Meta-Warriors, in general, could not.

BleakWarrior was one of the ones who could not.

The Gland Master, however, followed the traces of burnt flesh through the Intersecting Differentials of the planet's interior until, soon, he perceived the approach of a node. Other smells then came to his attention: the smell of fear, adrenalin and the breathless excitement that signifies combat.

The Gland Master emerged right in the thick of it, his body reforming as an organic whole among batons that flew to the left and right of him as he adjusted himself to the melee. He slipped his Spoons from their specially adapted sheaths and whirled among the members of The Toll like a nervous disorder. Above the furore, he could hear the sound of the Dirk as it deflected the impetus of meted blows with staunch reposts.

"Together, BleakWarrior," he cried over the stress of his efforts, "we will eliminate our antagonists. And then—"

The Gland Master embedded a Spoon in the forehead of one of The Toll. The man fell with the rigidness of a tombstone.

"And then," cried BleakWarrior, "the Dirk compels you to converse."

BleakWarrior was inspired by the arrival of a more hated adversary—so much so that the Dirk began to carry the fight to the linear aggressors, who were adept as fighters but wholly lacking the quality of rage. And, soon enough, their wounds were numerous enough to disable the effectiveness of their assault; and the Dirk and Spoons laid waste to them with definite measures.

BleakWarrior and The Gland Master stood back at a distance from one another, panting heavily and dripping blood, sizing each other up for weaknesses they didn't have, like wholesale distributors of mourning.

"You want to converse, you said," said The Gland Master with a faint trail of a smile across his lips.

"I have a question for you, hated foe," said BleakWarrior.

"A *question?*" The Gland Master spoke the word like he was issuing a curse. "And you expect me to answer it?"

"To answer it—" BleakWarrior made a melancholic gesture with his hand—"or die."

"Ha!" scoffed The Gland Master. "You think I'm going to bend to your will like some whore to the measure of your cock?"

"The question is not mine alone."

The Gland Master spat on the ground and snarled:

"Ask it, then, and be done with you. My Spoons are ever-anxious for your blood, as I am for your glands."

BleakWarrior ignored the taunts and said, "Wielder of spoons, I wish to know the answer to the question: what are we and why? I petition you for guidance, or for whatever knowledge you possess, or for suggestions you might offer me where bolder forms of truth are lacking."

The Gland Master raised his head on the end of his neck and scowled.

"What miserable piece of rot is this?" he said.

"The kind that requires a simple and specific answer," said BleakWarrior.

The scowl of The Gland Master transformed into a mocking smile.

"What makes you think I care?" he said, as if with pride.

"I'm not asking you to care," said BleakWarrior.

"You miss the point," said The Gland Master. "I choose not to care because I don't want to know." The Gland Master shook his head and grinned like the main feature of a freak show. "I enjoy my glands, BleakWarrior, and wouldn't have it any other way in life."

BleakWarrior eyed The Gland Master with a defeated look which, slowly, was accumulating into rage.

"How can you *not* want knowledge?" he said, through hardly parting lips.

"Because I know I'll never get it," said The Gland Master.

"Then you will perish beneath the knowledge of the Dirk," said BleakWarrior, "whose scorn for you is well-informed with visions of your termination."

"Lay on, BleakWarrior, and tarry with my Spoons for all your glands are worth my leaking."

With bodies strewn between them, The Gland Master and BleakWarrior prepared themselves for a more demanding encounter. A dusty vortex meandered across the surface of the Hill of Banes.

And then they began.

A member of the Toll had seen from a distance the destruction of his fellow members and was watching in subdued wonder (members of The Toll were not given to displays of over-excitement) as the killers—two of them—began a violent struggle between themselves.

"In the name of the Great Thirst, who are these people?"

But he didn't stop to give an answer. Instead, he turned his muskin and headed in haste to the nearest encampment.

The Toll must learn of these custom-breakers, who had violated every rule of *The Ancient Rote of Tongues*.

The Gland Master considered the possibility that his reach had exceeded his grasp for the day.

BleakWarrior was getting the better of him.

The flash of the Dirk was a sinister streak of punishment that defied the methodology of the Spoons with its preposterous cohesion. The Gland Master applied himself to a different technique; but the Spoons were forced to work tirelessly against the dizzying array of angles and thrusts accomplished by the Dirk.

A question occurred to The Gland Master as he backed away from the unmitigated madness of a fiend who'd attained his uttermost pitch of battle mania.

"Was it wise of me to have departed so readily the unfinished bounty of Burn Freak's glands . . . ?"

No, he thought, it certainly wasn't.

With an unexpected fleetness of foot, The Gland Master turned and ran from the Dirk's ingressions upon his person. The tactic was a good one. BleakWarrior was befuddled by its suddenness and too much in the throes of madness to respond with the obvious countermeasure of giving chase.

But not for long.

"Return at once!" cried BleakWarrior. "Return at once and face the interrogations of the Dirk!"

Which only inspired The Gland Master to run all the faster towards a crag he had in mind for his evacuation from the scene . . . reaching it sparingly and casting himself from its propitious height. He hit the ground with a smooth disintegration of his molecular form and function . . . and proceeded to retrace the malodorous trail that had led him from the City of Honours, where Burn Freak's glands awaited his pleasure of finishing them off.

Big Sister had lifted her calfskin skirt over the stanchions of her thighs and now straddled, rubbed, gyrated and smeared herself over the rotundity of Little Sister's breasts. Her juices oozed over Little Sister's nipples. The nipples were stiff as knuckles in the aftermath of a fist-fight. The oily softness of Big Sister's minge was reaching a point where fisting itself might be an option.

In the meantime, the mutual exchange of their moans and gasps was all-encompassing. So much so that, when The Gland Master crawled from the skylight, they were too engrossed in the midst of their embrace to notice his arrival.

Until he said, "Delightful emissions, my dears, for which I will receive my enrichment for the day—if not for the entire week!"

Big Sister rolled off Little Sister's upper body. The two of them stared. With their Weapons discarded at an unreasonable distance, their faces wore the look of kittens bundled into a sack, filled with stones and thrown into a river.

The Gland Master drew the Spoons from their specially adapted sheaths and prepared to exterminate them quickly and efficiently in accordance to his preferred methodology.

"Sister, fuck. He's going to eat our fucking glands!"

Big Sister scrambled away from his oncoming form—uselessly—which made him laugh. The Spoons were raised like pincers ready to strike. The Gland Master's head stood out on the end of its neck like a creature after carrion.

Which made it an easy target for the contents of the alchemical container which Little Sister now flung in his face—Burn Freak's acid—which hissed and spat and sizzled like a receding tide.

The Gland Master bellowed like a cow in a snake pit. He

let the Spoons drop as he clutched and clawed and scraped at his face, which fell away in his hands like the skin of a heavily soused tuber.

"Don't let him fall!" cried Little Sister.

And Big Sister didn't. She grabbed The Gland Master and stuck a knee in his back, then threw him over the peak of the roof like a sack of beans. In the meantime, Little Sister had retrieved the Long Sword; Big Sister retrieved the Short Sword.

"The fucker must die!" cried Big Sister.

"But not too quickly!" cried Little Sister.

"Not too fucking quickly at all!"

And the people on the streets of the City of Honours ran in panic, screamed and stood transfixed as a mangle of body parts rained among them, slapping hard against the marble slabs, and spilling their blood in ribbons over the insipid whiteness.

BleakWarrior descended into the crevice where he hoped to find a stream to satisfy his drooth after the fruitless exertions of the day.

There was a dried up trail of sand that might have been a stream at certain times of the year, but this wasn't one of them.

BleakWarrior sat on a rock in the orange haze of the dimming sun and considered the full extent of his misery.

It ran long and deep as the stream that wasn't there.

Then there came a sound, like moving earth, which BleakWarrior at first mistook for an outward manifestation of physical and mental fatigue; but its continuation suggested otherwise.

No longer ignoring it, BleakWarrior looked up at the Hill of Banes and saw about a dozen members of The Toll come galloping over its broad ridge on muskins whose pace was cumbersome but unrelenting in the manner of stones.

BleakWarrior smiled wanly and said, "With fullest

recourse to my wrath, and miseries abating like the streams of drier places, madness compels me to remain companionless, wherefore these men will suffer the exactness of my pain, which I will make their own."

BleakWarrior drew the Dirk.

And rose to meet them.

The Sisters of No Mercy had fled from the City of Honours like eels through gaps in an underwater system of tunnels. They were lying on a field of grass in the midst of the Major Plains in the Midlands of Shinnach. Beside them lay an alchemical container containing several sets of glands which they had ousted from the routed body of The Gland Master.

"That went well," said Big Sister, chewing upon a juicy stalk of grass that tasted, and felt, like a piece of wire.

"Not that well," said Little Sister.

"No," said Big Sister, "not that fucking well at all. It's a fucking disgrace we lost the bitch's acid."

"Not a disgrace," said Little Sister, correctively. "I mean, we got ourselves some deadly sets of fucking glands, no?"

"We did," said Big Sister.

"And it's not every day that you manage to get some deadly sets of fucking glands to save your Middle Sister, Sister."

"No," said Big Sister, "it isn't."

"I'd say that today has been a great success."

"I agree," said Big Sister, "a really fucking great success."

"I mean, we've got one deadly testicle and three sets of deadly glands, Sister. How good is that?"

"Not bad," said Big Sister. "But it's a pity about the bitch's acid."

"Yes," said Little Sister, "it is."

"It would have been a really great fucking addition to our collection of restorative anti-potions."

"I know," said Little Sister, "but not *that* good."

"No," said Big Sister, "not that fucking good at all." She

let out a heavy sigh and twisted the end of her wiry stalk of grass. “So who’s next on the hit list, Sister?”

Little Sister unravelled a piece of parchment where the names were scrawled beside tersely written descriptions of them.

“Well,” she said, “there’s some fucker here who uses his feet for Weapons.”

“Feet?” Big Sister screwed up her face like she was swallowing bits of broken glass. “We’ve got to take his fucking feet to feed our Middle Sister?”

“No,” said Little Sister, “his liver.”

“Liver?”

“Yes.”

“Not his feet, then?”

“No.”

“But how do you know?”

“Because of his name,” said Little Sister.

“What’s his name, then?”

“Liver Dye.”

“Dye?” said Big Sister. “Dye? What kind of stupid fucking name is that?”

“It’s the kind of stupid fucking name of our next victim, Sister.”

“Oh,” said Big Sister. “Well let’s go get him, then.”

“OK,” said Little Sister, “let’s go.”

“I’ve got to say,” said Big Sister, tossing away her stalk of wiry grass, “that I’m heartened by the fact that we don’t have to take his fucking feet.”

“So am I,” said Little Sister, not really sounding very heartened about anything. “So am I.”

Book 2: In the Research of Purposes

7. BleakWarrior Leaves the Isle of Norn

Though his knowledge was limited—to the point that he was deeply concerned by his lack of it—he was nevertheless able to inform me of certain tendencies among the Meta-Warrior class of being in relation to their linear counterparts.

It is common practice among Meta-Warriors to ally themselves to linear humans so long as there is something to be gained in favour of their campaigns of hatred against one another. They are accustomed to forming secret pacts with powerful dignitaries, or controlling them through blackmail or threats. Or sometimes they choose to conceal themselves in linear groups or institutions, with an aim to exploiting the people or powers that, from those sources, fall within their grasp.

More often than not, they will form or fashion cabals or cartels among themselves which will sometimes involve the recruitment or collaboration of linear functionaries, which are not so much based on trust as on the devious cunning of the superior strategists among their number.

BleakWarrior

—The Private Testimony of Achlana Promff, Priestess of the Church of Nechmeniah

BleakWarrior was on the Isle of Norn seeking passage to the mainland. Political tensions between the clans of Upper and Lower Norn were verging on war, and BleakWarrior wanted nothing to do with it.

More to the point, BleakWarrior had been involved in a conflict between rival linear factions who were acting under the coercion of Meta-Warriors, now vying for power and preparing themselves for the impending upheaval.

More to the point, still, BleakWarrior had engaged in a bit of killing that had alerted his presence to a couple of cabals who were now out looking to kill him.

To make matters worse, both the Storm Brokers Union and the Board of Shipwrecks had employed linear means of tracking him down by marking him out as a wanted criminal. Up and down the length of the Isle, his name was being touted by Free Traders of Interest, while a reward was on offer for information that would lead to his arrest. It was bad enough having Meta-Warriors on your tail, but a rabble of linear humans was unbearable—like being pursued by a nest of wasps.

An audacious wretch, capable of crimes of an unmentionable caste, with eyes the colour of unpolished nougats of precious stone. Beware the hypnotic influence of their bilious texture; for they are liable to corrupt the mental faculties of whomsoever succumbs to their allure. But let it be known that the Board of Shipwrecks and the Storm Brokers Union are offering, jointly, a reward of a hundred skegs for his successful apprehension . . .

He had heard the Free Trader of Interest say it himself, and thought it a fair, if foppish, description of the Warped Lenses. Too fair, in fact. Which is why he had tied a silken scarf around his face and was carrying a stick in the guise of a mercenary whose sight had been lost in the midst of some dangerous affray.

It was a ridiculous disguise, given that it was so pitifully obvious. But it would serve him well in the town he was in now—a port on the coast of Upper Norn called Stormway—which was as good a place as any to find a berth for the mainland.

Better, in fact, because its inhabitants were a miserable brood of seafaring folk who were hardened to a point of extreme reticence. So much so that they minded their own business with a commitment to silence that was almost admirable (BleakWarrior was reminded of a Monastery in the southern glens of the Girnan Howe where the monks had sewn their lips together with copper wire to prevent them from speaking. The people of Stormway didn't require the copper wire to prevent them from speaking. But their dourness had produced a facial distortion of craggy lips and sullen brows which reminded BleakWarrior of certain breeds of wailer-monkey on the Isle of Smir).

Stormway itself was a huddle of granite facades infested with seagulls that shat all over its mossy roofs and scavenged its streets for fish or crabs or whatever boons had fallen from the creels they used to carry them in. The people of the town referred to the gulls as rats with wings; but BleakWarrior enjoyed the way they disturbed the peace with their incessant wailing and aggressive reactions to the linear twits who tried, and failed, to shoo them away.

BleakWarrior didn't understand why they didn't lay traps and eat the gulls instead. But that's the kind of people they were: gormless, as well as uncommonly ugly.

Which was yet another reason to hasten across the Sea of Sores to some coastal village on the eastern seaboard of Fiddith Fa. And, from there, he would take a southwest route through the Vale of Fiddith, then west through the Feylands of the Yaw. Then he would turn south across the Fetid Mountains (where he hoped to avoid the Machinists of the Faltering Steppes) before beginning his descent into the rich and fertile valleys of the Quagan.

The Quagan was abundant with hilltop towns and lowland cities, but BleakWarrior was only interested in two: the City of Praxis and the City of Prelations, which is where he would find the Meta-Warrior he was looking for now.

It was Blooded Up who told him, before he allowed the Dirk to do its worst against her.

"In one of the Twin Cities of Physicians, in the lands of the Quagan, you will find a Meta-Warrior called The Ever Decreasing Circle of Choice."

BleakWarrior grunted.

"The Ever Decreasing Circle of Choice has a vested interest in science and, under his linear name of Doctor Vile, is known to the linear scientocracy as a pioneering brain specialist. If anyone can tell you what we are, BleakWarrior, he can."

"But you can't?"

Blooded Up laughed.

"I'm a killing machine, BleakWarrior, with little more intelligence than the turtle I ate for supper the other day."

"Turtles are rather cunning in their own way."

"Cunning enough to avoid the soup plate? I think not, BleakWarrior. And yet," she said, "my lack of wits doesn't prevent me from thinking that your promise not to kill me rings hollow."

"Hollow?" BleakWarrior frowned. "I asked for information in exchange for your life, and all you have given me is a name. Names are nothing without faces. *Names* are hollow."

She smiled sweetly. "If you like, I can give you more than a name. I can give you anything. Anything at all."

It was a pathetic attempt.

"You have nothing to give me I cannot take," said BleakWarrior.

"Take me, then," she said.

"I will," said BleakWarrior. He pressed the Dirk against her throat. "*After* you are dead."

Welter of Impermanence was obsessed with the perfect kill for which a certain amount of *pain* in conjunction with *death* was necessary.

On that basis, she had considered awarding herself points on a scale of one to a hundred in relation to the perfection of an assassination and wondered if, by following this strategy, a superior value of killing was obtainable.

Probably not.

Nevertheless, the immaculate standards of her extermination techniques—of which there were around 36 for painful killings and 10 for ultra-agonising stupors—allowed for a wide variety of possibilities as regards reaching the quietus of the ultimate hit.

Today she was hoping to improve on the previous best score she had never given herself in the belief that the setting was highly favourable. A gauze of mist had drifted in from the sea like a slab which reduced the streets of Stormway to a dismal pallor of low visibility. The cries of the gulls offered a good screen of disorderly commotion to diminish the chances of being heard.

Welter of Impermanence fingered her Utensils with an awareness of her desire to use them. But she had no desire to squander the tactical advantage of her situation (albeit, at this point in time, she was favouring the use of the Corkscrew or the Skewers).

"Patience," she advised herself. "Your time will come."

It did.

BleakWarrior, faking a limp or a shuffle (she wasn't sure which), appeared through the mist. Welter of Impermanence followed after him with supreme caution. She quickened her pace when she saw him turn into a deserted alley between the squat facades of smokehouses running along the shore—then stopped when she saw another figure creeping after him.

A figure she recognised.

A figure that was Nowhere Bound.

Nowhere Bound's expression of vacancy was more terrible than the fury it masked.

He stood and watched the fake stumbling figure of BleakWarrior disappear into the dankness of the alley.

"Later," he said, and turned to face the interloper, whose neck he would wring with the extreme satisfaction of a qualified neck-wringer.

The interloper eased between the smokehouses. She had half a grin that lit her face and another half that was clouded in bad humour. He recognised her as an operator of the Board of Shipwrecks who had a stupid name he couldn't remember. It was time, therefore, for her to die.

"Just what do you think you are doing, stranger?" She spoke in tones as thin as morning ice.

Nowhere Bound flourished his garrotte.

"Aw," he said, "you're so cute. I like it when the tongues of cute people pop out of their mouths like big thick purple sloppits of bile."

Welter of Impermanence inclined her head:

"And I like to see the brains of people who don't have any spill out of their ears like dribblets of frogspawn."

She produced a set of skewers that made it very clear that, in her case, actions spoke louder than words.

Nowhere Bound looked horribly blank, almost as if he had fallen in love.

"So what about when the eyes of cute people fill up with blood as the air in their lungs begins to dwindle and their eyes begin to bulge like pustules ready to burst with projectile splatter?" he said.

"Nice," said Welter of Impermanence, who may or may

not have raised an eyebrow. "But not as nice as when the eyeballs are dislodged by the pressure of prickets in the brain that eject them from their sockets and allow them to dangle on striplets of threads like an ill-born puppetry."

Nowhere Bound let his arms fall by his side. The blankness on his face had increased to a definite ardour. Welter of Impermanence did the same. She, too, had felt the lust that slid between them like mortar between two bricks.

"I think," said Nowhere Bound, "that we should join forces."

"I think that we should have sex."

Nowhere Bound swallowed.

"What about BleakWarrior?" he said.

"There's plenty of time for him."

Welter of Impermanence took a step closer. Nowhere Bound did the same. Welter of Impermanence stood on her tip toes and offered her lips. Nowhere Bound stooped and offered his. Welter of Impermanence lifted her hands up to his shoulders—squeezed them—then lifted her hands up to his cheeks.

And calmly embedded the Skewers into his ears right up to their tips—enough to drive his eyeballs from his sockets as she had predicted.

Nowhere Bound gave a little whine, as if a tiny pocket of trapped air had been released from the pit of his stomach. His eyes dangled like flowers on the ends of drooping stalks. His brains dripped out like frogspawn. Welter of Impermanence removed the Skewers from his pivoted head and, finally, let his body drop.

"I suppose it's true, then," she sighed, pocketing the Skewers in hidden slits. "Love conquers everything."

In the meantime, BleakWarrior had found the proprietor of The Ma Grin Deep Sea Fisheries Holding, who was called The Ma Grin.

"Yes," she said, "you can take a berth with the *Silver*

Darling which leaves within a half an hour. Time is of the essence." She chuckled through the black rivets of her teeth. "And so is money."

BleakWarrior grunted and dropped several little hard white balls into her hand that looked like nougats of ivory, and were. But their name, as currency, was skegs, and these were the last BleakWarrior had in his possession.

"One moment," said The Ma Grin.

BleakWarrior paused.

"You're the one they're looking for, aren't you, with the amber eyes?"

BleakWarrior grinned and lifted the veil from his face so she could see the Lenses. The Ma Grin drew a breath and stared as if expecting something hypnotic to happen.

Nothing happened.

"Right, old hag," said BleakWarrior. "That'll teach you not to believe everything you hear."

She eyed him warily, then smiled through the debris of her teeth.

"Hah," she said, "what difference would it make to me anyway? I'm half as mad as I am sane, regardless of whatever tricks your eyes might play on me."

BleakWarrior's face grew hard.

"Do not reckon the extremes of madness with your linear eccentricities, old hag. The difference is one of water to the manner of stone."

The Ma Grin's mouth fell open to reveal the full extent of her dental rot. BleakWarrior didn't take the time to make a closer inspection. He was hastening off with a shuffling manoeuvre that differed entirely from the one he'd used upon his arrival. His lack of facility for perfecting his disguise allowed The Ma Grin to rouse herself from her momentary bewilderment; and her coarse laughter floated after him like a distortion in the eardrum.

The Ma Grin returned to sup on her pot of beer after he had departed from the yard that served as her central office.

Her abrasive mirth was quickly staunched by her addled brain. She was still sipping from her pot of beer when the scrawny woman with the movements of a reptile appeared through the gate of the yard that served as her central office. The Ma Grin eyed her with a business-like scorn. The scrawny woman approached her and said, "I'm looking for a crippled man who wears a veil across his face, like this." She made a motion to convey the appearance. "You have the look of a woman who might have seen him."

The Ma Grin chuckled and supped from her beer as if the scrawny woman had amused her with a bawdy jest.

The scrawny woman frowned and, suddenly, produced an egg whisk which she held before The Ma Grin's beetroot face.

"This, as you can see, is an egg whisk," said the scrawny woman. "Note, however, how the blades are forged to an exceptional degree of razor-sharpness. This is perhaps the strongest indication of its proper use, which has nothing to do with whisking eggs."

A look of worry spread across the face of The Ma Grin like a rash of the pox.

"Yes," the scrawny woman said. "I want you to tell me everything I need to know."

"About an hour ago, he was here," said The Ma Grin.

"Here doing what?"

"Seeking passage to the mainland."

"What part of the mainland?"

"Northern Fiddithia."

"What part of Northern Fiddithia?"

"The Town of Healing Sores."

"And did he get it?"

The Ma Grin nodded.

"And when does he leave?"

The Ma Grin glanced at her time piece and shook her head.

"Gone already?"

The Ma Grin nodded.

"Well," said the scrawny woman with the Egg Whisk, "I reckon you've just made the biggest mistake of your entire life."

She grabbed The Ma Grin around the cheeks and chin so that her mouth fell open, then drove the Egg Whisk down The Ma Grin's throat. She adjusted the posture of her body, pinning a knee against The Ma Grin's chest. Then she whisked and whisked until The Ma Grin's tongue and tonsils were shredded. Then she shoved it deeper into the oesophagus, which was grizzled through years of exposure to beer. And she whisked and whisked with firm gyrations until a welter of blood foamed up from The Ma Grin's withered lips like a geyser.

The screams of The Ma Grin were barely audible given that her vocal chords had been curdled into a throaty pulp that was filling her lungs with stringy lumps of liquid gore.

Whether she was dead or not when Welter of Impermanence had left her lying in the yard that served as her office was besides the point.

She would die soon anyway.

To be sure, it wasn't the cleanest kill that Welter of Impermanence had engaged in, but she reckoned it was good on account of style.

But none of this—nor the extermination of Nowhere Bound—could excuse her overall failure to obtain the intended hit of the day, for which she awarded herself an imaginary zero.

Welter of Impermanence slipped her Egg Whisk into its place of concealment in her utility suit. Two choices now lay open to her: to continue her search for BleakWarrior or return to the Board of Shipwrecks and admit her defeat.

Welter of Impermanence straightened her back—there was a mute crack of settling vertebrae—and commenced her negotiations for a boat that would take her across the Sea of Sores to Northern Fiddithia.

8.
The Circle is Out for the Counterpain

The Ever Decreasing Circle of Choice had the finest set of teeth in the whole of the continental mainland. When he smiled, it was like a row of exploding stars that had been converted to ice, and their uniform brightness was perfectly unnerving. There were rumours of certain peoples among the southern island groups who had developed the highest standards of personal hygiene and dental care. But rumours were rumours. In the case of The Ever Decreasing Circle of Choice, his teeth were as clean as the organs of a chaste young linear female kept in chemical vats for their anatomical preservation.

He was smiling now, with a chaste young linear female stretched naked before him on the slab, her body squirming in the witless panic of a helpless victim.

"It's all about choice," said The Ever Decreasing Circle of Choice. "I do not presume to hold your destiny in my hands." He regarded her with the infallible sincerity his position demanded. "The choice, therefore, is entirely yours."

He drew a metallic stake from the sleeve of a robe that was fastened together by a girdle arrayed with an ominous range of surgical instruments, syringes and swabs, and tubes containing discoloured liquids. From the other sleeve he drew a metallic hammer with a tiny head and slim handle.

The girl stared up at him, now rigid as a stick insect with

fear. She looked as if her eyeballs wanted to leap from their sockets which, from a scientific point of view, would have been interesting. However . . .

"I can assure you that you would hardly feel a thing. A couple of stiff taps to the temple—" He struck the stake with the metallic hammer to demonstrate the point.

She shook her head feverishly—a definite *No*.

"Very well." The Ever Decreasing Circle of Choice slid the stake and hammer back up his sleeves. "Then I thank you for donating your body to the purposes of my research. I will, of course, do all that I can to preserve your life for as long as possible."

He selected a syringe from his girdle and held it up to his eyes to examine the needle. He pinged it a couple of times and grunted as if to express his adamant denial of a minor professional concern. Then he smiled his magnificent smile and said, "Shall we begin?"

Counterpain was an acquaintance of Dominatrix Kerl, one of the most notable practitioners of her trade in the whole of Clawland.

"Do it!" cried Counterpain.

And Lady Kerl obliged, with an expertise that was the basis of a reputation that was second to none.

Counterpain mewled like a cat being dipped in a cauldron of boiling oil—a sure sign that he was enjoying himself. But it wasn't for the sake of pleasure that he craved the stimulus of pain. It was for the replenishment of his precarious physical condition, which was necessary for the sake of causing pain in others.

Like himself.

But not like Dominatrix Kerl.

Nevertheless, it was one of her traits (immensely appreciated by the bulk of her clients) that she allowed herself to endure the abuses she administered to them—albeit, with an exquisite touch they were desperately lacking.

Counterpain, however, was an exception, which is why he was an acquaintance (not a client) of Dominatrix Kerl. She provided him with her services free of charge on the condition that he obliged her with the identical treatments she offered him.

"My turn now," she gasped, and promptly positioned herself on all fours, her arse in the air like a piece of fruit that was ripe for the picking.

Counterpain, breathless, and bleeding from the parts of him where Dominatrix Kerl had applied her skills, did what he was told. The only difference was that he did it gently (linear humans were more vulnerable to the robust usage of a stalk of rosebush, replete with thorns, rifting up and down the anal cavity). Kerl, of course, was oblivious to his capacity to endure the most ferocious onslaught of physical arousal. She regarded him, merely, as an extreme case. For him, however, it was more than a therapeutic acquiescence to libidinal urges that were overwhelming to the point of demanding their release. It was a question, rather, of life or death. His preference for auto-destructive methods of stimulation was not a preference but a necessary means of metabolic renewal—which was a necessary means of making sure that, whenever he came face to face with his enemies, it was they, rather than he, who would die.

"It's not that I want you to suffer." The Ever Decreasing Circle of Choice removed the siphons from the various parts of the chaste young linear female's body, tending her as if she were his own child. "That's why I gave you the anaesthetic, you see?" He paused and looked at her. "You *do* see, don't you?"

If she had nodded, he wouldn't have known. Her head, along with the rest of her body, was firmly strapped to the slab so that her movements were kept to a minimum of utter stillness.

The slab, it was true, was cold and hard, and The Ever Decreasing Circle of Choice regretted the discomfort it must be causing her. It is not that he was particularly concerned about the girl's happiness. Nor was he acting under the ethical constraints of his position as a leading practitioner in his field. The stringent binding of the body to the slab was necessary in order to obtain the right kind of purchase with his incisions and probes, which were matters requiring the utmost delicacy on his part.

The biological and chemical resources of the human body, moreover, were by no means infinite. It was therefore necessary to prolong the lives of specimens for as long as possible (given, also, that the process of acquiring them was both difficult and expensive). Thus, an appropriate measure of care and attention had to be taken which, ultimately, provided a degree of relief from the stresses and strains of their dedication to the demands of progress.

The Ever Decreasing Circle of Choice gazed upon the chaste young linear female with a patriarchal staunchness to the cause of her well-being that may have been mistaken for a callous indifference to the eventuality of her doom. He wiped away the glistening trails of wetness from her eyes and nostrils and injected her with a sedative, fearing that, in the aftermath of her recent traumas, her heart might burst. It was with a degree of satisfaction that he watched her drift into an inviolable slumber. He stroked her brow for a moment: then, with phials full of substances he'd extracted from her waning form, he hastened away from the operating chamber into the adjoining clutter of his laboratory.

The laboratory was awash with a dim glow issuing from an electric bulb that hung from the ceiling like an enormous teardrop. The bulb was fed by a fat cable that wormed its way through hollow walls from a wind-powered device on the rooftop garden of The Circle's villa. The current hummed melodiously over the distorted angular vestiges of his subterranean workspace and had the effect, on the mind, of a protracted lullaby or incantation. The Ever Decreasing

Circle of Choice had often speculated on the possibility that the effect of the melodious hum had contributed positively to a fuller realisation of his genius.

"But what is genius?" he would immediately accost himself.

And this, indeed, was the ultimate purpose of his inquiry: to discover and extract the essence of genius so he could somehow use it to reinforce his own.

"Nay, Dr Vile," he would reply, "there can be no such thing as an elementary condition of neural energies we recognise as genius. Nor can we hope to remove this quality from its inner solutions without ruining the subtleties of its existential worth."

"It remains to be seen," said The Ever Decreasing Circle of Choice. "According to my calculations, a palpable neurochem is likely to exist; albeit, it is currently unobtainable due to its minuteness."

"Ah!" he exclaimed. "Then you are pursuing an aim without a focus. In other words, you are pursuing a miracle!"

"Enough!" he cried. "Your perpetual negativity is too much a burden on my ambitions. My aims are just."

"To the extent that a waste of time is just?"

"There are times, Dr Vile, when I despise you."

"You despise nothing," he said, "and there are those among our number who would see this as a flaw—a weakness—which they would soon exploit at your expense. It is a problem, sir, that you refuse to hate."

"I am not a bar brawler, Dr Vile. I am a scientist. As such, my priority is to discover the essence of genius."

"And the essence of yourself?"

"Is not a concern where the discovery of genius is forthcoming."

"*If* it exists."

"I have convinced you often enough that it does."

"And I have convinced you often enough that it doesn't."

"Then we are both right!"

"And both wrong!"

The Ever Decreasing Circle of Choice paused for a moment to restore himself to a medium of calm and, savouring the soothing evocations of the melodious hum, set about his work with his customary fanaticism.

The overall weirdness of the laboratory was enhanced by a vast apparatus of scientific hardware that formed bizarre constructions across several benches that furnished its misshapen enclosure. Beakers and flasks bubbled and foamed on tripods over languorous flames. Funnels dripped sparse amounts into massive jeroboams. Desiccators suckled moisture out of slackly-formed orbs that reformed and flopped like a manufactured force of entropy. The whole thing was held together by stands and clamps that were interconnected by glass burettes and rubber tubing. It hissed and throbbed like an artificial creature, cloying the air with a noxious smear of yellow gas, with vapours spilling from its gaps like an ectoplasmic phlegm. Putrescent clusters of fungal growths, reams of slime and gelid saturations clung to the brickwork of the laboratory like a primordial matter. The Ever Decreasing Circle of Choice adored the aura of stagnation that pervaded his environs: its clammy texture—the redolence of its organised shabbiness—the fluctuations of its teeming rot.

Aware of the fact he was happier here than anywhere else, he removed one of the phials from his belt and deposited its contents into an alembic dish that spat and fizzled with nefarious concoctions. He adjusted parts of his instrumentation, then removed himself to an adjacent room that sufficed for an office.

The Ever Decreasing Circle of Choice sat himself at an ancient desk, wiped his hands on a calfskin cloth and, folding it neatly, put it to one side. With an exaggerated flourish of his fingers, he took up a quill, dipped it in a pewter ink well, and, with a studious attention to detail, added a new entry to his scientific journal.

I believe, he wrote, *that I am very close to perfecting the plasm. I have already exposed myself to the effects of my initial formulae, and I am happy to report that the sense of euphoria I received was utterly compelling.*

Overall, the plasm requires the proper extraction of the hormonal properties of a chaste young linear female combined with extracts taken from my own blood samples. The result is a chemical admixture that exerts a powerful influence over the sensory receptors of taste and smell; and, to this extent, it acts very much like the pheromonal secretions that influence the behaviour of certain animal or insect species.

Aside from perfecting the plasm, my next endeavour is to find some way of introducing its influence into the ID network. It is my intention to acquire a different class of being from which to elicit the quality of genius so dreadfully lacking in our linear counterparts. I feel certain that . . .

The Ever Decreasing Circle of Choice paused.

"I feel certain that . . ."

"I feel certain that my brain is ablaze with so many precocious inclinations, Dr Vile."

"For which I suffer."

"For which I do indeed suffer."

And The Ever Decreasing Circle of Choice lay down his pen.

And sighed.

Dominatrix Kerl's bordello was appropriate for the purposes it served. It lay well-hidden in the backstreets of the City of Transactions that sat on the banks of the River Claw in neat rows of commercial blocks and bustling depots, treasuries and secluded bank vaults.

The bordello consisted of various rooms and corridors immersed in the seductive gloom of semi-hallucinogenic bowls of incense. Its lobby displayed the brighter elegance of freezes showing naked forms in dignified poses that were rarely struck by the visiting guests in the upper floors.

When Counterpain left the building, he was in for a nastier shock than the ones he'd received from Domanatrix Kerl. Outside, arranged in a semi-circle at an unreasonable distance from the entrance of the bordello, stood The Scrawler with her ragged pack of juvenile linear misfits, The Scribes.

The Scrawler brandished her Quill with the sort of posturing that suggested she wanted to use it. The Scribes were wielding their writing tools in a manner suggesting they wanted to do the same.

As much as Counterpain would have relished the indiscretion of hundreds of intimate lacerations upon his body, there were limits even to his tolerance.

These limits were called *Death*.

Counterpain bolted back through the lobby of the House of Kerl and sped up the stairs. The Scrawler and her Scribes came after him, squealing with a pubescent glee that was somehow more disturbing than ordinary bloodlust. The Scrawler ushered them on with maternal encouragements and the brisk but loving commands of a teacher in charge of her favourite class.

Counterpain was running through the sprawl of corridors looking for a stairway to the roof he didn't even know was there.

It wasn't.

But there was a window made of frosted glass at the end of one of the corridors. It reared before him like a magnetic attraction, and Counterpain let himself be drawn wholeheartedly.

"You fucking bunch of linear freaks," he shouted back at the gleeful Scribes.

And he slowed his movements so they could see him just as he was about to fling himself through the frosted glass onto the street or yard or outhouses below. It was a stupid gesture he couldn't resist.

And, as he speared himself through glass, he hoped in the name of all that hurts that the fall was enough to be properly fatal. He would look kind of stupid languishing in a rosebush or impaled on a railing after vocalising his defiance in a way that seemed even more childish than they were.

But, as it happens, he found himself falling onto the flagstones of the wine garden where Dominatrix Kerl liked to entertain her guests before degrading them with the delightful pleasures at her disposal.

There were three or four guests there now, Dominatrix Kerl lounging among them while a couple of rented paramours served them spiced wine and raw fish eggs. Whether or not they had seen Counterpain diminishing into the flagstones was, for him, a total irrelevance.

But they had.

And they sprang to their feet in consternation, exchanging looks by way of acquiring an objective confirmation of what they had seen. Their consternation turned to terror when The Scrawler and her Scribes came spilling out onto the wine garden in their haste to assess the success or failure of Counterpain's Leap.

It had, of course, been successful; and The Scrawler and her Scribes were livid with indignation. It seemed only fitting, therefore, that they should avail themselves of Dominatrix Kerl and her handful of guests.

"Children—" The Scrawler clapped her hands twice to gain their attention. "Let us provide these people with an impromptu demonstration of our writing skills."

They saved Dominatrix Kerl till last, subjecting her to a myriad of inscriptions until she started to expire like a leaking fruit.

Some of the phrases that contributed to her demise were highly appropriate to her station:

Terror is the certainty of suffrage!
Desire was the bondage of my life!
The Oppressor Was Myself!

Others were more general:

Where once I was I am no longer.
Time is merely a shadow of space.
Language is violence.

Dominatrix Kerl died as she had lived, suspended in a slipstream of pain and pleasure at the behest of a fanatical brood of ardent sensualists. She bled through the language of her body and was written out of existence like a piece of history.

It was widely agreed among those who had cherished her services that she would be as sorely missed as she had made them suffer.

In a journal entry entitled "The Analysis of Misfortune," Dr Vile wrote:

Plainly, there is no such thing. Nor yet do we proceed along a predestined path, as many of our religious fanatics would have us believe. Fortune depends upon a wilful manipulation of circumstances in order to make them work in our favour, which is a process requiring an intuitive grasp of possible outcomes as yet undetermined by the passage of time. So it is not, by any means, an easy undertaking: nor does it depend on the frivolities of chance. Simply put, the capacity for transforming the undisclosed eventualities of life into a single "object" of controllable distinction depends on (the prevalence of genius in the mind of) the controller.

Given, then, that I have optimised the effectiveness of the plasm to an infallible pitch of its imminent use, I am confident of extending my "thought-cast" over the abstractions of destiny, which is now made viable by my invention—yes! —of the Sensorial Platacaster.

I have tested the Sensorial Platacaster upon myself to the extent of eliminating the technical imperfections which have partially reformed my physical appearance (my mouth, it appears, is slightly misshapen, and my nose enlarged. My teeth, however, are largely unaffected by the mishaps—caused, I believe, by a minor flurry of electrostatic malfunctions). It remains for me only to project the plasm with great force through the inverted materiality of an elected body of solid matter, for which the floor of my laboratory will provide an adequate platform. I have enclosed the Platacaster within an unbreakable thermoplastic container which will also serve as a means for impounding my attracted specimen. I will then subject my specimen to a series of investigative procedures which I have devised in conjunction with several approaches: psycho-chemical, sensorial, neuro-electrical and biotic.

It remains for me, in my eagerness to embark on these impending phases of my research, to expose myself to the sedations of the melodious hum. It is vital that I retain an attitude of patience in awaiting the arrival of my quarry. The activation of the Sensorial Platacaster is already underway. My excitement is total. I am, I admit, rather a—

“Fool!” cried Dr Vile.

“Enough!” he returned.

“But think, man, think. For all the time that you spend on these outlandish courses of action, you could have already devised a range of toxins to use with cataclysmic purpose against your foes.”

“Be given to understand that I regard your protestations as an irrelevance.”

“But if you concentrated your efforts on the production of deadly alchemical preparations—”

“Enough! I will not dabble in pottages and broths like some Fiddithian witch doctor.”

And, with that, Dr Vile composed himself and attended to the operations of the Sensorial Platacaster. Seeing that everything was in order, and that its automatic functions were performing adequately, he returned to his desk and reviewed “The Analysis of Misfortune” (perhaps for the fifth or sixth time that day). Finding that it met (yet again) with his approval, he leaned back on his chair, submitted himself to the melodious hum and, with an implement specially designed for the task, polished his teeth to an impossible sheen of icy whiteness, almost to a point where you could hear them.

The feeling is neither one of ecstasy nor excruciating pain. It is neither pleasurable nor discomfiting. It is more a kind of abandonment of sensory perception as it is normally felt, except perhaps in the province of dreams.

But a Random Leap is not a dream event. It is a sub-intimate contact with reality where the existential separation of differing states no longer applies.

The rush of the disbanded molecular structure of the body through atomic minutia produces a feeling of mental and physical disintegration that never acquires the obliteration of death but retains, instead, a proportionate degree of distance between the contingencies of form.

Randomised particles maintain a loose coherence through the indirect routes of meta-solidarity: but the condition is one of flux rather than amalgamation, of nuance rather than mutability.

Darkness and light, colour and texture, shape and substance, are replaced by a sensation of liquid airiness which pertains neither to liquid nor air. The emotions become a suspension of rudimentary concerns that are distilled to points of primeval clarity: fear becomes terror; contentment becomes elation; sorrow becomes despair; anger becomes fury. All are combined—and the mind enlivened—by a supreme alertness to an impossible calm of controlled hysteria.

And then . . . to be cast adrift in this condition is to suffer the expectation of its permanence as a disbanded sense of selfhood versus a protracted hope for the Random Leap to come to an end. It is the perpetual mobilisation of a phobic distress that will not resign itself to its closure until *after* the event, whereupon the experience is a germ in a compost of absolute horror.

In the stupor of his passage through a maze of IDs, Counterpain receives the impact of an attraction that spears him with a shocking need to partake of its source. He undergoes the normalisation of his physical and mental resources—the reassertion of which draws him from the vacillations of the Random Leap to a definite node.

Counterpain emerges from the anti-closure of the node into a place of containment in which he can barely move. The effect of the attractant is overpowering, and Counterpain feels the appalling erotic fierceness of an immediate need for raw sex. He searches for nakedness, for nubile succour, for delicious carnal offerings and profusions of youthful flesh. Instead, he sees a pallid face with incoherent features—a twisted mouth, a bulbous nose, bespectacled eyes that stare at him through a tiny door in the invulnerable hold of his enclosure.

Counterpain realises that something has gone very wrong—yet his penis soars with insatiable stiffness, as if something has gone very right. He considers the prospect of humiliations he has never known, which offers him cause for lunatic optimism.

But his overall mood, unalterably, is one of *dread.*

9. A Week in Pursuit of BleakWarrior

Meta-Warriors are without conscience and will seldom adhere to the concept of loyalty. Their precarious relations are fashioned out of an expedience of mutual gains that cannot last.

The cold logic at the core of their submission to these temporary measures is frightening for its lack of adhesion to any moral or ethical foundation. They are like animals devouring their young in order to accommodate the needs of the species as a whole, although this analogy, too, is insufficient to describe them.

Meta-Warriors have no interest in themselves as a social unit or as individual members of a cooperative group. Cooperation is limited to destroying the group they belong to, which is utterly contradictory of everything we know or suppose about Nature. And it is this, above all, that I cannot fathom: that they are completely devoid of any instinct for survival which, in other species, often results in extreme behaviour which, nevertheless, is an integral part of Nature's economy.

It is not the preservation of the species but its

elimination that moves them—that they should pare themselves to a manageable quantity of combatants, then battle it out, until only one is left and . . . what then?

"What purposes do you serve?" I asked my visitor as we talked into the night, the candle burning to its lowest ebb as the dawn came on.

He looked at me with stark Lenses that glinted, I think, with bitter humour.

"I serve nothing other than the consequences of life itself."

And he put his hand in mine, searching me with an intensity that set my cheeks alight and heartbeat racing.

I realised, then, in spite of myself, that I was desperately hoping that he alone—that he at least—would survive.

—The Private Testimony of Achlana Promff,
Priestess of the Church of Nechmeniah

Welter of Impermanence held the tongue of Captain Farigot in the grip of the Salad Tongs and gave them a twist. Farigot screamed, though the effect was more of a hideous rasp.

"Now," said Welter of Impermanence, "let's try again. Your passenger wearing a veil like this—" She made the appropriate gesture. "Where is he?"

She released her grip to allow him to speak.

"I don't know," he panted. "I swear it. We landed here at seventeen bells. He disembarked without so much as a word of thanks. It's the last I saw of him."

"He said nothing of his plans?"

"Nothing. I swear it."

"I'm afraid that's not the right answer."

The Salad Tongs were one of Welter of Impermanence's

favourite Utensils and were ideally suited to the purposes of interrogation. It's no surprise, therefore, that she was immensely skilled in using them.

Reasserting her grip, and using his chin for leverage, Welter of Impermanence expertly disgorged Farigot's tongue from the pit of his mouth. The manoeuvre was similar to ousting a root vegetable from a wet clod of earth, where a certain amount of rotation was applied in equal measure to a controlled but constant use of force.

Lying on the deck of the *Silver Darling,* puddled in blood, the tongue resembled the hatchling of some horrible insect that would grow more beautiful as time went on. On reaching the full extent of its maturity, it would doubtless begin to reassume the sickening aspect of its initial condition. But none of this was of interest to Welter of Impermanence, who preferred to maintain her focus on the job at hand.

Speaking of which.

As she waited for Captain Farigot to bleed to death—having no intention of bringing his suffering to a swift conclusion—Welter of Impermanence considered her next move.

It seemed unlikely that BleakWarrior would linger at his first port of call on the Fiddithian mainland. Having rid himself of his outlawed status on the Isle of Norn, he would nevertheless be wary of pursuit, as Welter of Impermanence herself had proven a wise precaution.

It was time, then, to open up a few lines of inquiry, beginning with the obvious haunts of inns, bordellos, the Office of Arbitration, and so on.

First things first, however.

Inspired by the thrill of violence and the arousal of gore, Welter of Impermanence felt an urgent need to masturbate at the soonest possible opportunity. Apart from the fact that it would relieve her excited senses, it would also restore a measure of calm she was currently lacking.

She rummaged among her places of concealment for a

Utensil to help her accomplish the task. The Cheese Grater—rubbed sparingly across the thighs, nipples, neck and clitoris—would do the job as well as anything.

Welter of Impermanence couldn't help thinking, as she masturbated over the expiring form of Captain Farigot, just how much he reminded her of something in life. Something she wanted. Something that Just. Wasn't. There.

Reading the Clouds was reading the clouds. In them, he saw messages that descended upon him with the aimlessness of moths.

"Moths," his dead lover once told him, "cause fear in linear humans because of the unpredictability of their flight. They are a living symbol of the absence of will in the motions of nature. They are life without coordination, drawn to the deadly smear of the flame in darkness: insensible to the arrival of their doom."

In time, the messages would settle on the veneer of his perceptions and burrow into his head like maggots feasting on a corpse.

"Linear humans despair of maggots," his lover had said. "They are a literal metaphor for the inevitability of decay that offends the human sensitivity to life."

Soon, the maggoty thoughts would reach a core of understanding and begin to form a clear pattern of ideas, derived from facts, that Reading the Clouds could act upon with the certainty of following a prophecy. They were not, however, prophecies, but the cognitive assimilations of circumstances that elemental bodies, such as clouds, were capable of garnering from the scenes of the world unfurling below them.

In every molecule of water, drawn from the earth by the warmth of the sun, there was a chemical enunciation of spatial and temporal particularity that had the clarity of a communicative symbol. To combine these molecules en masse was to begin to construct a kind of language that

Reading the Clouds was capable of translating into a psychodynamic tablature of comprehensible significations.

Clouds, for him, constructed narratives that contained information about what was happening on the planet surface from which they had been extrapolated. Reading them meant that Reading the Clouds could second guess their scenes and plots, identify their themes and summarise their characters who revealed themselves (as expansive rifts or flurries or gluts or perturbations) in the vaporous actions of the clouds. Reading the Clouds was able to anticipate their intentions, assess their whereabouts, analyse their tropes and intercede upon their plots with a range of deconstructive measures.

Like he had done with The Shambling Maw.

The Shambling Maw was sniffing out whores in a town called Happenstance on the Shinnachian side of the Ridge of Thaws. Reading the Clouds had read of The Shambling Maw's unsatisfied lusts, which had announced themselves in fat, precipitous clusters of cumulonimbus that came sagging over the horizon like overfed cattle. The Maw had been six months at sea, with cabin boys to serve for his amusements. But the flicker of lightning was equal to his annoyance with their lack of use. Reading the Clouds saw that the evaporations of The Maw's mood expressed a preference for buxom women who were well-worn to a point of moral and anatomical looseness. He wanted orifices well-stretched; soiled bodies; forceful impregnations; and a rough handling of buttocks and breasts, including his own.

Reading the Clouds hated the unsubtle shallow depths of The Shambling Maw's obstreperous masculinity—his boorish disavowal of the perverse—his sneering attitude towards erotic diversions.

So much so that he had snuck up on The Shambling Maw while he was in the act of fucking his whore and inserted The Crook between his madly pumping cheeks. He rammed The Crook up the Shambling Maw's anal passage, thrusting it through his guts and gullet until it sprung from his mouth in the manner of a ritual killing.

But there was nothing ritual about it.

It was a fitting end to a character so badly written upon the pages of the world.

Welter of Impermanence heard word of a man with amber eyes who had purchased a muskin and was heading west for the Vale of Fiddith, seeking passage, no doubt, to the Feylands of the Yaw. There was nowhere else to go heading west through the Vale of Fiddith, unless you were planning on staying there. But no one did, except for The Creepers of the Vale.

Welter of Impermanence had disposed of her informer using the Cheese Grater (still pungent from its previous use), taking his muskin for herself. He was a touring musician who played an instrument that resembled a dried up snake. On closer inspection she saw that it was, in fact, a dried up snake.

She cast it aside and rode hard beyond the periphery of the Town of Healing Sores. On reaching the Vale, a dry wind blew dust in her face with an irritating constancy. Welter of Impermanence wrapped a scarf around her face, leaving slits for the eyes, and quickly found that it stifled her breathing.

She tore off the scarf and let the dust blow in her face instead.

The muskin, meanwhile, was strong and hard between her thighs and, again, she felt an intensive need to masturbate. The rubbing of its back against her pubis produced an effect of arousal that would possibly perform the necessary actions all by itself.

Clearly, her excitement, first, of the murder of the snakeskin player and, second, of her desperation to catch BleakWarrior was making her over-anxious and erotically charged.

But, most of all, it was making her angry.

"BleakWarrior," she decided, "will suffer a death of

express brutality which will take me as close to the perfect kill as I can get. It's not right that he should die by ordinary means of expert bloodletting."

He wouldn't.

And she suddenly surged towards a state of orgasm that was as disappointing as the means of arousal itself. A muskin was an inelegant breed of animal that was well-adapted to long and difficult journeys over long and difficult stretches of terrain. It was not, however, well-adapted to the purposes of sexual gratification.

Which is why there hadn't been any.

Reading the Clouds lay on the Tepid Rock. The sky was awash with the scuppered rhythms of an erratic prose. The sun burned a hole through a pallid gauze of altocumulus like a blur of ink on mottled parchment. It was bright and bald in the manner of an amendment to the warped extravagance of dusk, like a new law that would never be granted.

The altocumulus had risen over the southerly rim of the Faltering Steppes, peculiarly dense and unable to form an even separation of its vapours. Crosswinds ran counter-wise to its broken uniformity; its consistency was disrupted by wavelets of gloss, like creases in a suit of armour.

It was evident that the formation had elicited a rupture from within the material order of the linear world, showing traces of inverted matter which the air had absorbed and then transformed into a visual stress of disorderly cloud-analogues.

"Inversions," muttered Reading the Clouds, letting the word spill from his lips like a resin.

And he knew at once that these were the secondary effects of a Random Leap or a Leap of Cynosure which didn't accord with any normal process of metatomic reorganisation.

Nevertheless, the Leap had been encrypted in the troposphere for Reading the Clouds to unravel to a point of where and when it had occurred. A closer study revealed to him its source: the City of Prelations.

But that wasn't all.

There was an emphasis of downdrafts in the north that caused a portion of the altocumulus to sag without rotundity, but with a ragged aspect amounting to a deeply held expression of ire. Reading the Clouds decoded the lack of pattern and discovered indications of cool bitterness and rage arising, he believed, from Northern Fiddithia—but he couldn't see the exact location.

Reading the Clouds allowed his exposition to broaden:

A tonal neutrality; a moribund dryness; an elapsing dash of female orgasm.

The Vale of Fiddith.

And, from there, a succession of tropes marking the activities of a killer.

"Sex and death."

And, somewhere within this heady mix, there were further traces of something more powerful—an underlying intonation of obsessive candour—an unconscious realisation of bliss—but buried too deep within the troposphere for anyone to comprehend beyond the fact that it was there.

Reading the Clouds allowed his mouth to sag open in evidence of his perplexity.

"I have never seen anything like this," he said.

But then he allowed his attentions to shift to something else of interest—something occurring within range of his location: a mild contortion of iridescence; an utterance of melancholy . . .

"The colour of despair."

BleakWarrior emerged from the Vale of Fiddith. The Feylands of the Yaw lay open before him in long tracts of wooded marshes spreading west that, to the south, became a blur of hills.

He was relieved to have avoided the attentions of The Creepers of the Vale, who patrolled the Vale with a mind to extracting “feelings of worth,” as he had heard it said, from passing strangers.

None had been taken.

Laws of a kind were resumed in the Feylands of the Yaw (which had been annexed by the Shinnachian Dynasty), meaning that, until he reached the Fetid Mountains, the travelling for BleakWarrior would be easy, quick and uneventful.

Except for the hills, which were liable to produce a few surprises on the way.

But, in truth, the journey for BleakWarrior was proving to be a terrible strain for all the wrong reasons. It was only mildly tough (and therefore dull) and was littered, rather than crammed, with moderate dangers (which never surfaced). The traversal of several stages of isolated but easy terrain was uninspiring, with exceptions by way of the hazardous bogs of the Feylands of the Yaw. The steep ascents of the Fetid Mountains would also provide a sufficient need for caution coupled with arduous bursts of physical energy.

But, other than that, the landscapes were less unkind to the body than to the roving eye, remaining murky for long stretches under shanks of mist, and dwindling over relentless folds of monotonous greenery. The distances were characterised by occasional steadings and vaguer types of human habitation (abandoned forts and hunting lodges; poachers’ huts and cabalistic retreats). The Shinnachian presence was limited to marker stones denoting an irrelevance of worthless territorial gains (the place was more of a vacuum than a colony, BleakWarrior reflected).

Overall, the approach to the Quagan from the north-east route was largely mundane rather than rapt in the splendour of its isolation. The biggest challenge for BleakWarrior was to brace himself against the boredom of his steady progress—which is more than can be said for the progress of others . . .

Welter of Impermanence was well within the confines of the

Vale of Fiddith when three of The Creepers came upon her. They walked their muskins slowly down a long slope, then settled in the ravine where they awaited her arrival.

The Creepers of the Vale were a magnet for the very worst kind of human outcast who had taken refuge in the hinterlands of Fiddith Fa, where they were able to carve out a life of secreted bliss, far and away from the prosecutions of the law against them. To a man, woman and mongrel dog, The Creepers had been ostracised by the societies that had suffered them, which they had abhorred—an underclass of sadistic malefactors comprising rapists, child killers, backstabbers and incestuous brutes—all of whom were stolidly marked by a rare gift for mindless cruelty.

That same cruelty had become a method and means for social cohesion which they had solidified further by communal tenets of vicious wrongdoing against others, according to which they prided themselves on depriving innocent passers-by of self-esteem and self-worth, by subjecting them to degradations which were exceptional even for them.

Welter of Impermanence could see, as she approached, the dirty cloaks of The Creepers stained yellow after so many years of hard living in remote locations. Their faces were expressionless, disfigured with scars, and bearing the look of haggard men who were used to getting their own way.

They wouldn't.

The one who spoke was slightly older than the other two.

"What are you?" he said. "A woman or some sexless freak?"

Welter of Impermanence replied:

"I've got nothing of any value for the likes of you."

"We're not robbers, you stupid bitch," he replied.

"We're mind fuckers," said a younger one.

"And body fuckers," said the other younger one.

The Creepers laughed as if it should've been funny.

It wasn't.

Welter of Impermanence said, "My body is not for the taking of strangers."

"It is the way of The Creepers that the bodies of women are saturated with our seed," said the older one.

"The only thing that's going to get saturated . . . are these."

Welter of Impermanence produced a set of carving knives from her places of concealment, each consisting of a different length and sharpness—each consisting of a different kind of pain or death.

"There are times," she said, staring at The Creepers as if turning them to stone, "when I'm so angry that *everyone must die.*"

BleakWarrior had crossed the hills that preceded the Fetid Mountains without incident, which surprised him given that they were known locally as the Hills of Bad.

The name of the Hills of Bad referred to two things: first, that they were bad and, second, that they were governed by a Grapoloid of distinction whose name, according to custom, was Bad.

Bad, however, wasn't one Grapoloid but many. In other words, Bad was the name given to whichever Bad had managed to wrestle power from the previous Bad who had wrestled power from the Bad before it (or him or her, or whatever they were, which was a matter of some debate among linear humans). Grapoloids were simple creatures in this respect, in that they enjoyed wrestling power from one another by whatever means, foul or fair, were appropriate for their social order; but, in other respects, they were as bad as the name of their leader suggests.

If not worse.

And, for anyone who encountered them, certainly no better.

Welter of Impermanence was midway across the hills that preceded the Fetid Mountains when a convocation of Grapoloids set upon her with a mind to causing her the perfunctory injustice of eating her alive. They had been attracted by the scent of her latest masturbatory endeavour, which involved the creative use of the Corkscrew, which she was now obliged to use for her protection rather than the acrimonious release of her libidinal tensions.

"I am Bad," snarled one of the Grapoloids as they rounded on her with their wet and snivelling snouts pressed in the air like modern art forms.

"Of course you are," said Welter of Impermanence, cool as a reptile in the mud.

"You die in bad fashion," said the Grapoloid called Bad.

"Hungry, are you?" said Welter of Impermanence.

"Bad hungry," said Bad.

"In that case," said Welter of Impermanence, "if any of you lay a finger on me, I'll make you eat them."

Her bravado drew a mixture of growls and guffaws from the pack, who were full of a rapacious hunger that, one way or another, was about to be satisfied.

"Our fingers make a good stew out of bad girl rider. Bad girl rider tastes good and warm. Bad girl rider smells good and warm as bad girl sex."

"Hmmm," said Welter of Impermanence, "you're not wrong there."

She whirled the Corkscrew in her hand. The Grapoloids flinched. They circled her warily on fragile legs. Their powerful arms, of which they each had two sets, were far less fragile than the legs that supported them on equally powerful upper bodies.

"You know something?" said Welter of Impermanence. "Whichever one of you comes near me first is going to get screwed." She whirled the Corkscrew to emphasise the point. "I think that, maybe, we should come to an agreement. I think that, maybe, we should think about eating this muskin of mine, instead of me."

"Muskin big and bad," agreed the Grapoloid called Bad.

"That's right," said Welter of Impermanence. "But not as bad as I can be if you refuse to accept my special offer."

The Fetid Mountains were so fetid that, by the time BleakWarrior had reached the Ridge of Thaws, his muskin had died and he, himself, was stinking like a dead animal.

Passing through the Ridge of Thaws, where the air grew cooler, the smell was dispersed. But:

"Still yourself," said Reading the Clouds as BleakWarrior emerged from a schism of rocks. "One more move and you'll be ripped apart by slings of wire."

"Slings of wire?"

"Mechanisms that propel short lengths of wire attached to weighted bolts on either side," said Reading the Clouds. "If they shower upon you, you will be riven."

"Then I am to be riven, it seems."

BleakWarrior drew the Dirk.

Reading the Clouds looked on.

"I never read this," he said, his voice betraying a hint of wonder.

Stillness settled between them like frost.

"Well," said BleakWarrior. "Am I to be riven or . . . ?"

Reading the Clouds whistled through his teeth. About a dozen men stepped forward from the surrounding cover of shrubs and rocks. The men were carrying tubular devices that coiled around their arms and chests, then rose above their heads in broad funnels that presumably launched the slings of wire their leader had referred to.

BleakWarrior looked suitably unimpressed.

"I would certainly laugh at these mechanisms if they were not so deadly. Your men look like they are caught in the grip of giant glymphs."

"Glymphs that launch an awful venom," said Reading the

Clouds. He regarded BleakWarrior with curiosity. “What is your name?”

BleakWarrior glared.

“Names,” he said, “are for those who need them.”

Reading the Clouds angled his head. He wore a look on his face of deliberate calm, with a degree of intrigue stirring underneath.

“Who are you?” he said.

“No one,” said BleakWarrior

“How can you be no one?”

“Because I am nothing.”

“How can you be nothing?”

“Because I prefer to be ignored.”

Reading the Clouds stared.

“Come with me,” he said. “I wish to ask you questions.”

“Questions are for questioners,” said BleakWarrior. “I prefer to fight and, if I fight, I prefer to win or die.”

Reading the Clouds studied BleakWarrior as if discovering a new species of insect.

“I would prefer it if, today, you did not die,” he said.

“Am I to be your prisoner?”

“You are to be my guest.”

BleakWarrior sheathed the Dirk.

“Then I warn you,” he said, “that I am not the kind of guest who is satisfied so easily by meagre offerings.”

“My offerings are good,” said Reading the Clouds, “and for the weight of my sorrow so much the better.”

Welter of Impermanence had abandoned her muskin to the Grapoloids. They fed upon it with such ferocity that they were unaware of her escape.

Except for two, who pursued her relentlessly until she was forced to turn and take them on.

It had been easier than she thought. One of them approached and started lurching its arms in an attempt to grab her by whatever part of her body seemed within range.

Being grabbed by a Grapoloid was generally a bad idea. Their arms were so strong that they could rip you apart without even trying to (which they often did on occasions of breeding with members of their own herd). But Welter of Impermanence managed to deflect its grasping hands with countermeasures before slamming the Corkscrew into the back of its neck, flipping her body so that the Corkscrew screwed deeper into its cerebral cortex—if it had one.

The other Grapoloid, which was having problems staying on its fragile legs after the rigours of the chase, was in no condition to resist the use of the Corkscrew upon its jugular—which, indeed, produced an effect of wine being spilt from an uncorked bottle.

Welter of Impermanence's escape had been successful due to the limited ability of the Grapoloids which she had exploited to satisfactory effect. The downside was that she was having to ascend the clammy steeps of the Fetid Mountains on foot, which meant that her skin was lathered in a layer of slime, rather than sweat, which was actually making her feel quite sexy. Neither could she help but notice how much she smelt like a girl wrapped up in bondage straps; and this was the last thing she needed when powering her way through the oily ferns that glistened wet from the dripping foliage overhead.

Humidity clung to the Fetid Mountains like a lubricant. The slopes were thick with an organic welter of sprawling variations of fecundity and decay. There was an aura of prototypical distinction between emergent species that took the principle of diversification to extremes that hardly seemed worth the bother.

Nature didn't care much for the practical disadvantages of freakishness as a basis for the propagation of life as a whole. And this, thought Welter of Impermanence, is surely what was meant by the condition of "savagery."

"Savagery," she decided, "is just another way of saying I don't care what I'm doing as long as I'm getting it properly done."

Which was as near as she would get to a philosophy. Which is why she strove upward and onward while willing herself with furious diligence to ignore the full extent of her arousal.

Until she reached the cool upstanding shafts of rock of the Ridge of Thaws, whose phallic rigidity proved too much for her to resist.

She was masturbating with a manic insistence on getting it done when the Machinists of the Faltering Steppes found her there, half-naked and wanton. It would have been embarrassing if she'd cared about things like that.

She didn't.

She did, however, care about her life, which is why she agreed to let herself be captured. There were too many Machinists for the Utensils to cope with. Not to mention the strange devices they wore about their arms and chests—probably weapons—the kind of weapons that were best avoided by a half-naked and wanton traveller whose fury beat in her breast like a starving animal.

BleakWarrior was led through a pass in the broad slabs of the Ridge of Thaws onto the grassy expanses of the Faltering Steppes. Miles of luscious pasturage unfurled before his eyes like a vision. Depressions of land formed rivers and streams that ambled and glistened like the hygroscopic trails of gargantuan slugs. A half a dozen villages smoked and steamed in wooded enclaves where the Machinists had built their homesteads alongside the factories, workshops, foundries and mills of their post-industrial rural mission.

Ignoring the villages, Reading the Clouds took BleakWarrior to the Tepid Rock which stood alone on the open plain some distance from the Township of Cowls.

They sat on the Tepid Rock with skins of wine and scraps of meat which they roasted over a fire while the stars shone over them like the visual impact of a severe concussion.

"You are not of the linear masses," Reading the Clouds

observed. BleakWarrior made no answer. "I read of your arrival in the clouds, which I am capable of decoding with an expertise that is as natural to me as fucking."

"You are not of the linear masses yourself," said BleakWarrior. "I knew this as soon as I laid eyes on you."

"And by what peculiar means are you able to see?"

"I see by looking."

Reading the Clouds gave a smile that emerged as a twitch.

"It is true," he said, "that I must look to the skies to read the plots of the world as they unfold before me. But my reading allows me to ascertain the advantages of counterplots to utilise against my foes."

"Then why allow me to live when the advantages fall so readily in your favour?"

Reading the Clouds gazed into the flames.

"I was intrigued by my inability to decipher your character with my customary accuracy. I read in you my own fancies of an intrepid suffering which knows no boundaries beyond the longitude and latitude of pain. I expected you to comply to the disadvantages waged against you with a disdain for life that is proportionate to your sorrow. Instead, I found a quality of rage that contradicts your tendency towards self-ruin. And, then, in the evidence of your person, which the clouds adapted to their form, I perceived a despondency which transpired against my judgement as a force of will akin to the wreckage of madness."

"Not all of us are what we seem, Reader, however the seeming."

"And for this," said Reading the Clouds, "I am shaken to the core."

"And so you should be," said BleakWarrior. "You adhere to assumptions which have their basis in likelihoods which are not, however, identical to the circumstances as you foresee them. They are indicative of our reactions to truth, but definitive of nothing more. You are vulnerable to the chaos of those, like myself, whose inclinations have the ungovernable tendency of moths."

Reading the Clouds looked up sharply.

"Moths?" he gasped.

BleakWarrior turned the Warped Lenses full on Reading the Clouds.

"You are turning the pages of an unwritten book," he said, "anticipating the stages of plots that are bereft, as yet, of the decisive outcome of the actions they portray. It is a dangerous game you play—to second guess the revelations of a trickster—a teller of tales—who is liable to change the orientations of their plots with the randomness—" BleakWarrior gestured towards the fire—"of flames."

"It is true that I act upon the likelier twists of circumstances I cannot know," said Reading the Clouds. "But here is where I depend on the logic of choice, where choice is a product of reason more than spontaneity."

"The matter of choice is limited to the biased appeal of what is worth choosing. Where is the logic in that, Reader?"

Reading the Clouds withdrew a skewer of meat from the flames and watched it sizzle with an expression of mild astonishment—the evidence of some deeper contortion.

"Not long ago," he said, "a linear woman was the focus of my aspirations, who died by the actions of her own hand. I had saved her from her abduction by a group of reiving Morrow Men, who found her strolling in the woods of the Fetid Heights, while I myself ascended them in search of a Meta-Warrior called Dim Licker of Skin."

BleakWarrior grunted. He'd heard of him—bad things, mostly.

Reading the Clouds went on:

"I had been following a grim-looking trail of nimbostratus that brushed against the Fetid Heights with a lingual roughness that one would expect from the presence of Dim Licker of Skin. But, suddenly, I was distracted by an updraft of spiralling vapours that betrayed an invigorating mix of poetic intelligence with animal cunning."

"Morrow Men," said BleakWarrior.

Reading the Clouds nodded and went on:

"I found them leading a woman they had captured by a rope around her neck, who had left no trace of herself in the atmospheric detail of the scene. She had resigned herself to death and, in doing so, had erased herself from the book of life, prior to dying . . .

"The Morrow Men chose to flee from me as I waded among them with expert lunges of the Crook; and then, she and I were left alone, and our bodies were drawn together as if by the ineluctable desires of communing microbes . . .

"Aye," he said, his eyes as wide and deep as abysses, "it was as if there had been an alignment between two stars of equal force. A bond between us formed as if by an alchemical fusion of our innermost parts of native sex and personality.

"She was a Machinist of the Faltering Steppes, she said, and she bid me to return with her to her brethren, which I did; and when they learned of my ability to factor the weather, upon receiving demonstrations of my infallible techniques, they implored me to remain with them as Monitor of Intrusions. I accepted my appointment on the grounds that my love for Honeycomb ran so deep in my veins that I was bound to her as if by a magnetic force, so much so that it had killed her."

BleakWarrior filled his cup with wine, passed the bottle to Reading the Clouds who accepted and said, "I admit that her suicide was not foreseeable in the mental drafts of nature that are my concern. And yet, in retrospect, I recall the brooding colours of dusk that preceded her death—signs concealed (not of themselves but) by a lack of my alertness to them."

"But why," BleakWarrior asked, trying but failing to suppress his thoughts of Achlana Promff, "did she do it?"

"Because my love was too great a violence against the

delicacies of her nature," said Reading the Clouds. "I believe that we, as Meta-Warriors, are too intense for linear souls to withstand the bareness of our heat, when so they are exposed."

BleakWarrior stared into the flames. The Warped Lenses shone with a warped intensity that might have been a reflection of his innermost brain pattern.

"It is not the loss of something known and loved that I crave," he said, "but the knowledge of something unknown and hated."

"How so, BleakWarrior? Where is the value in satisfying so reckless an aim?"

"Are not all aims reckless?"

"Only when the eye of the beholder is at fault."

BleakWarrior's smile was harsh:

"The eyes of *this* beholder are laden with faults, though some would call them excellences."

"Then I refuse to interfere with the courses of your craving. You will pass unmolested through the Faltering Steppes."

"Your accommodation of my needs will not be forgotten."

"Nor yours of mine."

"Then let us drink till there is nothing left for us to wish for."

BleakWarrior conversed with Reading the Clouds into the long hours of the night. Plumes of smoke rose from the flames between them, glazing the darkness like words without the substance of meaning.

Before dawn had broke, BleakWarrior departed into the nocturnal lustre of the Faltering Steppes, with a mind to reaching the luxuriant lowland valleys of the Quagan, whereupon Reading the Clouds had said, "I have read in the clouds a rupture emanating from the City of Prelations which occurred with an alikeness to a Leap of Cynosure but with striking imbalances underlying its mien. There, I think, you will find the one you are looking for—in a villa that reeks of degradations, which have addled the distant portions of the sky for as long as I have seen them. Know also that there are others in that city whom the sky remarks as capable of performing harm: I bid you to be beware of them with strenuous warnings, BleakWarrior."

And Reading the Clouds returned to the Township of Cowls where a second prisoner had been taken by the Machinists who, according to his commands, had dangled her from an elaborate mechanical contrivance called the Weakener.

BleakWarrior set off across the highland prairies of the Faltering Steppes where the windswept grasses moved left and right like waves across a green ocean. He was accosted by flying insects but bitten more by unbidden thoughts of Achlana Promff, which he wished (without success) to subdue.

She had left for him a letter in their delegated place of assignation. BleakWarrior had broken open its seal, unravelled it, and read it with unstoppable haste:

> I am being investigated. Our communications must cease. My diaries have been confiscated and are being examined. I have written too much of you. Flee at once. I will be arrested and questioned and, after that . . . I have degraded my Church. I will be drowned in a bucket of my own blood for punishment. The Wing of Enigmas will hunt you down as an abomination. They will cut you up and unravel you, impinge and probe while you are warm. Be gone from this place without delay. Remember that I love you—that I will protect you all I can—or I will die trying.

BleakWarrior had torn the letter into little bits, chewed on it and swallowed—devoured it whole as he might devour his own life—and resolved to never think of Achlana Promff.

Never again.

*

Hanging from one of the stupidest assemblages of ropes, ratchets, springs, sprockets, winches, tines and scaffolding she'd ever seen, Welter of Impermanence fought to contain her need to masturbate, which had already filled her with an uncontainable hatred of her captors, whom she had nevertheless attempted to mollify with a look on her face like some stupid unsullied orphan girl who'd got lost in the woods.

The strain of her desire to masturbate was greater than the strain of her calibrated position of discomfort on the Weakener. So at least it counted for something. But worse was the fact that they had stripped her naked so that her nipples stood out from her breasts as if the wind should suck them.

"No one will suck them."

Her inflated lips yearned to be breeched by some solid implement taken from its place of concealment in the utility suit which, together with her Utensils, the Machinists had taken away from her.

And worse than that, her legs were spread at just the right angle for delving her fingers into the accumulating dampness of her crotch; but, needless to say, her hands had been tied on raised arms that caused her breasts to thrust outwards with an involuntary brazenness that, under other circumstances, might have been quite pleasing.

"The first person who offers me the opportunity," said Welter of Impermanence, "will die."

But, in truth, she knew that the opportunity might never come and that her situation was less than encouraging.

Welter of Impermanence had been suspended from the balcony of a civic building of some importance, whose arabesque mouldings set it apart from the sombre timber edifices of the town as a whole. The town itself was patently ugly, harmonious rather than ramshackle, but in a way that soured the spirits rather than raised them. The people buzzed about its streets as if drawn by the steadfast appeal of believing (without knowing) that they were absolutely right about everything.

Which also made them dangerous.

Welter of Impermanence studied closely the inhabitants who paid little attention to her, save for the stinging glances they threw at her like livid sparks. She saw in their faces the deadpan cruelty of their arrogance, and it frightened her.

It frightened her because she might never get the chance to wipe that look from off their face.

Forever.

10.
A Week in Pursuit of the Essence of Genius

The Ever Decreasing Circle of Choice wrote in his journal at the end of the day:

The Sensorial Platacaster has produced its first success! What more can I say than that my specimen is typical of the species—utterly unique, uncommonly robust, with a body to match and a mental sensibility that verges on the sociopathic!

I began my experiments this morning in earnest using the psycho-chemical approach, which has already produced some exciting results. Suffice to say that I have learnt his name. Additionally, I have gathered some facts regarding his character and history.

The procedure was exactly as I had planned. I injected him with a Tell Me! solution whereby he responded to my questions with a compulsive need to furnish me with the absolute truth. The most important aspects of our discussion were as follows:

Me: "What would you consider your foremost attributes?"

Counterpain: "My capacity for physical endurance is undoubtedly my most outstanding trait. This is especially true in the case of sexual interaction with humans, or animals, through which I receive the reinvigoration of my vital parts."

Me: "Eh, which parts exactly?"

Counterpain: "All of them . . . I think."

Me: "I see. And to what extent is this a necessary function of your existence?"

Counterpain: "To the extent that, without it, I would surely die."

Me: "Interesting! And do you suppose that it also pertains to the more subtle depths of your persona?"

Counterpain: "Undoubtedly."

Me: "In what way?"

Counterpain: "In that I am also adept at inventing ways and means of killing people through a highly developed range of sadomasochistic techniques, which are mostly of my own devising—though help has been solicited on occasions by, uh, special acquaintances."

Me: "And can you provide me with examples of these techniques?"

Counterpain: "I would prefer to offer you demonstrations."

Me: "All in good time. For the moment, I would prefer verbal illustrations only."

Counterpain: "I see . . ."

And, here, I will spare you the details, which are assuredly colourful, and which are demonstrative, too, of a creative zeal which is attributable, no doubt, to an underlying quality of genius—which, in Counterpain, is not at once discernible but evident, nevertheless, on a number of counts (amounting to three).

I will now press on with further stages of my analysis, beginning with a methodology which I refer to as "sensorial." I will be assessing Counterpain's psychological reactions to physical tests which will allow me to quantify his general mental relations with the external world. Among my chief concerns are the emotional repercussions of his intolerance to pain, inasmuch as he might have any, which is, of course, a matter of some debate, for which I must now embark on the strictest scientific procedure.

*

Using a variety of instrumentation and some ministrations of my own concoction, wrote The Ever Decreasing Circle of Choice in his journal at the end of another day, I have successfully subjected my specimen to a series of physical tests, the results of which, according to my best estimates, are either profound, meaningless or decidedly absurd for their inaccuracy.

I began my experiments with a few sessions of force-feeding my guest with a sickly array of comestible items—thistles, urchins, aphids, worms, raw cephalopods and the boiled tongues of dogs. My aim was to assail him with a prolonged exposure to digestive disorders of which the chief inducement would be a sustained mauling of the bowels. I accomplished this task without much difficulty, whilst avoiding the threat of intestinal damage of a more serious nature. Counterpain was unable to prevent himself from vomiting up at least a half of what he had eaten, which did nothing to prohibit the stupendous gut-rot I was hoping for.

His response, however, was to crave more of the revolting items on offer, in view of which his discomfort, he said, was "mildly exhilarating."

I noted immediately a tendency of psychosomatic role reversal, whereby his reaction to affliction was translated, not as repugnant, but as wholly pleasurable. This, I concluded, was the earliest indication of his genius, which enabled him to convert his gastronomic shocks into a marked appreciation of their individual stimuli.

Similar results were obtained when I subjected him to a cruder analysis by dislocating his arms from their sockets and returning them again without means of facilitating a generous execution of the manoeuvre. While the extent of his pain was considerable, he nevertheless interpreted the injunctions of my controlled assault as "uniquely compatible with my love of the dramatic."

It was then that I decided that a more subtle

approach was required for pushing Counterpain to the limits of his endurance, whereupon I exposed him to the operations of an award-winning mechanical contrivance called the Bone Rippler.

The Bone Rippler is a simple device that is first attached to a section of the wearer's body where the bones are most prominent and, hence, more sensitive to the actions of its mechanism. The head, knees, elbows, hips, shins and knuckles are areas of particular vulnerability, albeit my preference is for the coccyx or the vertebrae at the top the spine. The deployment of the device is coincident with the general sensitivity of the wearer to the touch of foreign applications (the head works best for those who are more resistant to bodily interference, while the vertebrae work best for those of a more nervous disposition. In the case of Counterpain, I attached the device to the lower parts of his shins and toes).

The remarkable thing about the Bone Rippler is that it generates a sound at an ultrasonic frequency which causes the bones to vibrate at a consistent pitch of tolerable irritation which, sustained over time, becomes totally infuriating. The trick of the device is that it renders the subject senseless through the gradual accentuation of its worsening distress and, so, avoids the discourtesies of direct violence, whereby damage is limited to a transitory discomfort which instantly subsides upon the machine's deactivation.

However: the effect of the Bone Rippler on Counterpain was to raise him to a height of spiritual reverie which provided him with "a euphoric awareness of the sheer extent of our inability to comprehend the exact purpose of our existence beyond the fact that it is impossible to comprehend it!"

It is evident, then, that stimulations which should have alerted his brain to a negative interference with his body were accepted as positive contributions to his physical and mental well-being which were subsequently reinforced, instead of weakened, by the effect of the interference in question.

Remarkable, is it not? and equally significant in terms of the discoveries that await me.

Speaking of which, I will now press ahead with my plan to psychoanalyse the adaptability of Counterpain's brain to a series of neuro-electrical interjections which have never before been tried on live specimens of his calibre.

Questions, questions, questions, wrote The Ever Decreasing Circle of Choice in his journal at the end of yet another day (or was it the beginning? For he had become, by now, so deeply engrossed in his experimentations that time itself had lost the diurnal essence of its flow). Subsequent to the neuro-electrification of selected parts Counterpain's brain, I have stumbled on certain discoveries that have perplexed me by a considerable margin of double my sense of incredulity!

For instance:

The insertion of sub-cranial implants into the frontal lobes has provoked, in him, some startling reactions which began as follows:

Me: "I am about to raise the voltage of the

electrical charge which will produce an invigorating effect on the mental values arising from your personal history."

Counterpain: "My what?"

Me: "Your memories."

Counterpain: "Oh. And will it be stimulating?"

Me: "I should think so, yes."

Counterpain: "Will it make me feel happy?"

Me: "Ha! My dear fellow, I'm about to load your brain with a 100 volts of electrical mayhem. I should think it will make you very happy indeed."

Counterpain: "Fire away, then."

I did, turning the dial of the applications box to about three eighths of its fullest measure.

Me: "Please describe your thoughts and feelings as the voltage is increased."

Counterpain: "Now?"

Me: "Yes."

Counterpain: "Right. Well, my mind is becoming awash with a welter of impressions that are decidedly colourful."

Me: "What kind of impressions?"

Counterpain: "Naked ones."

Me: "I see. Then please describe them to me with as much attention to detail as possible."

And Counterpain, caught between gibbers and slurs, began his recital—

Of naked men and women who populated his mental landscape—fornicators (no surprise there) who assailed each other with willing seductions and a mutual investigation of one another's deepest lusts. He spoke most vigorously of their general tendency to congregate around a half-luminous mental aperture of visible distinction; and his name for it was the Oily Well.

"The oily what?" I asked him.

"Well," he said, and proceeded to speak of bodies dissolving in a turgid mass of wet holes and belligerent phalluses, elapsing into the Oily Well like cosmic milks into a void.

And I watched in awe as the electrical charge fed into Counterpain's brain like the branches of a small tree. His body strained with intensifying might against the bonds that bound him to the rack—the veins on his arms pulsing like snakes; his muscles taut as a mathematical equation. As I increased the voltage, the bonds began to strain to breaking point, forcing me to reduce the voltage to one eighth of its force in order to contain him.

It was clear to me, then, that I must prepare myself to extract the fluids of Counterpain's hippocampus and inject them into my own by way of obtaining a similar degree of superabundant animal vitality. Not to mention the possibility of acquiring a comparable sense of sexual disorientation which, from a scientific point of view, was sufficiently worthy of further study.

In the meantime, how else was I to summarise

these comprehensive marvels than by crying out with a shake of my fist:

"It is surely all in the hippocampus!"

And I closed my eyes to bask in the warmth of my ecstasy of purpose, then opened them again with a vague sense of alacrity when:

"Mean you do what?" spluttered Counterpain, who was now having difficulty in formulating coherent speech patterns.

"Well," I said, intently stroking my chin in a manner that seemed fitting, "it is apparent that your experiences have contributed to the creation of an archetype that is the neurological fulcrum around which your absorption of pain is able to generate a psycho-centrifugal surplus of regenerative energy."

"Party type?"

"Yes," I said, "the Oily Well! This image, which your brain has devised of its own accord, defines your experiences to a point of—"

"Not you are knocking about?"

"It's really very simple. Instead of processing your memories to a point of individual literal clarity, your brain has collated them into a collective symbol which acts as a psychic inducement to your—."

"But real Oily is the Well!"

"I beg your pardon."

"A Symbol is not. Originated I in the Well Oily. In my real it appears but is as dreams as you and I."

At this point, I hastened to cut the voltage in order to restore Counterpain's order of speech. I wiped away the slavers from his lips, and asked:

"Are you saying that the Oily Well is real? Are you saying that it is an authentic recollection? Are you saying that it is something you have actually experienced?"

"I was in there for centuries," panted Counterpain, his tongue flopping around his mouth like a bisected worm, "until the Gainful Maiden came to me to escort me from the midst of my delirium. She massaged my tender parts until I was predisposed to a linear awareness of myself. She bade me drink from the Oily Well. Its contents filled me with an illimitable sexual fervour, which is the basis for my lifework now."

"What lifework now?"

"Killing people."

"What people?"

"People," said Counterpain, his head blling into an unconscious tumble, "like you."

*

The operation slab, wrote The Ever Decreasing Circle of Choice in his journal at the end of the sixth or seventh day, is now fully prepared for a biotic session of surgery on my specimen, who is currently enjoying a delectable array of nutritious victuals, including supplementary ministrations of vitamins, minerals and anabolic steroids, which will put him in good stead for his forthcoming traumas.

It is my intention to put him under heavy sedation (amounting to a catatonic unconsciousness that lasts for days) which will assuredly prevent his reactionary metabolism from functioning properly. It is vital that he is reduced to a condition of pseudo-apoplectic numbness in order to contain the excitement of which he is capable which, should it go unmonitored, may lead to an apoplectic haemorrhage of actual proportions.

Far be it from me to risk the man's life prior to extracting whatever I can extract from him . . .

But enough talk!

Counterpain has eaten well and now lounges on the floor of his cage like an overfed floozy. I will administer a narcotic that buries him deep in the catacombs of sleep, whereby I hope to acquire the decisive fluids that permeate his frontal lobes.

In the meantime, there is much for me to ponder as regards the implications of the Oily Well, which requires of me an exceptional bout of heavy thinking. Soon, I will be constrained to making choices amounting to life or death decisions which, for all that they inspire me, compel me to the daunting task of choosing wisely and, above all, choosing well.

11.
The Brain Exchange

Never had a fusion of order and chaos been accomplished with such casual actuality among the linear peoples as in the City of Prelations, where dust in the air is a rouge in the lungs, dusts that were legion, and gaseous potencies, with a thousand radiant smells appending to extravagant victuals, punished flesh, chemical profusions, the exorbitance of steaming vats, lubrications and mechanical functions, electrical rupture and the tang of burning rubber, water tempering overheated parts, the sweat of hard labour, the pungency of live dissections—the excessive preoccupations of a culture whose destruction and creativity were simultaneously upheld as a definitive condition, both permanent and ephemeral in its flirtatious relations with extreme dangers, which it undertook unconsciously and, so, with a ruthlessness that assured it of an impressive ratio of manifold successes.

The momentum was one of onward motion, as inevitable as a tide on the shores of knowledge, which it erodes with inexhaustible thoroughness, until something happens—an outbreak of fire, a catastrophic plague, civil unrest—that will never happen, because the whole place, the whole people, is far too sure of itself to allow for the stagnation of outright failure.

Calamity refuses to fall upon those who least expect it; and the Quagan expected *nothing*.

It didn't matter if their discoveries were useless or impractical, for which they retained a novelty value of the fascination *in itself*. They amalgamated the nominal divisions of order and chaos into a self-propagating paradigm of existential bloody-mindedness that was distinguishable for its absence of moral cohesion that moderates behaviour.

And this is what made them special—the fact that they didn't care about the consequences of what they were doing as long as they were getting it properly done.

To this extent, they were like Meta-Warriors bereft of a definite purpose (of killing their foes), whose only validation was an illusion of progress that, in the end, was negligible because it was more like a form of entertainment than a way of life (like the ribald comedies of the decadent theatre groups of the Republic of Noth, except for the fact that the Quagan were writing scripts that were cruel enough to be real).

BleakWarrior nodded by way of acknowledging the objective accuracy of this thought. He could understand why a Meta-Warrior like The Ever Decreasing Circle of Choice had embedded himself in the midst of the Quagan as one of their foremost practitioners. The Quagan had offered him a platform for his expeditious deeds which he could utilise with impunity while disguising himself as a prominent member of its resident scientocracy.

"An excellent ploy," BleakWarrior admitted. "But I wonder if he has so engrossed himself in these linear practices that he has forgotten what he is—and why."

BleakWarrior passed a row of pig heads roasting on spits that dripped viscous amounts of fat into rows of flames that idled beneath them.

"My emotional positions," he thought, "are as pig heads over the flame of my madness."

But the flame of madness didn't idle.

The flame of madness roared.

The quadrangles and arcades of the City of Prelations showed a shoddiness of inaccurate construction that was a measure of how the enormity of a scientific free-for-all commanded the city's interests. It was the architectural equivalence of the favour given to issues of magnitude over the smaller concerns of the slaves and navvies who hammered and scrubbed with nervous industry—aware of the retributions that hung over them like a surgeon's knife, poised to make its first incision, were they to fail to carry out their tasks with satisfactory resolve—which they did with the slapdash efficiency of a people working under the constraints of tyranny.

Among the shabby droves of underclasses were the artisans and suppliers, chefs and courtesans—an indigenous workforce of privileged public servants and servicers—whose objective in life was to aid the scientocracy, with an awareness of their position as inferior but necessary parts of the entire rigmarole.

The commotion of the City of Prelations was brutal and senseless. But it was also full of an excitement of living on the edge of modern life that attracted scores of affluent visitors from foreign parts, who were not made welcome so much as tolerated. Most of these visitors were regarded with an incidental scorn for their outlandish dress or were vigorously ignored for their incessant gawking.

Which is not to say that they weren't being watched.

The eyes and ears of interested parties were ever-alert to the intrusions of guests who circulated their city streets, some of whom were like secrets said in low whispers, striving to be heard.

The Brain Exchange was frequented by aspiring scientists (many of whom had already failed) who were intent on hiring the services of licensed theoreticians who were also among the most scantily dressed young scholars in the whole of the Quagan.

The prostiticians, as they were called, had been tailored to specific areas of scientific and mathematical competency in order to serve as a learning resource for those who required it (usually because they weren't up to the task of learning whatever it was by themselves). Studies had shown that an additional exposure to erotic stimuli was conducive to cognitive activity, while other studies (largely dismissed) had argued that the sight of naked flesh was a perilous distraction.

Custom at the Brain Exchange, therefore, thrived, which made it as good a place to gather information as any.

"What do you wish to know, friend?"

A girl had approached BleakWarrior almost as soon as he'd sat at his table, her breasts like large apples edging out of her cleavage—like beacons guiding a ship to a safe anchorage on a stormy night.

"I require a hard-hitting beverage to soothe my rattled nerves," said BleakWarrior.

"It comes with the service," the prostitician said, and stood like she was waiting for further instructions.

"I would prefer to drink first," said BleakWarrior, "before availing myself of your obvious talents."

The girl shrugged and turned away. Within moments, a young man dressed in fishnet thongs arrived with a large carafe full of a dense and murky liquid. He laid it on the table, poured a glass, and departed without a word.

BleakWarrior took a gargantuan swig from the dense and murky liquid and found his head was aglow with drunken fervour. A smear of warm gloom flooded the Brain Exchange like an infection. Sludges of different coloured light shone from a pulse of small flames through kaleidoscopic glass encasements. The gloom was a multifaceted and muggy transparency. Potted plants emitted a semi-visible cloud of spores that enlivened the mind to a subtle level of plenary understanding. Talk among the clientele was lively and verbose, and BleakWarrior stood out for his solitary brooding, which was starting to grate with the prostitician who'd come to serve him earlier.

She came back to him with a look on her face like sour milk and said, "You really look as if you need my help."

BleakWarrior stared passed her and said, "I require a physician for my head."

"What?"

"It is my wish to undergo psychiatric therapy. I need a doctor—a brain specialist. Where might I find one?"

"That's not really what I'm here for," she said.

BleakWarrior settled the Lenses on her and gave it the full glare. The prostitician shifted on her feet and registered a smile that had all the charm of a hairline fracture.

"What about Dr Vile," said BleakWarrior. "I've heard he's good."

"Meribold Vile?"

"Where can I find him?"

"He's available by appointment only," said the prostitician.

"I'll make one," said BleakWarrior.

"There's a two year waiting list," she said.

"That's not what I asked," said BleakWarrior, allowing a trace of menace to creep into his voice.

"The Twin Spikes," she said. "That's his villa. Just follow the Major Boulevard heading west, go passed the School of Essential Sciences, then follow the road for the Half Snar. You'll recognise his villa because of the Spikes. The Twin Spikes. That's what gives his villa its name."

BleakWarrior paid the girl and finished his murky draught.

He slammed his mug on the table—heads were turned that turned away when they met the clammy glimmer of the Warped Lenses.

And he was gone.

To what extent can a Meta-Warrior comprehend the futility of its actions? To what extent can it bear the emotional repercussions of what it is, without knowing what it seeks or why?

It has been said of Meta-Warriors that rage is a measure of their underlying grief—not for the loss of anything before them, but for the loss of what they are working towards: themselves.

And yet, could anything be more perfect than the flaw of their ambitions that runs counter-wise to the linear grain of common governmental order? Could anything coincide more directly to the point of a specific purpose? To exist with an immunity to linear abstractions is surely to retain the simplicity of a pre-existence which is purer for its essential rudeness, where the loss of an already forfeited existence is done at the expense of nothing not already lost. It is the recovery, merely, of a preceding absence, made absolute by the fact that it still courses a living vein.

Meta-Warriors are not among those who suffer the distractions of an awareness of questions like these. Being, for them, is not a creed. No conviction is stronger than doing what is necessary without knowing why.

As to an instinct comes the demands of purpose, Meta-Warriors do what is necessary, *because they needed to.*

—Lord Hecticon, *Aspirations*

Mega-Negation gathered the Dead Rock Chapter of The Breaking Wave in the luxurious grounds of his observatory on the outskirts of the City of Prelations. Exotic teas were served on a leafy terrace overlooking the Valley of Grins. Fan cake was served on silver platters. A taciturn mumble of conversation spread among the Dead Rock Chapter members like a murmur of bees.

Mega-Negation positioned himself on his chair and made a signal for them to cease their blether and hearken to his address. The air was warm in the afternoon sun. Everyone stopped their blether and listened.

"Dr Snapper, Dr Breath, and Dr Thorn," began Mega-Negation. "We have had word from a prostitician operating under our command that an unlikely stranger was seen brooding like a stick insect in the locality of the Brain Exchange. Her suspicions were aroused by the fact that he declined her offer of technical assistance, which of course defeats the purpose of his being there. Instead, he asked her *questions* about a physician of some renown, whose name you might recognise as Meribold Vile."

The Doctors registered their disbelief in the form of a gasp. Mega-Negation allowed them to do so before going on.

"As executioners of our will to do damage to offending parties, I propose that we adopt a series of special measures attending to the highest standards of efficiency and stealth, with which to pursue our primary goals with a relentless determination to meet them. As a matter of course, and in view of our accessions to doing what we do best, I would ask you to conduct an investigation of the stranger's presence, with due care of potential dangers, and to capture him forthwith. I trust that my demands are equal to your approval."

The members of the Dead Rock Chapter grunted their assent in accordance to the demands of protocol.

"We are honoured that you ask," added Dr Snapper, and bowed.

"Good," said Mega-Negation. "Well, Doctors, I believe that this concludes our business for today. It remains for me only to petition Dr Thither for the use of one of his remarkable birds. Lord Hecticon must learn of our devotions to his cause, for such as we have made of them our own devoted causes . . ."

Happy Snapper was a bone specialist who carried a set of pliers that were big enough to wrap around a human leg. Breath of Death Air was an expert in chemical and gas applications. Thornographer was a sex therapist who specialised in acupuncture and asphyxiation techniques.

In addition to their Weapons of Choice, they had equipped themselves with serrated hooks, rip coils and potential energy weapons loaded with stupor darts, spike balls, razor wings and feather-toned impact prongs. They had swapped their gowns for combat frocks with an outward resemblance to the casual raiment of researchers pursuing a subsidiary class of scientific inquiry. The frocks were lined with copper foil to deter the penetrations of sharp instruments with reasonable forbearance. But it was the look in their eye as they left the precincts of the observatory that betrayed the extent of the dire tidings they would bring to whomsoever would bear the brunt of them.

Unto the shore that stands before them falls The Breaking Wave.

12.
The First Day of Retributions

It is true that I have no way of knowing if the quintessence of genius rests within my grasp; but I feel that it does. If not, then my experiments have surely been of great benefit to my cause. To have pieced together a psychological profile of my guest, which has prompted me to extract the fluids from his frontal lobes, has been useful to me to say the least.

In the first place, it has provided me with an insight into the workings of his mind which has provided me, in turn, with an insight into the workings of my own. There is something inordinately complex about our psychology, something that runs much deeper than I thought. In the context of science, complexity is a basis for uncertainty which, in itself, is a basis for extreme danger. To infuse the brain with additional fluids is the surest way of causing its irreparable harm, which I know to be true under normal circumstances of linear transaction. In the case of myself, I had thought to retain an immunity against collateral damage because of my Demi-Thurganic resistance to standard biochemical disruptions. It is apparent, however, that there are certain risks that must be assessed in relation to the likelihood of their occurrence. There is no telling what would happen to me if things went wrong; and I suspect that, by injecting myself with the serum, I might transform myself into a virtual monster.

Which brings me to another point.

Let us be sure that, in our case, we are dealing with a special kind of mental fabric—rather than faculty—which has evolved, I believe, from a precursory level of material substantiation. What I mean to say is that the Oily Well is real (that it happened) in more ways than one, and that it coincides with my own experiences of peculiar recollection, which in the past I have attributed, falsely, to dreams; whereas it seems clear to me now that these dreams are not the symbolic reproductions of our innermost fears and states of mind.

No.

These are things that happened as occasions of the fullest immersion of existential states, which exist, now, as inversions of a primary state of existential definition (which is to say that the concrete reality of the Oily Well was internalised as if through a vacuum between two versions of the same world). I may even go as far as to suggest that the Oily Well is a totemic memory deriving from an initial phase of sensory interaction with concrete forms which has undergone its existential transformation.

But, for the moment, allow me to catch my breath, for I am both enthused and dumfounded by this discovery in ways I cannot express without adequate reflection.

In the meantime, let us consider the serum.

I have decided upon the formula of the serum and am lacking only the realisation of its blend. My laboratory is prepared for the procedure, and it remains for me only to prepare myself for what is to come.

Speaking of which, it is interesting that I find myself in the position of being faced with the kind of choice that, normally, I reserve for my linear specimens. A part of me, certainly, wishes to proceed without the encumbrances of caution; but, as a scientist, I know that sound methodology is the cornerstone of good science. In short, then, I require a period of intensive thinking to allow me to weigh the possible outcomes of my . . .

Just a moment . . .

I think . . .

I think that . . .

I think that there is someone . . .

Something . . .

I think that there is someone trying to . . .

It appears that I may have to abandon my current entry due to the unannounced arrival of a visitor. He is a strange looking man who shows himself to be of a remarkable appearance, not least because of the amber encrustations that cover his eyes. I have never seen anything like those eyes; and, indeed, yes, I fear I must bring my entry to an abrupt close. My visitor is approaching at the very moment I write. Quickly as I can. He seems to be in a violent humour. He is holding before him

The Dirk pressed hard against The Ever Decreasing Circle of Choice's throat, forcing him to fall back against his chair which slid back against the wall of his study with a faint crunch of wood against plaster.

"I'm sure we can come to some kind of agreement," exclaimed The Ever Decreasing Circle of Choice, "regardless of the terms. You seem to me like a reasonable man, a man of substance. Need I mention the fact that you hold a certain advantage against me in the form of a knife? I won't deny it, no—that would be foolish. But it prompts me to ask if you would consider several propositions which immediately spring to—"

"Quiet."

"Of course. You will not hear another word from me. Not one. Albeit, I am somewhat surprised that my servants didn't prevent you from entering my villa without my consent. I must decide upon the appropriate punishments. I am also concerned about the manner in which you were received by my valets. May I ask if—"

"Your servants are dead."

"Ah," said The Ever Decreasing Circle of Choice, "then I hope they didn't oppose you or encourage you to violence. Let me offer my sincerest apologies. I will, of course, have their corpses flayed and eaten by dogs. I have built a contraption that caters for this very function. I can assure you that I will do everything in my power to—"

BleakWarrior pressed the Dirk against The Ever Decreasing Circle of Choice's throat. His head tilted back against the wall until it stopped tilting.

"Let me assure you that you will do everything in your power to help me," said BleakWarrior.

"It was always on my mind to help you," croaked The Ever Decreasing Circle of Choice, "and I was already making plans to that effect. I can see that you're a man of . . . exceptional needs. And how might I be of assistance, exactly? I feel bound to say that I am a brain specialist. I may be unable to assist you in matters pertaining to, ah, other parts."

"I'm not here because you're a brain specialist," said BleakWarrior. "I'm here because you're a Meta-Warrior."

And, for the first time since his arrival, The Ever Decreasing Circle of Choice was utterly speechless.

"I prefer to call us Demi-Thurgans," said The Ever Decreasing Circle of Choice, now sitting at his desk with his hands folded one on the other, his elbows spread, his head slightly inclined to one side in his customary position of professional consultancy.

"It is a good name," said BleakWarrior.

"Thank you," said The Ever Decreasing Circle of Choice.

"And now you're going to tell me what it means."

"I am?"

"Yes."

"Ah, well, simply put, it's a question of terminology appropriate to the natural sciences."

"I want to know what it means," said BleakWarrior.

"Ah, well, that's a different matter. And a tricky one."

"Tricky? Sailing knots are tricky, Circle, and the information I require is not a sailing knot."

"Ah, yes, naturally, of course. But you will also understand that there are certain codes of practice to be observed."

"I don't follow codes of practice," said BleakWarrior.

"No, no, I didn't mean you. I was referring to myself." The Ever Decreasing Circle of Choice gave a weak smile. "You see, knowledge is precious—very precious—and it has to be earned. It cannot come without a price."

"The price," said BleakWarrior, "is your life."

"Ah, yes, but these matters are delicate."

"Delicate? Flowers are delicate, Circle, and the information I require is not a flower."

"I mean," said The Ever Decreasing Circle of Choice, "that

they are—well, what I mean to say is that they are . . . private."

"Private?"

"For my ears only. And for yours. But not for anyone else's."

BleakWarrior turned the Lenses on The Ever Decreasing Circle of Choice. The Lenses glared.

"What are you getting at?" he said as smooth as glass.

"Well, I thought we might come to an agreement."

"We already have."

"Ah. But what if I asked you to offer me something that would furnish me with the right kind of motivation."

"The right kind of motivation for what?"

"For answering your questions."

BleakWarrior held up the Dirk.

"This is all the motivation you're going to get, Circle."

"What I mean to say is that, ah, with the right kind of motivation, I feel I might be able to tell you more than you actually think I know."

"And what, other than death, do you want me to offer you?"

The Ever Decreasing Circle of Choice lowered his head and whispered:

"Your promise not to tell anybody."

BleakWarrior took a deep breath and said, "It has been my life's work to search for information, Circle, and, for what I receive, I'm hardly likely to give it up so easily."

The Ever Decreasing Circle of Choice appeared relieved.

"In that case," he said, "I think we can—"

And he was immediately cut off by a scream too weak to be anything more than a rasping cough that quickly degenerated into a fading moan that wafted from the direction of the laboratory like one of its bad smells.

BleakWarrior was on his feet, Dirk in hand, rushing to the source of the pathetic appeal.

"Wait!" cried The Ever Decreasing Circle of Choice. "It's only my patient! Don't harm him!"

But BleakWarrior was through the door of the study into the laboratory where he saw . . . nothing.

Then he saw a door from where the sound now came like water running down a plug hole.

"What is that?" BleakWarrior demanded, raising a hand and pointing.

"It's an adjoining chamber where I perform my operations on slabs that are equipped with leather restraints," said the Ever Decreasing Circle of Choice, as if that should explain everything. "Follow me. Say nothing."

And the Ever Decreasing Circle of Choice rushed passed BleakWarrior as fast as a weasel and, slowing his pace, stepped into the chamber with BleakWarrior behind him like a hunting dog.

"Glad to see you again, sir," said a voice from inside. "I wonder if you would be so kind as to bring me a cup of water."

BleakWarrior entered and saw a figure strapped to a slab that had been tilted upwards to provide a degree of comfort for the person who was clearly in no degree of comfort at all. The person appeared wholly brutalised after an outlandish fashion of tremendous gashes cut across a shaven head that looked as if they were intended to be decorative, which made them more hideous than they already were.

"Who," said BleakWarrior, pointing the Dirk, "is that."

"That," said The Ever Decreasing Circle of Choice, "is my patient, Counterpain. Counterpain, may I present to you, ah, Dr Bleak."

"My pleasure," said Counterpain.

BleakWarrior stared at him through the Lenses as if hoping he would begin to boil. He scrutinised him hard and, sure enough, began to see him for what he was.

"He's one of us."

"Yes," said the Ever Decreasing Circle of Choice, "he is."

BleakWarrior rounded on the dilapidated figure of Counterpain with a look on his face like he wanted to devour him without knowing where to start.

"What have you done to this ruined specimen?" he said.

"Ruined?" Counterpain sat up uselessly against his bonds.

"Calm yourself, calm yourself." The Ever Decreasing Circle of Choice made a gesture to encourage BleakWarrior to silence then quickly fussed over Counterpain, laying him down and smoothing his brow as if administering comforts to a small child. "Don't worry. You're absolutely fine. You need more sleep, that's all. What you're feeling now—the way you look—it's absolutely normal for someone in your, ah, condition."

"But I feel marvellous," said Counterpain. "I just can't remember who I am."

"Yes, yes. A temporary amnesia caused by my, ah, surgical reparations." He turned to BleakWarrior and, with desperate cordiality, said, "Would you care to join me in the study for a refreshment, Dr Bleak? I have the very finest selection of imported wines from the Isle of Smir. Allow me to offer you a sample while Counterpain continues his, ah, recovery."

"I would be delighted for Counterpain to continue his recovery," said BleakWarrior.

They departed from the operating chamber and, immediately, The Ever Decreasing Circle of Choice began to flap.

"Please, BleakWarrior. You mustn't disturb him. It is imperative that he remains in the best of moods."

"You have reduced him to a mood of imbecility."

"I am a scientist, BleakWarrior, and Counterpain is a subject of my research."

"You are a Meta-Warrior, and so is he."

"What of it?"

"A Meta-Warrior should die like one."

"Since when, BleakWarrior, have you acquired scruples?"

"Not scruples, Circle. It is a matter of principle."

"A matter of principle? Have you discovered religion?"

"Madness is my religion."

"And where, I wonder, does madness coincide with matters of principle."

"It is a matter of principle that Counterpain's guts should lie in strings about his feet, his belly torn, and his head accosted by our Weapons."

"I have accosted his head with my experiments, BleakWarrior, and it is because of this that I may be able to help you."

"*If* you are able to help me."

"I think I can."

"We shall see, Dr Vile," said BleakWarrior, with the trace of a snarl across his lips. "We shall see."

The Ever Decreasing Circle of Choice sat at his desk, gazing intently at BleakWarrior as if searching for something that wasn't there.

"I will begin by considering the question: what are we?" He crossed his legs, pressed his fingertips together and closed his eyes. "It is difficult to say. We share the same appetites as linear humans but are unrestricted by their moral biases, which are redundant elements of our psychology but, in their case, act as a formal measure of difference from the world of beasts."

"Ever Decreasing Circle of Choice," interjected BleakWarrior. "I am aware of the linear weaknesses that are absent from our personality. I would petition you to keep directly to the point."

The Circle opened his eyes and frowned—then nodded once, smiled and resumed his discourse.

"Well, BleakWarrior, I will say this: we are abnormal; and, while we share the same appetites and abilities as linear humans, we exceed them by a dramatic margin. But note my emphasis on *abnormal,* rather than supernatural. It is my earnest belief, BleakWarrior, that Meta-Warriors do not exceed the laws of nature but rather bend them, somehow, out of shape. We have undertaken a separate development from the human genome and are measurable by our *difference* rather than superiority."

"This is all very well," said BleakWarrior, his head at an angle, looking at nothing, "but how does this relate to this term of yours?"

"Demi-Thurgan?"

BleakWarrior nodded.

"'Thurgan' is a word that is used by the Quagan to describe any of the elements or conditions of nature that are not sentient or human. Soil particles, water or gas, amoebas, fibres, pieces of grit, lizards, rocks, trees, centipedes, rivers, buildings—you get the idea. 'Quagan,' on the other hand, refers to anything in the world that is sentient or human, which is what the Quagan call themselves. The basis for the scientific canon of the Quagan begins with the separation of nature into the Quaganic and Thurganic order of states (while the zero order of states refers to everything in its entirety).

"I have devised the phrase 'Demi-Thurganic' to account for a third order of states which describes the condition of Meta-Warriors as an evolutionary manifestation of Thurganic qualities which have somehow acquired the Quaganic distinction of self-awareness."

"And how have we acquired it?"

"I don't know. All I can say is what I believe—that we have emerged from a preconscious condition of materiality into a conscious one without knowing it."

"And why are we compelled to kill, to fight, to destroy each other by the direst means of retribution?"

"Again, I don't know. All I can say is what I believe—that we are emissions of sentience adjusted to the mobility of human form, compelled to act with empowerment against comparable forms that act against us. This, I think, explains our profligacy in areas of sexual and violent conduct. Our aim is to overrule our rivals with acts of violence or a sexual domination of their minds and bodies. We devise ourselves in opposition to anything that stands against us. We are natural in the purest sense—a force of will that stops for nothing—not even itself. You and I, BleakWarrior, are exceptions."

"Why?"

"Because we have stopped."

BleakWarrior stared for a long while and said, "And we have evolved, you say, from the basis of grit?"

"That's one way of putting it."

"And how is this possible?"

"Metaphysics," declared The Ever Decreasing Circle of Choice. "We have evolved from one order of material existence into another."

"How?"

"Impossible to say. I think, however, that we have somehow been forced out of our natural elements by an exertion of metaphysical will that has turned us into anthropoid projections of our innermost states of materiality, which have undergone their metaphysical transformation into innermost states of mind."

"Then we are not as souls that walk within sleeves of flesh?"

"No. Our condition is one of metaphysical strangeness without the essence of spirituality. We are metaphysical in our relations with the linear world, capable of entering an interspatial intimacy with its physical structures. We are not as distinct from its molecular properties as the linear species of animals and plants. We are, if anything, more natural than they are—"

"You're talking about Random Leaps."

"Yes," said The Ever Decreasing Circle of Choice. "And, indeed, it's interesting that the impact of a Random Leap, in linear terms, must ordinarily result in death, which I believe is necessary to keep us living through one extreme of existence to another—and beyond. It is in fact possible that every time we accomplish a Random Leap we are undergoing a moment of death that enables us to live through the consequences of the processes we are defying."

BleakWarrior grunted and stared through the Lenses as if into the blankness of his own heart.

"Forced out, you say," he said, suddenly.

"What?"

"You said that we have been forced out of our natural elements."

"Yes."

"By who or what?"

"Our Mentors."

BleakWarrior raised the Lenses and stared at The Circle straight in the face.

"You mean The Bard?" he said.

"If The Bard is the one who comes to you repeatedly in your dreams—to guide and instruct you—then yes, that's who I mean."

"And you think he has . . ."

"Forced you from your natural element."

"Are you sure?"

"No," said The Ever Decreasing Circle of Choice. "There are certain details that escape me."

"Such as?"

"I don't know. But I believe that our Mentors are a latent force of metaphysical will that inhabits a Thurganic plane of existence in the natural world, which is not outwardly sentient but is, however, inwardly equipped with a pre-awareness of itself, of which we are a materialisation in human form. And, so, I believe that we are projections of the metaphysical will of our Mentors, who have imagined us into life, as it were, through an existential reversal of our Thurganic condition of pre-awareness . . . Are you following me?"

BleakWarrior hesitated and nodded once.

"Good," said The Ever Decreasing Circle of Choice, "because here comes the difficult part.

"We are aware of our Mentors only in the sense that they exist as evasive mental images that appear to us in our dreams and reveries that we hardly recall from the obscurity of our half-remembered thoughts. But who are they, BleakWarrior? Who are they and why?" The Ever Decreasing Circle of Choice leaned closer. "Given that our Mentors exist inside of us as memories of defining import, I believe that they are an inner reflection of our*selves* and that we have imagined our*selves* into existence by adapting ourselves to a Quaganic plane of materiality." The Ever Decreasing Circle of Choice lowered his tone to a sombre depth. "We are the realisation of the thought of ourselves which originates in the thought of our Mentors. We have acquired a conscious knowledge of our existence which we have always had without ever being aware of it, and that is all."

"But how can our Mentors develop a sense of themselves from the basis of grit?"

"I don't know," said The Ever Decreasing Circle of Choice. "It is possible, for example, that nature possesses an awareness of itself without self-knowledge. And, to this extent, I believe that Meta-Warriors are an expression of nature's self-knowledge in its full variety of forms."

The Circle looked up at BleakWarrior who stared through the Lenses without saying anything.

"Of course," said The Circle, "these are only theories. It would be good if, somehow, we could put them to the test."

"Yes," agreed BleakWarrior, "it would."

For a while they were silent. The Ever Decreasing Circle of Choice looked at BleakWarrior, questioningly, then asked:

"You have these dreams of which I speak?"

"Of course."

"Recurring dreams of a particular nature?"

"I do."

"And obscure but vivid memories that play around the edges of your consciousness like violent sparks?"

"In abundance, yes."

"These are not dreams, BleakWarrior. They are memories of your existence before the existence you know now—states of mind in their moments of birth—a distant forging of your character.

"It occurs to me that to access these memories would be to understand them, and that to understand them would be to provide ourselves with a key to understanding who and what and *why* you are. Or," he added, "at the very least, it would provide us with a key to understanding more about your origins than you do now."

"What I know now is next to nothing."

"Quite." The Ever Decreasing Circle of Choice leaned back on his seat and nodded. "Quite."

"Electricity is the essence of everything."

"Everything?"

"Yes."

"How?"

"Because our minds consist of electrical impulses that underlie their entire function."

"In that case, I agree with you."

"Good. So," said the Ever Decreasing Circle of Choice, "here is what I propose to do . . . I have already engaged in several experiments upon linear specimens using a method of electrical injection which has produced a series of interesting results."

BleakWarrior held up a hand.

"Let us cut to the chase," he said. "You wish to apply these methods to me."

"Yes."

"And to what effect beyond those you already know?"

"You, BleakWarrior, are a Demi-Thurgan. I have never had the, ah, pleasure of applying my method of electrical injection to a specimen of your calibre. Except for Counterpain, of course."

"Counterpain?" BleakWarrior stiffened as if in response to an insult.

"Don't worry. My objectives in the use of Counterpain were different, and more dangerous. Don't tell him I said that, by the way. But I can assure you that, done properly, the method of electrical injection is free of risk."

"And what does it involve?"

"It involves the transmission of electrical currents into the brain through the strategic application of copper wire conduits."

"And to what effect?"

"To the effect of stimulating your neural energies to intensive levels which will expose your primal memories to our clear and comprehensive scrutiny." The Ever Decreasing Circle of Choice made a triangle of his fingers and waved them up and down, slowly, in synchronisation with his speech.

"If you allow me to do this," he said, "I may be able to reach the taproot of your memories and gain access to the epoch of your pre-awareness."

"And how do we proceed?"

"My usual approach is to put my specimens into a semi-conscious slumber in order to arrest their inhibitions of panic and fear which, in your case, is perhaps unnecessary."

"It is."

"I would suggest, then, that we put you into a sort of waking trance where you will remain in full possession of your senses, but with an inward rather than outward focus that allows you to convey your emerging mental content with absolute rigour."

"That is acceptable."

"Good. It will be necessary for me to bore little holes in your skull in strategic points in order to insert the copper wire conduits. These will be connected to a small generator of fixed voltage which provides the source of the electrical charge. I can assure you that it is perfectly painless."

"Pain is irrelevant," said BleakWarrior. "But I will take the appropriate precautions for ensuring that you are in no position to resort to foul play."

"This is a scientific matter, BleakWarrior, which requires my adherence to professional codes I do not care to break."

"We shall see," said BleakWarrior, eyeing The Ever Decreasing Circle of Choice through the Lenses with an enigmatic appraisal of his words and worth. "We shall see."

And The Ever Decreasing Circle of Choice resisted an urge to visibly shiver.

The Ever Decreasing Circle of Choice began to assemble his apparatus and lay out his tools.

"You ask, how could it happen? What is its purpose? What is its aim?" The Ever Decreasing Circle of Choice shook his head with a steadfast uncertainty. "I don't know, BleakWarrior, and I can only offer conjectures based upon reasonable judgements that may or may not pertain to the thing in itself."

"Such as?"

"Well," The Ever Decreasing Circle of Choice sighed, "let us say this: the creation of reality and consciousness are not accomplished in separation but are reliant on one another for their existential validation. Reality is nothing without its registration by a conscious entity, while consciousness is nothing without a sense of itself in space and time. And, of course, there are many forms that reality can take from its position of virtual absence, depending on the ways of the mind that perceives it for what it becomes."

"Reality is a construct and we are the constructors," said BleakWarrior.

The Ever Decreasing Circle of Choice gave a broad smile that revealed the full magnificence of his dentistry.

"A construct, yes," he said, "which in the event of its construction is capable of emerging in many different forms according to the constructor. There are no architects of reality, BleakWarrior. No deities, no gods. The thing that separates us from the linear species is that, while they imagine an imposition of order on the chaos of the world, we imagine nothing. We are merely the reflection of an unconscious construct that we have created without being aware of it."

"I understand what you mean," said BleakWarrior. "A linear human regards itself as a creation, not a creator, whereas we regard ourselves as nothing and, in regarding ourselves as nothing, we *are* the reality that we conceive."

The Ever Decreasing Circle of Choice sighed.

"Oh, how I've missed the benefits of good conversation with someone of an equal mind. But, yes, BleakWarrior, I do believe that we are, in fact, bereft of purpose and that the question is largely redundant, given that reality has no purpose beyond the fact of its existence, which we, as Meta-Warriors, seek to destroy by destroying each other.

"But consider this, BleakWarrior, for I have theorised long and hard: We are the thought of ourselves conceived by our Mentors, with a power to act according to our needs—yes?" BleakWarrior nodded. "Now consider this also: Every thought that comes into existence aims to be the dominant thought above all others. It aims to be a state of mind or, more to the point, it aims to be an *ideology*. It is my belief that we are battling against each other in order to become the dominant thought among our kind and, from there, by the elimination of our rivals, to position ourselves as the ideologue *above all others*."

"This makes sense," said BleakWarrior, "without making any, if what you say is true. But," he continued, "if I speak for myself, I feel no need to dominate anything. I only feel the need to know."

"To know is to dominate, BleakWarrior. Knowledge is power."

"If that is true," said BleakWarrior with a bitter smile, "I would not be surprised."

BleakWarrior allowed the Dirk to hover around the zone of The Circle's testicles as he bored small holes into BleakWarrior's skull and inserted the wires.

"Any inappropriate moves on your part," BleakWarrior had said, "and your suffering will be equal to mine by twice the measure."

"BleakWarrior," said The Ever Decreasing Circle of Choice, "in spite of the fact that your aptitude for mathematics is wildly incoherent, I am inclined to believe you."

The Circle continued fiddling with his apparatus for a few moments and said, "There, the filaments are in place. I will now raise the dial until you feel a vibratory numbness spread across your cranium. I think you will find the sensation to be vaguely thrilling. I have been told that it has a sedentary effect, similar to certain types of recreational drug, but that it is accompanied by an underlying sense of euphoria. By gradual stages, you will be lulled into a sort of waking trance that will cast a light of self-awareness over the darker portions of your psyche."

"I am beginning to feel it now."

"Good. I am ready to take notes. Let us aim for a spontaneous transcription. You must allow yourself to speak your thoughts without thinking. Simply repeat them as they come to you. Repeat your thoughts, BleakWarrior, and I will write them down as I receive them from you directly."

"Are you ready now?"

"Yes."

"Then prepare yourself, Circle, for the First Day of Retributions."

The wind skirls around the perimeter of ruined walls, finding cracks, probing the fiery gloom. Sparks spiral upwards from the smelt, spinning madly into the nothingness of darkness and wind. The glowing coals pulsate like the hearts of small birds. The moulds upon them boil with virulent heats. The Bard introduces the blood and bile of animals to their metallic lustre. He takes his harp from its hook on the wall and, with nimble fingers, elicits words from the timbre of its strings:

"In this, the essence of beasts apportions life to our pursuit of others' doom. Like wine that courses the living vein, our tools are enlivened by the vital matters that inhabit them."

He hangs his harp from its hook on the wall and works the moulds to the equilibrium of their mix. The look of determination dawns in his eye like the glimmer of a star on the shores of a ruined world.

He takes his harp from its hook on the wall and elicits words from the timbre of its strings:

"We retain the forces of life in the moulds of the blade, and the blade is called the Dirk. The Dirk is an extension of your personality. It lays to rest your doubts and leads you to the best of your conclusions."

The Bard hangs his harp from its hook on the wall and works the moulds and, in the days and nights to come, he takes up the harp and elicits words from the timbre of its strings:

"We are unlimited in our use of savage gifts. The metals of the Dirk are steeped in the yokes of seagulls' eggs. Seagulls know nothing of scarcity in a world that offers only scraps.

"The spleens of otters have been mixed with particles of quartz from the embattled hills. They take their place in the composition of the Dirk with an otter's thirst for joy and cruelty. The best kind of fierceness moves with impossible slickness against the tides."

The Bard hangs his harp from its hook on the wall and works the moulds and, in the days and nights to come, he takes up his harp and elicits words from the timbre of its strings:

"The mould of the Dirk is cooled in waters drawn from the Talking Well that provides the vital piquancy to the wines I brew from the fruits of the embattled hills. The Talking Well speaks of an everlasting grief. It speaks in a language of hidden rivers that emerge from the depths of the world's sorrow. The mould of the Dirk is cooled in the sorrow of the world that, when it strikes, conveys an everlasting grief to whomsoever it strikes against.

"These are only some of the interpretations of our craft."

The Bard works through the days and nights with relentless industry. BleakWarrior stands naked beside him and watches and listens to every keening aspect of their labours.

When they are done, the Bard takes his harp from its hook on the wall and elicits words from the timbre of its strings:

"Visions of madness are too great a strain on the regular orientations of consciousness. The Dirk will inspire you to a regular perception of your mental scene.

"The aim of savagery is to exist with the effortlessness of stone. You will return to the wilderness to confront the visions of your madness with the effortlessness of stone."

I travel over the barren land as naked as my birth. The wind is cold against my skin. My skin is as hard as the wind is cold. Haggard mists lie over the land like an aching in the heart that will not lift. There are no horizons. The wilderness is without the approximations of distance or locality.

The wilderness simply is.

I register the terms of my madness as objects of ordinary substance that emerge from my power to conceive of them as things that walk with thrashing limbs or things that crawl on sagging bellies or things of distorted lineage that chew on the blood-soaked bones of their murdered offspring.

These are the emissaries of my disorder.

Once, they menaced my alertness with the dislocation of my senses from repeated scenes of awe. Once, I fended them off with nothing more than my repugnance for them. Once, I succumbed to their enchantments with a personal alarm that shook me to the core of my bleakness.

I had no core: there is no core to bleakness. Bleakness is the periphery of an absence that envelops me like a warmth. But it is cold, so cold; and it rains against my body like gravel; and I begin to run.

I run over the land of my heart, the land of my own making, the land of my expression of myself without the result of meaning.

I run with a result of meaning to inscribe upon its emptiness. I return with the Dirk with an aim to straying aimlessly over the remoteness of the terrain.

Then they come: the Berserkers rushing at me from the crags, with spears to pierce me, swords to hack and whips to flail me, swung with might from blood-stained hands.

I take them all, one by one, slicing their bellies, spilling their livid guts like eels. I decimate their chests with an embroidery of lesions. I sever the knot-work of their veins. I untie them bodily from their bones with slick administrations of the Dirk. I slice their pates from their skulls. I sink my teeth into their muscles. I tear off chunks of flesh and spit them into the wetness of the moor.

I run against the wind and rain. I am full of the satisfaction of my fury.

Horned beasts, and shapeless masses of muddling skins, come sniffing from the shambles of the hills. They flick their long, abrasive tongues at me, with rows of barbs that shear the surface of my nakedness.

I fight them all, one by one, sinking the Dirk into to their sodden forms, slicing open their dangling sacks of throbbing tissue, waylaying them with staunch fists as stark as undressed stone. They grapple me with tentacles. They flay me with their caliginous limbs. I extort their tongues. I dismember them. I sink my teeth into their sappy carcasses and swallow their bile.

I run against the wind and rain. I am full of the satisfaction of my fury.

They come brawling from the mist, androgynous figures with leathery skins and squat heads and lipless mouths and worms emerging from their eyeballs. Their gnarled breasts are shorn of nipples. Their bodies are covered in warts and welds and the smear of raw filth. They are amalgams of sex, with flaccid cocks that swing like stockings full of boiled meat. They wish to defile whatever falls within range of their lust. They wish to rip things open and shove their cocks into the wounds, to fuck the innards. Their loins yearn to spread the seed of filth that defines them.

I deflect their battering fists and gouge them with dynamic fingers. I accost them with my manic strokes. I cleave their breasts. I mutilate their shambling cocks. I burst their bellies like bags of gelatine. I recoil from the odours that I disperse from their spilled guts like breakages of lizards' eggs.

I run against the wind and rain. I am full of the satisfaction of my savage gifts.

Into the blackness of night, where the mist dissolves in the grip of darkness, where the wind and rain are colder than the cruelty of a disease.

I see strange illuminations of a volcanic temper. I run towards them with the Dirk held fast in my grip. The Dirk is warmed by the blood and heat of battle. I am warmed by the blood and heat of battle. I am cooled by the wind and rain of night. I run over corpses burnt to a pitch of blackness. I run over corpses frozen stiff with the brittle rot of a rapid scorching.

The corpses have been blasted by the vile evacuations of LavaHead.

LavaHead looks down at me from the crest of a hill. It is the Hill of Scars. Magma gushes from his eyes and ears. Magma gushes from his nose and mouth. Lava spills over his shoulders and chest and culminates in the furnace of his loins. LavaHead's flesh is scarred and scalded by the flow.

LavaHead hurls globes of lava at me from his mouth. He spits lava at me from the eye of his belligerent cock. He drenches me in the traumas of his wrath. He will not come down to me from the Hill of Scars. Lava runs from the Hill of Scars and pools in the boggy channels at my feet.

I run up the dreadful slope of the Hill of Scars under a hail of volcanic debris. LavaHead waits for me in the blaze of his eruptions. The rain soothes me where I am burnt by the lava that strikes me like a spray of venom. LavaHead roars like a breaking rock. There are cracks in his body where lava leaks out in vicious trails. I swivel and dash between the blasts of his flaming downpour.

I fight LavaHead in the wind and rain on the Hill of Scars for many days and many nights of diminishing worth. My body bleeds with the burning streaks of my sundered flesh. LavaHead bleeds with lava where I cut him open with hazardous contributions of the Dirk.

I fight LavaHead in the wind and rain on the Hill of Scars for many days and many nights of diminishing worth. He does not weaken. I, in the satisfaction of my fury, do not weaken.

In the twilight of a day where the mist rises from the breach of the Hill of Scars, I see the wilderness of rounded hills that spread before me as bare as my fury. These hills are my strength. Once, I walked their heather summits for eons of torment. I know these hills with the intimacy of a wound in my body that will not heal.

LavaHead leans towards me to soak me in the oblivion of his gush. I twist away from the uneven courses of his spillage. I steer the Dirk between his rancour and plunge it through the mantle of his chest.

LavaHead groans like the collision of two plates of land. Lava spills from his disparted ribs and splashes into the bareness of my face. My face begins to burn like an everlasting sorrow. My eyes are blinded by a searing pain like the everlasting pain of grief. LavaHead keels over like an eroded stack. When he dies, the heat of the lava on my face is cooled by the wind and rain that blows against me. The lava drops off my face like scabs from the bloody welts of my personal history. My face is as clean as a dawning day. But the lava that burns my eyes now turns to a solid crust and remains within my sockets with the staunchness of an ancient mineral.

The Warped Lenses.

"Your visions of madness," said The Bard, "are contained by the discord of your feats. They will wrangle within you for as long as you wear the Warped Lenses; and, for as long as you wear the Warped Lenses, they will never wrangle without."

13.
Abysmal Silence is Not Golden

Happy Snapper span the pliers around his fingers with the ease of a meaningless trick which he did without thinking. He approached the gates of Dr Vile's villa and sheared the pliers through the coils of metal that clamped them shut.

The gates swung open on smooth hinges without a sound.

Thornographer took a step forward, paused, then cast an eye over the ill-kempt neatness of the gardens. There was no sign of life—no gardeners, servants, pets or visitors—nothing.

Breath of Death Air drew a pair of vials from the abundance of his pantaloons and stood beside Thornographer.

"Quiet, isn't it?" he said.

"Very," agreed Thornographer.

Happy Snapper came and stood beside them. He twirled the pliers around his fingers and started whistling a tune without a melody, then suddenly stopped and said, "I wonder if there is a particular reason for this abysmal silence."

"I believe that there *is* a particular reason for this abysmal silence," said Thornographer.

"I also believe that there is a particular reason for this abysmal silence," said Breath of Death Air.

"Shall we go in and find out for ourselves?" asked Happy Snapper as if proposing a leisurely walk in the city park.

They entered the grounds of Dr Vile's villa. Nothing

stirred. When they reached the front door, they rang a bell which echoed languorously through an empty hall. They rang it again. Nobody came to greet them. They rang again and, still, nobody came to greet them.

And this is when they decided that brute force was necessary.

There comes a time for The Breaking Wave when brute force is *always* necessary.

14. How Weakness Was My Source of Strength

The Hill of False Summits grips the horizon like a clenched fist. The uneven rotundity of its bulk rivals the sky with its overbearing proportions of heather and rock. Its purple cresses rise and fall and rise again through successive depressions of escalating gradient. With each accomplished ridge, no succour is given. Passing showers strike the terrain with the force of whips. The wind skirmishes like a berserker. Squalid prolongations of vegetable and mineral roughness accost the vastness with the diagonal rupture of upward form.

To reach a summit is a rule of ascendancy. But when the summits prove false, so the rule proves false unto itself, and the matter of ascending becomes a self-defeating purpose of invalidating the will to succeed.

On some occasions, Welter of Impermanence has abandoned herself to the apathetic rage of refusing to go on, drawn by the appeal of giving up, drawn by ever-decreasing stints of elevation, down through an underlying swaddle of mist, to nothing below—because the Hill of False Summits is also a Hill of False Beginnings.

But, mostly, she labours after the monotonous drag of hitting a final height that defies her arrival. A summit is breached that reveals another, until all summits are a series of thwarted perspectives over interminable tracts of sodden turf.

Many hundreds of years have passed. Movement through space is divested of the measure of time: eons without reference to passing events must cease to be eons.

Then, by gradual stages, the heather gives way to protracted slabs, receding like muddy water from a balding shore. The wind relents. The rain withdraws in a whirl of vapours. And, suddenly, the Hill of False Summits hardens its exterior to a critical mass—abundant with density—and lessens its curvature to a finite point of incrustation.

Welter of Impermanence heaves her languid body over stone, willing her defeated limbs to succeed with every fraction of culminating mantle. The Hill of False Summits affirms its falseness: it haemorrhages upon a summit that is absolute and, in contrast to the interminable postponement of its apogee, is ultimately true.

The Pioneer prattles over his maps. He inclines his head without looking at the approaching waif whose form resembles a thistle under the battery of a downpour.

"I know who you are," he says. "You will live to fight for better things than the disappointments you bear now."

Welter of Impermanence collapses in an upright heap, steadied by boulders. Her eyes betray no sense of satisfaction in the release of her burdens. She is convinced that the Hill is an external manifestation of her internal rancour; but she also knows that she is wrong.

A further supposition occurs to her of impending hardships, for which the Hill of False Summits was a hapless preparation. She gazes over the lofty clouds—which are indicative of fair weather—whose peaceful appearance strikes her as remotely insulting. She has endured too many abuses of nature to accept this respite with anything more than outright scorn.

"There you will see," says the Pioneer, sweeping an arm across his maps, "the variations of mountain and plain, the unkempt forests, the tillage of the fields, the fecundity of wetland copses, bracken on the silent moors, the waterways from highland crests, the roughness of the ridges over lowland swale, spurred rocks on coastal wedges, the debris of islands, the estuaries of mouthing rivers. Notice, also, the sprawl of a demolished whole, enclosed by oceans, and the stark huddle of architectural follies where the people thrive like maggots on the crust of open wounds."

The Pioneer turns to look upon Welter of Impermanence and reveals the vacant sockets of his eyes.

"I have scrutinised the world with an intensity of purpose that has rotted my eyes, for which you must impose yourself as the organ of my vision."

He hands her a cloth sack.

Welter of Impermanence opens it.

And sees the Utensils.

"I know who you are." The voice was soft as air against her cheek. "You will live to fight for better things than the disappointments you bear now."

Welter of Impermanence searched her muddled brain for an interpretation of the words; but they came without the weight of meaning.

The Machinists had taken her down from the Weakener and were carrying her to her allotted place of execution. She was aware of nothing. She saw and heard it with the blankness of an unconscious state that, later, would come back to her in brash but fleeting episodes of stunning clarity.

"Know that I have tried to persuade the Machinists to boil you in oil and flush your flesh from off your bones as if by moulting.

"But they have rejected my preference for the vats, which I know to be appropriate for your destruction. The Body Launcher is new to them and they are eager to appraise its worth. There is a novelty value about its use for which you are a principal tool of our research. Saps and entrails are expected to stain the heights of the Muckle Head, and blood to soak its abutments, in the outcome of your bodily libations.

"You will know that the Machinists must ascertain the failure of their pageantry, which you and I will recognise as patent farce."

Welter of Impermanence considered whether the voice was real or a delusion provoked by the stresses and strains of her preparations on the Weakener. But the voice went on:

"I know you for what you are, which prevents me from exposing you to the common understanding of our host, which risks my own exposure to them—even if, in essence, I am nothing. But I will dispiteously reveal myself to you for all that I am worth . . .

"I am Reading the Clouds, and reading them under the supposition that the clouds never lie, but will deceive us if we mistake their missives for labels of our own making: the deception, then, is truly ours. The satisfaction of killing rests in me with the warmth of an animal nestled in my breast. My lover is dead, whereupon I marvel over her absence with tears that wet my soul with acidic sorrow. My love for her was a flame in the darkness of her chaotic tendency. But words must fail. Words are nothing. Words must come without the gift of meaning, as they come to you now in the midst of your delirium.

"It is my opinion that meaning is like the spatial emptiness of cracks in stone which reveal nothing of the stone itself. The cracks do not exist except in relation to the substance of stone which determines them (not as spaces but) as cracks.

"I would ask you, then, why I lack the enthusiasm for life but fully retain an urge to destroy you with an instinctive purpose for which I have no name? To engage each other with words and weapons is beyond the measure of this, our present encounter. Listen well, therefore, to what I propose . . .

"Beyond the Ridge of Thaws, to the west of the easterly routes from whence you came, there lies a town of ill-repute called Happenstance. Hasten there when you are ready—I will read of your arrival in the scripture of the clouds.

"You will find me on the esplanade that overlooks the town beneath its highest walls: and, there, we shall meet and, when we do, then one of us, not now but then, will surely die."

Welter of Impermanence was loaded into the Body Launcher. She looked upon the faces of the people who watched. Their attempts to remain sombre struck her as evidence of their blatant hypocrisy. They lusted after violence with a desire to witness the brutal consequences of their actions under the pretext of following a festival rite.

The Body Launcher was activated with a suddenness that almost tore her soul from her body.

The mechanism adjusted through a series of rhythmic jolts. The launch pad jettisoned like the tongue of an exotic lizard. Welter of Impermanence was flung with extreme force over the tops of the trees towards the broad face of the Muckle Head. The crowd held their breath, their eyes sparkling with the wild expectancy of a messy collision.

And Welter of Impermanence passed through it, out of sight, as if disappearing into water. Above the silence came the sigh of Reading the Clouds. The Machinists stared at the Muckle Head as if waiting for something to happen.

Then it sunk in . . . Something already had.

15.
BleakWarrior Makes a Leap of Bad Faith That Feels Good

The Ever Decreasing Circle of Choice shuffled through the transcripts, highlighting pieces of text with a quill and drawing BleakWarrior's attention to them.

"A point of convergence, you see? A place where the two versions of your world find a point of intersection between their Quaganic and Thurganic opposition. Think of it as a vacuum that sucks both ways. It is the perfect paradox, BleakWarrior, which, in our case, makes perfect sense."

"And what can I do with a perfect paradox that makes perfect sense?"

"I've no idea. But it is my considered opinion that you must find a landscape that resembles the landscape of your mind—the landscape of your own creation. Tell me, BleakWarrior, in all your wandering, have you ever been in any place as remote and wild as that which you have described to me today?"

"I have been to many wild places," said BleakWarrior, "and done many wild things."

"Were any of them familiar to you?"

"Sometimes there is a sense of familiarity in the fact that the wilderness inspires me to be wild."

"I see," said The Ever Decreasing Circle of Choice, poring over the transcripts until, finally, he said, "There is something that strikes me . . . here." He pointed the nib of the quill at a messy juncture of his haphazard scrawl.

"What is it?" BleakWarrior leaned over the transcripts and peered.

"Your reference to the Talking Well."

"The Well that speaks of the world's sorrow?"

"Precisely."

"You suspect that the Talking Well is a point of convergence?"

"It has a definite symbolic association with the concept in mind, which leads me to think that it may exist quite literally." The Ever Decreasing Circle of Choice looked up from the transcripts. "There's something else, perhaps a coincidence but . . ."

"What?"

"Counterpain through there." The Ever Decreasing Circle of Choice made a loose gesture with his hand. "When I used my electrical treatments on him, he revealed to me a similar symbolic association. In his case, however, he described it as an Oily Well, which was a sort of hyperpoint of sexual confluence and bodily interaction."

"Intriguing."

"Yes," said the Circle, "it is. A well is a source, BleakWarrior—a source of something vital." The Circle shrugged. "It is something to aim for, BleakWarrior. But remember: we are wading through the mud of conjecture. The conjecture is good, but my first advice is to find a landscape that fills you with a sense of stark recognition." The Ever Decreasing Circle of Choice leaned back from his desk and folded his arms. "Find the landscape, BleakWarrior, then make a search for the Talking Well."

"And if I find it?"

"Climb into it and see what happens."

"This is interesting advice."

"Not advice. Suggestions." The Ever Decreasing Circle of Choice shrugged again. "If you enter the Talking Well—if such a thing exists—then perhaps it will take you nowhere. On the other hand, perhaps it will take you exactly where you wish to be."

BleakWarrior stared through the Lenses. The Ever Decreasing Circle of Choice shifted nervously on his seat.

"I will go, then," said BleakWarrior, "in search of the Talking Well."

"And if you find it, BleakWarrior, I ask of you this: come back to me."

"Back?"

"Yes. It would be of immeasurable benefit to my research to have news of your discoveries—whatever they might be."

BleakWarrior hesitated, then said, "I will see what I can do."

"Well, then," said The Ever Decreasing Circle of Choice, "I wish you the very best of luck in your search, which is the very best of luck to me." He took a deep breath and added: "There is one other thing I would recommend before you depart."

"What?"

"It concerns the implications of our theories in the event that they are true. I was thinking . . ."

"What?"

"Shhh." The Ever Decreasing Circle of Choice made a sharp motion with his hand for silence. BleakWarrior cocked his head, listened and, sure enough, there was a pounding of metal against wood coming from above.

"The door to my villa," said The Ever Decreasing Circle of Choice. "Did you . . . ?"

"The door is barred," said BleakWarrior.

"Someone's trying to break in." The Ever Decreasing Circle of Choice gritted his teeth in panic. "It must be them. It's what I feared."

"Them?"

"I must ask you to leave, BleakWarrior. Immediately. Our lives depend on it. If they find you here they'll kill us both."

"Who?"

"People you don't want to meet."

"People like us?"

"People who are *more* like us than we are."

"How?"

"They're scientists, BleakWarrior. Bad scientists. Very bad scientists with bad weapons."

"Scientific weapons?"

"I'm afraid so, yes." The Circle began frantically gathering up the transcripts. "I must destroy these immediately."

BleakWarrior clamped a hand on The Circle's wrist. The Circle froze.

"Where is your Weapon?" he said.

The Ever Decreasing Circle of Choice's eyes bulged like the eyes of a snared rabbit.

"BleakWarrior," he said. "It is a nasty habit of our kind that, wherever we go, we have a tendency to be noticed. The City of Prelations is no exception."

"I am accustomed to being noticed."

"What I mean to say is that the City of Prelations is under the control of a cabal. A very big and powerful cabal. And it is my considered opinion that, by standing up to them, you will die."

"Strange, then, that they haven't killed you."

"Not strange but practical. They are aware of my activities and wish me to continue unabated. It's a sort of understanding—an unwritten agreement, if you like. They believe that they will benefit from my research—which, if truth be told, they already have. But if they catch you here with me they will suspect me of colluding with a rival cabal—and this is something they will not tolerate. You must flee, BleakWarrior, or face death."

"I prefer to face death."

"I would rather that you faced your quest for the Talking Well."

BleakWarrior grinned or grimaced (it was hard to tell which).

"What are our options?" he said. "Where can I escape?"

"There are no windows in my lower vaults, no doors, no exits, besides the one you came down."

"Then we are compelled to fight. Good. There is no greater incentive than desperation."

"No," said The Ever Decreasing Circle of Choice. "Our choices have been reduced to only one."

"Which one?"

"The Sensorial Platacaster."

"Come again?"

"It's a device that taps the Interstitial Differentials of solid matter and mimics a node. But it can also be used to generate an artificial force of gravity that is equal to the impact of a Random Leap."

"A Random Leap?"

"Yes."

"Has it been tested?"

"Not in reverse, no. But it's our only hope. I must do what I can to appease our intruders with some clever bluff. You, however, must leave immediately. It is only a question of—ah, I think that's them. It appears that you were wise enough to lock the door to the lower vaults."

"I was."

"Then you may have saved our lives," said The Ever Decreasing Circle of Choice, and dragged BleakWarrior by the arm, saying, "Follow me, quickly now. Watch your head against the lintel—ah, too late. Are you all right? Quickly, in here." The Ever Decreasing Circle of Choice gestured towards some kind of bulky apparatus in the corner of his laboratory. "Let us hope we meet again in better circumstances, BleakWarrior." He opened the small but heavy door of a squat container that was barely big enough to conceal a dog. "And I would very much appreciate it if you came back to me with news of your discoveries."

BleakWarrior crawled inside the container which was extremely cramped and reeking of some attractive and repulsive smell that gave him an instantaneous and painful erection. Once inside, he found he couldn't move. The door slammed shut behind him and pressed hard against his heels. He was thoroughly trapped and it occurred to him that The Ever Decreasing Circle of Choice was in the position to do with him whatever he liked.

BleakWarrior had a sudden presentiment of being incinerated by jets of flame or liquidised in a shower of acid. The container had that kind of feel about it—of vulnerability to death by burning.

However:

"I have no idea if it will work," The Circle was saying from outside the box, his voice muted and barely discernable. "I have never tried it in reverse, so, ah, either you will be successfully projected in the manner of a Random Leap or else, ah, completely annihilated."

"You could have told me this earlier," said BleakWarrior.

"If I had told you earlier, you wouldn't have agreed to go in, would you?"

"Probably not."

"Well then, there you go," said The Ever Decreasing Circle of Choice, now cranking up the power handle of the applications box. "But do try not to worry. If all goes to plan, you will find yourself rising from the crust of some dim and distant corner of the world, exactly as you would in the aftermath of a Random Leap. Prepare yourself. I am about to hit the ignition switch."

BleakWarrior felt a sudden tightening around his body as if he were being immersed in glue. He struggled to breathe as the air became charged with an electromagnetic pressure of intense proportions. Then, with even greater suddenness, he felt himself being discharged through solid matter like a husk held up to a blowsy wind—his mind and body a multitude of enigmatic seedlings, and his thoughts dispersed like the microscopic disintegration of a small vacuum.

Then there came a series of vibrations that signalled to

BleakWarrior what he believed to be a fault in the activation of the machine. He braced himself for his potential obliteration from the arena of life and, in doing so, found it strangely satisfying to perceive of his impending departure. But the warmth of this presumption, and the phantom sense of relief it brought, quickly gave way to a raft of sensations that permeated his mind and body like an electric current through water molecules. The effect was one of galvanising his discharged form and giving it a sense of weight that caused him to instinctively stiffen as if to brace himself against an impact.

No impact came. Instead, there was a feeling of physical and psychic dissemination which had no pleasing attributes whatsoever. It reminded BleakWarrior more of a metallic tanginess layering itself within the nervous system and taking root as a chief determinant of his conscious thought processes. The feeling of dissemination was comparable to a Random Leap, it was true, but with a slowed down sense of mobility which utterly lacked the sense of momentum that a Random Leap normally generated.

Yet again, however, this feeling gave way to one of spatial lightness combined with a sense of travelling in suspension without being drawn towards a specific node. It was a frustrating and pleasurable sensation that felt like a sustained wave of emotional rapture that lessened, instead of intensified, the more it went on. But none of this could prepare him for what came next—a sudden infiltration of euphoric psycho-sexual bliss that appeared to come from outside of BleakWarrior's core reactions to the artificially induced Leap process.

Whatever it was, it passed through and beyond BleakWarrior's atomic substructures like a waft of warm air; but, more than this, the feeling of comfort it transported through him contained something more powerful—a force of desire that was charged with emotional and carnal extremes of lust; and within it, too, a feeling of contrary distinction, like a desire to do great violence resulting in seriously harmful consequences.

But something else dominated the characteristics of the allure—something so intoxicating that, almost without wilful effort, BleakWarrior allowed his dissipated atomic form to venture after it through the ID network. He was drawn as if by a magnetic force, compelled to pursue the euphoric waft whether he willed it or not, but sure he really wanted to.

And, with this apprehension of certainty lodged in his mind like a colourful species of tree frog, BleakWarrior wondered where the euphoric waft was leading him and asked himself, *why?*

Book 3: Attendances to Mayhem

16.
The Brotherly Devotions of Burning Hot Coals

The Gutter had a brother who was seeking to square the circle of revenge against the bitches who'd taken his brother out.

Burning Hot Coals.

Burning Hot Coals carried a pluriskin sack over his shoulder and wandered the streets like a drunk man looking for a bed for the night.

His mind, however, was perfectly clear.

As the sky is clear with an azure apparition of substance that effectively conceals the immensity of its depth—thereby protecting the over-wrought sensibilities of linear humans from the cosmic horrors of the void.

The same indifference to existence, including his own, formed the basis of the emotional composition and character of Burning Hot Coals. He was a void within the three-dimensional constancy of his body. Thoughts appeared inside his head like black holes.

He shouldered his way between scores of merry-makers who spilled from the wineries onto the streets like a human scree. He turned into a narrow opening between drinking dens and followed a narrow tunnel that led him into a secluded courtyard called Sapper's Nook. In Sapper's Nook there was a beauty salon called *Seeing is Believing*.

Burning Hot Coals stepped into *Seeing is Believing* where several women were receiving cosmetic adjustments to their faces, fingernails, feet and hair. One of them wore a look on her face like she thought she was more important than the others.

She was.

Burning Hot Coals walked up to her, grabbed her by the throat, swung her off her chair, and threw her onto the floor among her newly shredded locks. The other women ran shrieking from the salon like a flock of flightless birds.

Needless to say, it would be wise to hurry before the alarm was raised, though Burning Hot Coals was aware of the fact that it couldn't be raised so easily.

The Covenant of Ichor were an outlawed organisation who couldn't risk their exposure to the interventions of the City Arbiters any more than he could. They were also ideologically opposed to receiving assistance from a people they considered a separate species; and Burning Hot Coals—who was a man after his own kind—was liable to prove them right on that score.

Burning Hot Coals drew his knee across the chest of the leader of the local order and applied his weight. He slipped the sack from his shoulder and shook it open: smoke plumed from its sooty maw. He reached into the sooty maw and, when he did, you could see how his fingers were bloated and misshapen by uneven layers of mottled scar tissue. He withdrew a small lump of smouldering coal. It throbbed with a residual heat like a pulsating organ. He clasped the leader of the local order under the chin and squeezed her cheeks. Her mouth fell open like the entrance of a small cave.

"Where are they?" Burning Hot Coals spoke with a portentous matter-of-factness that sounded like his words were produced by grating his teeth.

The leader of the local order made a gurgling sound like her throat was full of glue.

"Where are they?" said Burning Hot Coals.

Again, the woman gurgled, which prompted Burning Hot Coals to slacken his grip in order to allow her to speak.

"Not here," she said in coughs and splutters.

Burning Hot Coals reaffirmed his grip and squeezed. He raked his broken nails into her cheeks until blood was drawn.

"Where are they?"

The woman's eyes erupted with tears and began to bulge.

Burning Hot Coals slackened his grip.

"City . . . of . . . Antiquities . . ."

Burning Hot Coals smiled through his absence of teeth.

"Fuck you very much," he said.

And he forced her mouth as wide as it could possibly get. Then he rolled the smouldering piece of coal onto her tongue and let it fall against her tonsils. Then he clamped her mouth shut and levelled his weight against her gut, forcing her to gasp—and, when she gasped, she swallowed the smouldering piece of coal, which didn't go down but stuck in her throat, where it settled and burned like an amalgam of fury.

The leader of the local order was unable to scream because she was too busy choking. Nevertheless, she had been very lucky that Burning Hot Coals had taken little time to interrogate her. His methods normally involved the insertion of red hot coals into other sensitive parts of the body, which he sometimes created artificially with the use of a metal spike. The metal spike was ordinarily used by shepherds for puncturing holes in the swollen bellies of sheep that had eaten the wrong kind of toxic hillside vegetation. The leader of the local order was already half-spewing, half-coughing up the piece of coal when Burning Hot Coals rose from the stink of her oral carnage and departed the scene with the sleekness of a rat.

He had, he reflected, been remarkably nice to her. But he was undeterred by his lack of gratification which he would assuredly redress upon the furtherance of his investigations.

The City of Antiquities would provide him with a far more interesting source for his amusements, even though he was entirely oblivious to the whole idea of being amused.

17.
The Node to Nowhere

Welter of Impermanence emerged from a mossy stretch of moorland where there was little to revive her from her depleted state. In time, however, she regained consciousness, then reason, then strength, and managed to raise herself on her elbows, spitting dryness from her lips, looking around, and wondering where she was until . . . an incoherent bleating, scattered balls of dung, wisps of wool . . .

The Girnan Howe was unsuitable for agriculture and more appropriate for the grazing of sheep.

The shepherds of the Girnan Howe were legendary for their resilience to the wind and rain that battered the moorland throughout the year with an unchanging regularity of temperature that hovered between mild humidity and chilly dampness. The faces of the shepherds were ruddy with weathering and their bodies robust after the manner of their constant hardships.

One of these shepherds was out tending his flock on the rain-swept isolation of the Howe when he saw a female figure approaching him through a gauze of mist, which he at first mistook for an eidolon of the moor called a Scarum.

Scarums were known to patrol the territory of the Howe

in search of shepherds to spirit away to the subterranean darkness of their ancient barrows, where they would cherish the shepherds as household pets, or boil them alive, or possibly eat them. This was said to be in revenge for having been driven off the surface of the Howe by earlier generations of humans who were jealous of their pale and perfect physiques and their magical ability to turn water into liquid gold.

The shepherd would have been terrified out of his wits if it weren't for the fact that the Scarum was naked. He eyed its approach with a keen regard for its lithe and sinuous aspect that brought a warm and weighty tension to the meat of his loins. But, by the time the Scarum had reached him, his lust had faltered. The shepherd suffered a brief panic at the thought of falling under some kind of spell, but it soon dispersed when the lovely form of the Scarum stopped before him and, in a stricken sort of way, bared its teeth in a smile and said, "I need clothes."

The shepherd removed his sheepskin coat, his undershirt, his boots and leather hose, holding them out as if afraid she might bite him.

"This is all I've got," he said.

The Scarum took the clothes and dressed itself.

"I need Utensils," said the Scarum.

The shepherd looked bemused.

"Begging your pardon," he said, "but I've only got a few things for tending the sheep?"

The Scarum breathed out, hard, then resumed the unnatural coolness of its demeanour.

"These clothes are nice," it said. "Supremely delicate but strong. A bit like me. But—" The Scarum leaned towards the shepherd who backed away—"where can I find a city?"

"A city?" The shepherd looked as if he didn't understand the question.

"A city," the Scarum confirmed.

"Why would you want to go to a city?"

"To find a place where they sell kitchenware of the highest calibre," said the Scarum, and blinked, once.

"But," said the shepherd, "what would a Scarum do with kitchenware of the highest calibre?"

The Scarum took a step closer . . .

The shepherd doubled up in the iron grasp of a fist around his testicles and wheezed as if drowning in smoke.

"Just tell me where I can find a city," said the Scarum.

The shepherd struggled to find breath.

"West," he said.

"West where?"

"The City . . . of . . . Antiquities . . . "

The physical and mental consequences of an artificially-induced Random Leap were such that BleakWarrior emerged from the node in a state of temporary devastation. He felt as if his body had been turned inside out and flayed from the soul upwards. He was disorientated in the extreme, with his head spinning as if propped on the end of a stick and twirled in undulating circles at high speed.

Progress through the ID network had been slow and painful to a point that it had lasted for hours instead of the fleeting moments it normally required for its duration. It had felt unnatural (which stands to reason) and had taken a toll on BleakWarrior's mind and body that reminded him of the final stages of dehydration prior to death. But, as he lay there on a surface of springy heather and soft grass, the lingering traces of the euphoric waft began to enliven him to a more solid state of his recovery.

As it did so, BleakWarrior realised that he felt as if he'd emerged from the ID network saturated in some kind of exotic love juice. This, at least, is the effect that the euphoric waft was having on him; and, as his body reassembled its full atomic state, he became richly enthused with a wild desire for sexual gratification that required an immediate seeing to.

But the arousal lessened as BleakWarrior began to visually engage the landscape he had emerged from—a wide open space of rough terrain, over which there sounded an incessant bleating. Sheep, he thought, are of proficient use for sexual purposes, as the habits of some of the northerly tribes had proven beyond dispute. But BleakWarrior was unable to reconcile himself to the prospect of aligning his sexual preferences to something that wasn't, at the very least, vaguely human. He therefore willed his sexual excitement to subside (although the impressions of the euphoric waft stayed with him without surcease) and, looking beyond the scattering of sheep, he prepared himself for an impromptu journey over the empty moorland.

After four or five miles of strenuous walking, he saw ahead of him the oddity of a robust and windblown linear human dressed only in small cloths, who was walking briskly over the moorland, leaning into the wind, and evidently in need of warmth and shelter. BleakWarrior hastened to catch the man up and, closing in on him, cried out:

"Ho, traveller."

The man wheeled round and, as he did so, lost his balance and fell awkwardly on his rump. BleakWarrior strode up to him as the man rose up and readied himself, it seemed, as if to break into a run.

BleakWarrior held up a hand by way of assuring the man he intended no harm.

"Stay yourself, man. I require nothing more than a quick word that renders my aggressions unnecessary."

The man complied, albeit he was clearly riveted with fear.

"I have no clothes to give," said the man, somewhat strangely, BleakWarrior thought.

"Nor do I require them," said BleakWarrior, angling his head at the man and asking, "What manner of misfortune has fallen on you? This is no place for idling naked under the setting sun and illuming stars."

The man shook his head.

"It was a strange and violent woman, sir, who robbed me of my vestments—a woman of such cruel temper, whom I mistook for a Scarum, that I could not refuse her."

"You let a woman rob you of your vestments?"

"No ordinary woman, sir. She inspired fear, much like yourself. I mean—forgive me, sir, but I am frightened of you."

"And were you frightened of her?" BleakWarrior was beginning to sense a chain of events falling into place; and somewhere inside of him the euphoric waft stirred like a phantom.

"Like a rabbit, sir. She came naked over the heath

towards me and demanded the clothes off my back. She applied force with such strength that I could not resist her. And when she asked me directions, I was happy to oblige by way of being rid of her. That was the way of it, nothing more nor less than that."

"Directions?" BleakWarrior straightened his head and applied the Lenses.

"To the nearest city, over yonder."

The man pointed in a direction that BleakWarrior believed was westerly—the opposite way from which he'd come.

"How long ago was this?"

"I don't know, sir. I'm afraid I have no means of telling the time out here. There's no need for it. But I'd say that she'd be five or twenty miles to the west of us by now, sir. More or less."

"And how long will it take her to reach this city of yours?"

"It's not my city, sir, but I reckon she'll be there by the break of day tomorrow, sir, if not before. She struck me as a good walker, of that I'm sure."

"You have served me well, man of the heath. Away and find your bed for the night. I must go and pursue this woman of yours."

"She's not my woman, sir. And I'd advise against it. She was a danger to me, sir—a danger to my life. And I'm a strong man by way of handling my sheep all days of the year."

BleakWarrior gave a bitter grin.

"Your advice is well heeded," he said. "But I must go and pursue this woman of yours, then match her strength or die."

The Shepherd looked at him pitifully, perhaps believing BleakWarrior to be quite mad (which was not a bad guess).

"Good luck to you, then, sir," he said. "I hope that she is more civil towards you than she was to me."

"That," said BleakWarrior, "is very unlikely."

And BleakWarrior looked westward where the clouds were gathering on the horizon like a stampede of bulls.

"One more thing, man of the heath," he said. "This city of yours, what is it called?"

"It's not my city, sir, like I say. But it's called the City of Antiquities."

BleakWarrior stared at the ground for a moment. He had been there before, several times, and knew the place reasonably well. He raised his head again and asked:

"And where am I now?"

The Shepherd gave him a curious look and said, "This is the Girnan Howe, sir. Good land for grazing sheep, and that's about all."

And BleakWarrior nodded once, turned about and went on his way.

BleakWarrior hastened over the moorland in pursuit of the mystery girl of the Girnan Howe—the same, surely, whose traces he had followed through the ID network and, now, beyond.

Even if he couldn't find her (and perhaps, judging from the Shepherd's descriptions of her, it might be better if he couldn't), BleakWarrior reckoned that a visit to the City of Antiquities would provide him with an opportunity to regroup his thoughts, find maps and supplies, and gather useful information to allow him to plot his next course of action.

Be that as it may, such platitudes of obfuscation were purely designed to subdue the true feelings of excitement he felt towards the possibility of encountering the girl, who had, it is true, left some kind of indelible mark on him. She had somehow infiltrated the core of his being in ways he could not properly digest, beyond the fact that he felt compelled to chase after her. And, even while he realised he would probably have to kill her in the end (if, indeed, they ever met), who's to say he was not wrong?

The thought of the euphoric waft was all that mattered in the meantime.

18.
Goring a Whore for Liver Dye

It was a city full of studious fakes—of architectural fits and starts of imitation—of historical seizures without the depth of actual history.

Its people were full of a fascination for antiquarian objects that was equalled by a desire to relive the ways of olden times which they idealised to a point of ludicrous unreality. Which also explains why the City of Antiquities, in itself, reflected a modern taste for nostalgic longings that were founded entirely on a misapprehension of the distant past.

Its artificial quaintness had become the sum of its everyday life, which meant that people were nice to each other in ways that people of the past never had been. They were also abnormally law-abiding and socially calibrated to the highest standards of common decency and a mutual respect for one another's private affairs. The inhabitants of the City of Antiquities were among the most morally coherent of the entire continent, which also made them among the most nauseating.

Nevertheless, they were often called upon by nature to satisfy an underlying range of lusts that infected them like the symptoms of a disease. Which is why they engaged in routine acts of naughtiness under the auspices of private clubs that catered for a wide variety of specialised themes from a wide variety of former epochs. It was all quite titillating without overstepping the boundaries of taste (in the sense that it was fun without tending towards all-out degradation).

And this is where The Sisters of No Mercy were able to undertake a clever plan of disguising themselves as an escort service, with an overall aim of attracting the attentions of one particular visitor.

Who wasn't a visitor.

But whose name, instead, was Liver Dye.

Liver Dye sliced a diagonal line across the belly of the lady who lay on his bed like a marble effigy of vanquished youth, parting the layers of tissue as easily as he had parted her thighs during the course of his seduction.

He whistled a silent tune through his lips as he prised her liver from its stubborn knots of ligature, easing it out with attentiveness as if trying to avoid a small explosion.

Liver Dye took a moment to savour the softness and warmth of the bloated organ (which, if truth be told, was unimpressive), then placed it in a box that was ordinarily used for storing soil samples.

He looked down at the woman who lay on the bed, her body now stiffening with the brittleness of coagulating body fluids.

She'd been healthy for her years and full of the roister of good living. Her hips and breasts were generous with flesh on slack rows of muscle. But her succulence was diminished by the rigours of age; and, to this extent, she would barely suffice for a satisfactory admixture of high quality foot balms.

"I must avail myself of younger donors," he said to himself as he toyed with the lady's wound with the tip of his knife, poking at her flaps of skin like an absent-minded schoolboy.

And he looked down at his feet, and his toes waggled like the heads of little underlings in need of feeding.

Clearly, they agreed.

News of another murder had spread across the city like a seismic rupture—this time, of a seasoned whore, who was actually a tourist pretending to be one.

"Well, well, well," said Big Sister, adjusting her corsets with the look of a woman who wondered why the fuck *other* women had ever worn such a thing. "Looks like our fish has partaken himself of another bite."

"Right," said Little Sister. "And this will be his fucking undoing."

"Speaking of which," said Big Sister, "I wouldn't mind undoing *this* fucking thing."

"I'll do it for you later," said Little Sister.

"As long as you make it worth my while."

"Making it worth your while, Sister, is what I was fucking born for."

Liver Dye siphoned the pigments from the disgorged livers of his victims in order to make a rust-coloured balm which he applied to his feet to stop them from withering.

His withering feet were a mystery to him. He had no idea why they withered, except for the fact that they did, and knew only that if they withered below a certain point of proper feeling they became so wrinkled and flaccid that walking itself became a difficult undertaking.

When his feet were at their most taut and supple, however, Liver Dye was so skilled in their use that he could break the necks of his enemies using a short, sharp spinning manoeuvre called the Double Metatarsal Loop. Other than that, he had mastered a hierarchy of stunning moves that could inflict a range of fatal injuries, including the Reverse Hack and Sack Rip, the Cranial Disintegrator, the Adverse Mangle, the Full Frontal Choke, and a special variation for women called the Backward Master's Flipper Dash. To say of Liver Dye that his feet were killing you was a statement of fact, as well as a hyperbolic plea for mercy, which Liver Dye was happy to prove beyond all claims of reasonable doubt.

Liver Dye's appearance was of an agricultural consultant engaged in field work activities that required his extensive travel from place to place (with visits to cities for commercial purposes or laboratory testing). A variety of stains on his attire showed evidence of periods spent in rustic locations. He wore a wattle hat in the style of a crofter and the facial tattoos (a bunch of grapes on either cheek) of an associate member of the Wine Maker's Union.

Overall, he was conspicuous in a mild but not alarming sense, and was instantly perceived as one of a dozen of his kind who were present in any given city at any given time of the year.

Apart from the fact that he wasn't.

The linear stereotype he projected was both a disguise and a means of forging intimacy with suitable donors, inasmuch as there was nothing unusual about a professional traveller satisfying his lonely whiles with women of a certain character.

In the meantime, the City of Antiquities was clearly an outstanding resource, above all because of its lack-witted City Arbiters (whose lack of wits was equal to their lack of numbers). Most of the City Arbiters of the City of Antiquities were retired from active service and were, in effect, hobbyists dressed in hideous pantaloons after an archaic fashion that had never existed.

Liver Dye would have a little time to play with before a successful muster of serious law-enforcement was able to match the strategic cunning of his transgressions, which he intended to enjoy with a wantonness he could rarely afford in his wider quest to maintain his feet to their full extent of ergonomic proficiency.

But such are the attractions of loose women made looser by methods of skilled disembowelment that the whiff of their death finds beastly nostrils, like those of Number 17, whose visitations to the City of Antiquities, which he intended to service his fondness for whoring, had instead unearthed an unexpected yield of pitted fruits from the muck of human scandal—his awareness of which dispersed itself through psychic routes and, so, unto the telepathic divinations of Lord Brawl, whereupon Lord Brawl at once discerned that the pickings were good for a few loose Bastards to pick upon . . .

In a nearby village, Sons 4 and 46 felt a shiver of words pervading their veins like filaments of ice. They dropped to their knees as if struck by news of tragic import.

"My sons!" The voice resounded in their ears like an echo trapped in a tomb. "In the service of my aims you have relieved me of my atrocious burdens, which I have wrought with equal sorrow unto myself as upon my dreaded foes. It is because of you that I bear so well the inky stamp of my intentions—but, aside from this, I summon you now with a mission demanding your staunchest dedication to our cause.

"I am assured of a presence in the City of Antiquities whose name springs to my lips in syllables of despair, such as I pronounce them, in my plainest speech, as *Liver Dye*."

The Bastard Sons emitted a gasp of interest which, whether or not it was feigned, was expected of them as a matter of procedure.

"The city lies within your approximate reach. Hasten there with all speed, my Sons, and you will find your Brother, 17, with plans amounting to the downfall of a sorrowless fiend who plunders female vessels for their precious load, which I abhor."

Sons 4 and 46 did as they were told and, on reaching the City of Antiquities, rendezvoused with 17 who eagerly awaited them.

With a nose like dogs, they scented the blood of the sorrowless fiend their Father had referred to them and, already, had worked out a way to put an end to Liver Dye's cranky-pranky disruption of the community—by removing his feet and making him eat them.

19. Love on the Heels of Certain Death

It was Liver Dye who started it after picking up a couple of high-class whores who told him they were—

"Sisters, motherfucker. Not fucking whores at all."

Liver Dye's face was like a blank page that was badly in need of being filled.

He had taken them back to his apartments, threw himself on his bed, tucked his hands behind his neck, felt the shaft of his knife beneath the pillow, and commanded them to undress.

They did.

Underneath the floral abundance of their costumes they were wearing underwear that didn't match the floral abundance of their costumes.

As Liver Dye put it:

"Why are you wearing those leathern bodices that look as if they've been designed for combat? And what are those?"

"Those," said Big Sister, "are our Weapons."

Big Sister drew the Short Sword. Little Sister drew the Long Sword. Liver Dye's face bore a sudden description of extreme disappointment.

"I am very annoyed about this," he said.

"Not as fucking annoyed as we are," said Little Sister.

"Not as fucking annoyed as we are at all," said Big Sister.

"But," said Liver Dye, looking at each of them in turn, "why all the anger?"

"Because, foot boy, anger is what we were fucking born for."

The City of Antiquities was in a state of emergency without even knowing it.

However . . .

Three of the Bastard Sons of Brawl were on the case. They wore masks in the style of an epoch known as The Hiding. During The Hiding, it was fashionable to maintain a public profile of visual anonymity in order to engage in lascivious acts without being recognised.

The masks were made of dark materials that covered the whole of their heads, with spaces or slits to accommodate the sensory and respiratory functions. The features of the masks were moulded in the manner of anthropomorphised beasts associated with qualitative states like wisdom, hilarity, drunkenness, slyness, looseness, joy or sexual potency. Number 4 was wearing a mask with elongated ears that reached over his head like a pair of drooping horns. 17 wore a mask that made him look like a licentious fish. 46 wore a mask that was non-descript, except for the O-shaped mouth that looked as if it was designed for the purposes of oral sex (and probably was).

The standard vestments that went with the masks were short cloaks wafting around the trunk of the body that hung immodestly over the thighs and buttocks (which were meant to be seen as an indication of a willingness to caper). The legs were furnished with silky red or purple tights (the colours of wickedness). The feet were clamped in dramatically high-heeled boots with pointed toes that made them look like instruments of torture.

The appearance of the Sons of Brawl was as three ill-proportioned chimaeras whose bestial upper bodies sat on the delicate, prancing stalks of birds' legs with deformed feet. They had never felt so ridiculous in their entire lives. And yet, the disguise was necessary, and would also encourage them to a greater release of violence due to the humiliating candour of their dress (which had come very close to reducing them to tears).

Notwithstanding the discomforts of the Bastard Sons of Brawl, the City of Antiquities was a perpetual carnival of eccentric tourists enjoying a wide selection of exotic revels. There were many varieties of pleasure from which to choose to satisfy a wide variety of uncommon tastes. The cabaret suites and fetish clubs were pointedly suave without being sleazy. The saloons and brothels were pointedly sleazy without being suave. There were taverns and alehouses of every type, from bucolic to bawdy, and restaurants to cater for every type of gastronomic hauteur.

An extravagance of marvels were on display in the city's multitudinous architecture where, sometimes, entire streets or blocks of buildings had been uniformly modelled on the particular trend of a particular epoch. Or sometimes it was more of an admixture of contrasting incarnations of historic urban settings. Either way, the architectures were transgressive of each other's styles so that no one style was able to dominate the overall prospect.

But none of this would be worthwhile without effective street-lighting; and, to this extent, the municipal bodies of the City of Antiquities were very accomplished masters of the arts required.

The streets were lit according to their thematic emphasis—mostly brightened by the standard technologies of lamps and lanterns, but with occasional kernels of seediness requiring the throbbing glare of specialised pyrotechnics: candles, braziers, sulphur bowls, bonfires and other sources of an antique or cabalistic flavour. One or two establishments had been wired with circuitry to enable the bald luminosity of electric valves; but these were confined to anomalies, such as the Aquarium, where the lurid effect of the valves had been successively exploited through the clever use of light filters and restrictive flutes.

As a visual spectacle, the tourists themselves were hardly secondary to the City's architecture; nor were they upstaged by the illumination of the streets. In general, they dressed according to the overall theme of their prevailing fancy and tended to congregate in appropriate areas of thematic confluence. But it was not unusual for variant themes to begin to overlap as the night wore on; and, at such times, it was as if a hundred different festivals from a hundred different times and places had converged on a single point of universal revelry, which was hugely enjoyed in spite of the incongruities of its multifaceted falseness.

In the face of a welter of uninhibited human glee, it was impossible to gauge the full extent of disgust that welled in the haggard breasts of the Bastard Sons of Brawl. Suffice to say that it made them want to cause bodily harm even more than they already wanted to—but that, after all, is why they were there. But their struggle to contain themselves was taking an ungenerous toll on their patience, inasmuch as they could be said to have any.

"I can hardly walk in my stupid boots," complained 4, as they bludgeoned their way through swathes of merry-makers.

"I can hardly walk in mine either," said 17.

"I can hardly walk in mine either," said 46, "but I *will* make a point of using them to repeatedly stamp on the head of the remover of livers."

"Good point," said 17.

"Father says," said 4, "that we have to make sure that the liver remover doesn't get into a position where he can attack us with his feet."

46 gave a knowledgeable grunt.

"His feet are well-known to be deadly," he explained. "We must be sure to confine his feet to enclosed spaces."

"What kind of enclosed spaces?" asked 4.

46 shot him a glance as if to assess his stupidity.

"Walls, sculleries, alcoves, corridors." He thought for a moment and added, "Staircases."

"Cluttered areas," interjected 17, "with furniture."

"Furniture?" 4 frowned.

"Chairs and tables," said 17. "Anything that offers us a temporary barricade against his feet."

"It's all to do with range," continued 46. "We must keep him at bay by remaining outside of the range of his feet."

"How do we know when we're within range of his feet?" asked 4.

"Because of the length of his legs," said 46.

"But," said 4, "how do we get close enough so we can kill him?"

46 shot him another glance.

"We use our skills," he said. "We must remain outside the range of his feet whilst making sure that he falls within range of our weapons."

4 bit his lip. He had the look of someone who wanted to ask more questions without knowing how to.

In the meantime, they had been monitoring Liver Dye's movements and were on the point of taking significant action. He had proven difficult to find, and difficult to track, and was, by nature, an elusive beast with the instincts of a sand lizard.

The strategy of Liver Dye was simple but effective. He would switch his rented rooms on an ad hoc basis, leaving behind a trail of plundered bodies with their bellies cut open and livers removed. He chose his rented rooms in the busiest quarters of the town where the commotion of the crowds was at its height, so as to shield his activities from public notice.

After several days of studious observation, however, the Bastard Sons of Brawl had got him firmly within their sights.

They had followed him to his current apartments, where he had newly returned with a pair of high class whores in crazily abundant floral dresses.

"Let us wait for a while," 46 had said. "When he's fully engrossed in removing the livers of his whores, that'll be the time to go and get him."

"Right," said 4.

"I'm going to make him eat my stinking heels as well as his own feet," sneered 17, still struggling to cope with the cut of his boots.

They nested themselves in the throng of a bar on the other side of the street from Liver Dye's apartment block. The apartment had a spacious balcony and, as they looked on, one of the whores came on to it under the pretext of taking a turn of her pipe, but seemed to be making an assessment of the busy scene on the street below. Satisfied, she re-entered. The Bastards gave it little thought and satisfied themselves with fulsome draughts of house wine to settle their excited nerves.

"Let's give it another round of wine, then go," said 46, after allowing a little time to pass.

And, suddenly, 17 put a hand on his shoulder that caused him to twitch to such an extent that he almost hammered a fist against his brother's jaw. However:

"Look!" hissed 17. "The whores are coming out!"

And, sure enough, the high class whores were exiting the main doors of the tenement, looking a little flustered, it was clear, but not in the manner of the aftermath of rampant sex—nor, indeed, of having had their livers removed. One of them, in fact, looked badly bruised, while the other was bleeding from her nose and cradling an elbow.

"The whores have escaped his clutches and they flee!" said 17.

46 shook his head.

"Something is not right here," he said.

"What shall we do?" asked 4, looking like an abandoned child on the verge of weeping.

“We’re here for Liver Dye,” said 17. “Let’s go get him, I say.”

46 had narrowed his eyes through the eye-slits of his mask.

“Yes,” he said. “Let’s kill the remover of livers, just like Father wants us to.”

And they were gone.

And watching them from the corner of the bar was a blonde-haired girl of dishevelled appearance, her shoulders hunched as if in fear. She reached for a cocktail full of ludicrously coloured liquids, gripping it with twitching hands, her fingers shaking like twigs in the birl of an autumn wind. Her eyes peeped out from under a fringe, watching the costumed figures as they crossed the street like a dog pack. Clearly, they were intent on targeting the remover of livers and had been shocked to see the two sisters emerge from his apartment block.

“I wonder if they know who the sisters are,” she thought to herself.

Probably not.

There were so many of them here now, milling about the city’s streets, that she felt completely lost. And terrified.

“Just how am I going to manage to kill these brutes,” she whispered under her breath.

Then she drank from her cocktail like she really needed it.

And did.

The Sisters of No Mercy emerged from the apartment block of Liver Dye looking like they were part of a group of fetishists called the Broodists. The Broodists had existed in a period of high decadence where it was common to resort to self-abuse as a means of personal ornamentation. Broodism was not an uncommon theme in the City of Antiquities; and, because of that, The Sisters of No Mercy went largely unnoticed as they fled from the scene of the apartment block of Liver Dye—and this in spite of the disgruntled looks they wore on their faces that sat with their bruises like old friends on a stony beach.

The tussle with Liver Dye had been much harder than they'd anticipated because of the inconvenience of his adeptness as a fighter, notwithstanding the fact that he was naked and seemingly unarmed.

"How the fuck were we to know?" Big Sister moaned.

"We should've guessed it," said Little Sister. "Why the fuck else would he anoint them with liver oil?"

"I thought that was to stop them from fucking withering."

"Yes, but why the fuck would they fucking wither in the first place if they weren't his fucking Weapons?"

Big Sister thought about it for a few moments and said, "I don't know, Sister. Why?"

Little Sister shrugged.

"I don't know either," she said. "But it sort of makes sense."

And they harried their way through the overspill of revelry on the streets towards a quieter section of the town that was called the Normal Quarter because of the way in which the multifaceted thematic disorder of the city centre was suddenly transformed into sober rows of stores and shops where practical goods were sold under dull conditions of everyday custom. The Normal Quarter had been deliberately set apart from the city's main thoroughfares to avoid spoiling their antique flavour; while its own flavour was one of mercantile and residential blandness that provided a welcome retreat from the excessive pretensions of the inner town.

"I hope," said Big Sister, "he won't be able to use his feet to cut his way through the rope."

Little Sister shook her head.

"I was careful to wind the rope between his toes and

clamp his feet together from the heels upwards. Then I wrapped it thrice around his shins and under the soles of his feet, then up around his knees and thighs, then wrapped it nice and tight around his scrotum which—you know—is the point of leverage around which the whole structure of the knot is turned. If he moves, he'll more than likely rip his balls off."

"I know all that," said Big Sister. "It's just . . ."

"What?"

"*He broke my fucking nose, Sister!*"

Little Sister stopped and put a hand on Big Sister's shoulder. Big Sister looked tearful.

"It's OK," said Little Sister, "I straightened it out. It looks the same as before. It's a beautiful nose. Really, it is."

"It's all swollen," said Big Sister, the tears now welling in her eyes in little pools of wet light.

Little Sister stepped up on her toes and planted a kiss on Big Sister's massively bloated nasal tip.

"There," she said. "Better?"

Big Sister looked cute and smiled.

"Yes," she said, "better."

"Come on," said Little Sister. "We'd better get those fucking alchemical containers so we can get that fucker's liver in them. I can't believe the ones we had were out of date."

"Shit happens," sighed Big Sister.

"Damn right it does," said Little Sister, and led Big Sister by the hand through the quiet streets of the Normal Quarter towards a shop of some renown called The Domestic and Alchemical Hardware Emporium.

Burning Hot Coals carried his bag through the happy crowds with a look on his face like he'd like to fit a piece of coal into each and every one of their mouths and make them swallow it hard enough to burn a hole through the pits of all their stomachs.

He was dressed in charred accoutrements that made him look like a chimney sweep with a severe tendency towards unpremeditated murder. The description was fair, and was also enough to cause looks of consternation on the faces of the people who passed him by.

Burning Hot Coals didn't fit in. He stood out like a black spot in a line of vision.

But, more than that, he simply didn't fucking care.

The Bastard Sons of Brawl hastily entered the tenement block and ascended the stairwell. The heels of their boots clacked against the polished granite of the treads like an obsolete folk rhythm.

More suited to such plans of action without thought, 46, 4 and 17 jostled up the stairwell like birds bursting into flight through the tiny door of a cramped cage. They spat and cursed and thrashed their arms and elbows into each other's backs and sides and bellies, clacking their heels like hammers against a row of teeth. The rage in them was accumulating like froth in a bottle that needed to explode. 4 fell behind 46 and 17 but caught up with them just as they reached the door of Liver Dye's apartments. 46 and 17 paused as if to plot a coordinated entry. 4 ran right passed them and threw his stocky sprawling body against the door. The lock shattered, the door burst open, and 4 flew into the room and collided with a table that sent him spinning to the floor in a clattering heap.

46 and 17 whooped and laughed like hairy animals and rushed into the apartments in a frenzy of excitement. They had drawn their weapons from behind their flapping cloaks. They span on their heels and whirled their heads with an ungainly distension of limbs and necks. Their masks provided them with an aura of theatrical malice that was badly offset by the awkward gait of their bandy legs in the red and purple sheen of tights.

Not that it mattered. The Sons of Brawl were insensible to matters of appearance in the heat of a brawl.

But there was no brawl. There was no remover of livers. There was no aggressive resistance of unlimited foot-power to contest their arrival. The success of their mission seemed under threat; and the Bastard Sons of Brawl were quick to become unnerved and anxious by the unexpected elusiveness of Liver Dye.

46 and 17 were bawling orders at each other—"Through there! The scullery! The dressing chamber! Beware the privy!"—when 4, rising to his feet like a recovering drunk, drew his weapon (a double-headed hand axe) and pointed:

"The bed!"

His shout was loud enough to cause his Bastard Brothers to cease the commotion of their search. They followed the outstretched doubled-headed axe and saw that 4 (perhaps for the first time in his entire life) was right.

In the spacious room of the apartments they had entered, they had seen the bed—no doubt about it—but had failed to observe the undulating burden that lay beneath its silken sheets. They hastened to tear away the sheets from the bed with weapons raised in readiness to strike against a barrage of deadly foot manoeuvres. Instead, they froze.

Below them, naked and bound from head to toe, with his testicles caught in a hideous grip of complex knot-work, was Liver Dye. His mouth was stuffed with wet cloths, and the cloths bound by a strip of leather drawn to an exquisite tightness.

The Bastard Sons of Brawl stared at him in outright mystification until, finally, 46 said, "Remove the gag. Then his feet. Then we make him eat them."

From the back of Liver Dye's throat there came an involuntary whimper that, very quickly, became a scream.

"I need some cutlery," said Welter of Impermanence at The Domestic and Alchemical Hardware Emporium, which had taken her the best part of a day to find since her arrival from the Girnan Howe at the crack of dawn that very morning. "The best you've got."

The hardware specialist glanced up at her and didn't say a thing. He was fumbling beneath the counter of his shop. He continued fumbling and chose to ignore her.

"I need some cutlery," said Welter of Impermanence, in exactly the same tones as before.

"Up there."

The hardware specialist gestured towards a row of shelves that were out of reach. On the shelves there were rows of trays with labels on them—"Knives," "Forks," "Spoons," "Miscellaneous."

"What's in 'Miscellaneous'?" asked Welter of Impermanence.

The hardware specialist looked up from under the counter.

"Just what it says."

Welter of Impermanence looked at him as if she wanted to wring his neck.

"I want to look inside the trays," she said, evenly.

"Over there."

The hardware specialist gestured towards a ladder that ran along a rail on the wall. Welter of Impermanence went up to the ladder and moved it along the rail until it rested under the trays. She climbed up and started rummaging.

At first, the hardware specialist had chosen to ignore her in a display of macho indifference towards womankind which had no particular reason to exist. After a few glances, he began to take interest—first, in the degree of expertise with which she examined and tested the quality of each implement; second, in how she deposited her choices in various compartments of her attire; and third, in the way her buttocks moved as she delved among the various articles.

"Hey," he said, with an emphasis of authority (it was, after all, his shop). "Don't put them in your pockets. I can't see them." He came out from behind the counter. "You have to pay for those."

Welter of Impermanence carried on with her rummaging. She plucked objects one after the other out of the trays, running her thumb along blades, holding handles to her tongue to taste the alloys, holding them up to her ear as if to listen to their composition.

"If you can't pay," said the hardware specialist, "you'd better get out. Or—" He took a step closer and licked his lips—"There's other ways of paying. If you don't have any money maybe you could—"

Welter of Impermanence wheeled round on the ladder and caused him to jump.

"Okay," she said.

The hardware specialist looked confused.

"What?" he said.

"Whatever you want," said Welter of Impermanence. "Or maybe I can do whatever I want—" She held out her hand—"with this."

It was a bread knife. The hardware specialist let his mouth fall open.

"I—"

He didn't have time to finish whatever it was he was going to say.

Welter of Impermanence stepped off the ladder and let herself drop. She landed beside him, face to face, eye to eye, the tips of their noses almost touching. The hardware specialist felt a sudden cold shaft in his gut that quickly became a rod of pain. Then he felt it twist inside him like he was an empty space being infiltrated by a vortex. He tried to disengage himself from the vortex but it was too gummy. It was as if his innards had turned to a glue that clung to the vortex without being able to detach themselves from its ineluctable strength of magnetism.

Welter of Impermanence was standing with the bread knife plunged in the hardware specialist's abdominal tracts when the door swung open and two ladies dressed in voluminous frocks walked in and:

"Fuck me," said one, her eyes widening in appreciation of the gore.

"Fuck you, no, Sister," said the other. "Looks to me like she's the one whose doing the fucking."

"It looks like what she was fucking born for, Sister."

"Fuck me if I don't think you're right."

"I usually am."

"Don't I know it, Sister. Don't I know it."

Little Sister stepped forward and drew the Long Sword.

"Hello," she said to the girl who was standing holding a bread knife in the guts of the hardware shop's proprietor, "my name's Little Sister. What's yours?"

Welter of Impermanence, without moving, said, "My name is for my friends, and I don't have any."

Big Sister stepped forward and drew the Short Sword.

"That's OK," she said, "we don't have any friends either."

Welter of Impermanence pulled the bread knife from the guts of the hardware specialist and let his body drop. Blood pooled around her feet like an amorphous creature undertaking a bizarre metabolic expansion of its form.

"You'd better get out of my way if you don't want to end up like him," she said without emotion.

Big Sister nodded as if suddenly aware of something.

"Sister," she said, "I've got to say, I admire her style."

"Me too," said Little Sister. She pursed her lips and added, "She's kind of thin, though."

"Totally fucking thin."

"But not *that* thin."

"Not fucking thin at all."

"She's more like, scrawny."

"Scrawny is good."

"But not *that* good. She has, for example, got all the right curves in all the right places."

"I was just about to say exactly the same thing."

"Which makes me wonder, Sister. Just what are we going to do with a girl who's got all the right curves in all the right places?"

"Well," said Big Sister, "she wouldn't be missed, if you know what I mean."

"I know what you mean," said Little Sister. "No friends."

"Or good manners."

"That's OK, Sister. We don't have any good manners either."

"No, we've got them bad."

"Very bad."

"Very bad," said Welter of Impermanence, wagging the bread knife at them, "is what I was fucking born for."

"So, there we were," said Big Sister, "on our way to get our fucking containers after the old ones had started getting hairline cracks, cause they get brittle, see, when they're out of date, and only last a few months or years or decades—you never know which—cause they're made of fucking compounds that no one knows how the fuck to make. Except the people who make them, fuckers living in fucking caves or labyrinths or something, fucking around all day for centuries with weird alchemical shit that's older than I am—and here we are now, on the floor of the hardware specialist, all naked and ready to interact with a total fucking stranger."

The girl whose name they didn't know inclined her head with a sort of sardonic smile that Big Sister found quite sexy.

"Yes, we are naked," she said, and trailed the tip of her finger across Little Sister's ample belly. Little Sister gasped, shivered and threw her head back like it was triggered by a tripwire. Her thighs fell open like the gates of a lock that forded a canal. The girl whose name they didn't know's finger traced a line down her belly and toyed its way through the initial thatch of Little Sister's warming love cup.

"Make it yours," whispered Little Sister, and the girl whose name they didn't know was happy to oblige.

In the meantime, Big Sister watched the girl whose name they didn't know with heightened interest and absently played with Little Sister's broad nipples which grew stiff and alert as little sea urchins. Big Sister reflected on the fact that it was good to have found a willing companion to add to the mix. Without having to resort to using aphrodisiacs of a suspicious or specious origin, The Sisters of No Mercy were pleasantly surprised to find that the girl whose name they didn't know was very eager to respond to their demands for impromptu sex. It was clear, as they undressed, that the girl whose name they didn't know was also capable of providing them with expert stimulations which she was also keen to receive with perfect abandon.

With the blood of the hardware specialist dampening the floorboards beneath them, they got down to it without the preliminary drag of fully-clothed action.

"We don't like messing about," Little Sister had told the girl whose name they didn't know.

The girl whose name they didn't know, flicking her tongue across her lips, said, "Neither do I."

Under normal circumstances, Little Sister liked to sit back and give instructions, which led to the pleasure of being obeyed. But the girl whose name they didn't know was remarkably aware of what she was doing to the point that the instructions were unnecessary. With Big Sister on one side and the girl whose name they didn't know on the other, Little Sister spread herself on the floor and availed herself of a hefty pampering. Big Sister was pretty rough (not because she tried to be but because she couldn't help it) while the girl whose name they didn't know was pretty smooth. So the overall balance was like being buffeted by two winds from two different seasons.

In the meantime, the floor of the hardware store was lined with rough wooden timbers full of splinters that had been softened up by the spilled blood of the hardware specialist. The effect was such that splinters would lightly pierce or grate against the skin of their buttocks and thighs without causing discomfort, whereby the pain was inefficacious as pain and was, in fact, perfectly titillating. Encouraged by Little Sister's increasing waves of elated sighs, the girl whose name they didn't know was also heating up to a higher point of physical arousal. She slid her fingers into Little Sister's over-brimming centre of wetness, using the benefits of her obvious experience to draw the wetness from the warmth of its allotment. Little Sister began a rhythmic pant in unison with the gyrating motions of her hips. Big Sister caressed her neck and nipples and watched the girl whose name they didn't know expand upon her preponderance of miracles.

"I get to lick your pussy after this," she said with steady matter-of-factness to the girl whose name they didn't know. The girl whose name they didn't know looked up at Big Sister and nodded, slowly. There was a trail of saliva hanging from her lower lip.

"I *want* you want to lick my pussy after this," she said.

Big Sister looked pleased. Her own nipples were reaching out from the flat moulds of her chest, aching towards their maximum projectile of stiffness like limpets on a rock. She toyed with them a little herself, and said to the girl whose name they didn't know, "You like the look of my nipples, girl?"

The girl whose name they didn't know looked at the nipples and said, "Tell me who wouldn't?"

And so it continued until it was time for Big Sister and Little Sister to lay the girl whose name they didn't know onto the bloody timbers of the floor and subject her to a gentle ravaging. They pushed her legs apart and raised her pelvis to their lowering heads. The pubic tuft of the girl whose name they didn't know was a reddish colour that spread lightly across her crotch to much lesser effect than the dark eruptions of The Sisters of No Mercy's sweltering love-pits. Likewise, the mouldings of her clitoris and labia formed a dainty pink whorl against the fleshy brown folds of The Sisters' thick and meaty nests.

But what was most alluring in the appeal of the girl whose name they didn't know was the potency of her vaginal juices that spilled over the lips of The Sisters of No Mercy with a sublime and syrupy thickness that seemed to fill their brains with infusions of erotic wonder. The taste had a weighty tang that produced an effect of mild invigoration mixed with a prolonged sense of internal melting, like being absorbed by the outer shades of a celestial aurora.

The Sisters of No Mercy smiled, almost laughing, and mashed their sodden lips against the dripping honeycomb of the girl whose name they didn't know. They pressed the softness of their tongues to her needy grinding movements. The girl whose name they didn't know began to ascend the stages of an orgasm that, when it came, hit like breaking waves on a sun-drenched beach.

After which, The Sisters engulfed each other like amoebas engaged in a microscopic amalgamation. The girl whose name they didn't know lay on the floor in a pose of exhausted radiance, in part to conceal her underlying dissatisfaction; for she had already began to ponder the question of how she was going to escape the clutches of these gorgeous freaks.

And wonder if she really wanted to.

Afterwards, The Sisters of No Mercy felt delighted but strange. There was something about their manner, a subsiding bliss replaced by a hyper-active girlish excitement, that caused them to talk in uninhibited streams of gregarious babble.

"We know it's got properties," Little Sister explained to the girl whose name they didn't know, "but we don't know what they are yet. So, the plan's to get the thing out and cut it up into little pieces, then put it in an alchemical container like the one we—"

"Get the thing out?" interrupted the girl whose name they didn't know.

"With our Swords," said Little Sister. "Then, like I say, we cut it up into little bits and pack them into—" She raised the bag containing the alchemical container they'd snagged from The Domestic and Alchemical Hardware Emporium—"this, then take it with us to use as a reanimation feed for our Middle Sister."

"Middle Sister?"

"Yeah."

"You've got a Middle Sister?"

"Yeah," said Big Sister. "She's dead just now, but we're going to bring her back to life."

"Back to life?" The girl whose name they didn't know looked incredulous. "How are you going to do that?"

"By feeding her with shit like this," said Little Sister, raising the bag with the alchemical container and giving it a light shake.

"See," said Big Sister, "we're on a mission to get our Middle Sister back to life by feeding her with bodily extracts taken from people like us."

"People like us?" The girl whose name they didn't know looked worried.

"Fuck me, girl, you ask so many fucking questions."

The girl whose name they didn't know looked sheepish.

"Sorry," she said.

Little Sister nudged her shoulder with her own shoulder and said, "That's OK. But in answer to your question—of which there are so fucking many—yes, people like us."

"You mean like . . . humans?"

"Linear humans? No fucking way. I mean, people like *us*."

"Like you?"

"And you."

"Me?"

Little Sister nodded and said, "We know what you are, girl."

The girl whose name they didn't know chewed her lip and said, "But you're not going to . . . You're not going to use . . . "

Little Sister gave the girl whose name they didn't know a look like she was offended.

"Use what? Use you? Are you fucking kidding, girl? The only way we're going to use you is by advising you to come with us so we can have lots of sex with each other to help each other to expand our knowledge of how to kill people who want to kill us. See?"

The girl whose name they didn't know looked relieved, although she was actually wondering just how it was she was going to get herself out of this increasingly messy set of relations.

"So how did you know," said the girl whose name they didn't know, "that I'm like you?"

The Sisters of No Mercy exchanged a look and smirked.

"Fuck, girl," said Big Sister, "it was the way you were holding the bread knife in the hardware specialist's guts. We thought, How the fuck could a pretty little thing like that hold a knife in the guts of a pretty ugly thing like him without the slightest indication of showing she wasn't enjoying it? There was only one answer, girl. You were one of the people of mood, rather than habit."

"People of what?"

"Of mood," said Little Sister. "Unpredictable."

The girl whose name they didn't know didn't know what that was meant to mean, though she understood it well enough.

And that's when she decided to stop asking questions. Because she was fairly certain that The Sisters of No Mercy had meant what they said about not using her as a special feed for their Middle Sister. And, as they walked through the festive streets of the city, she sensed in them a genuine pulse of warmth that hit her like rays, a warmth she partly reciprocated, in spite of her need to escape their grasp, if *need* to escape their grasp is what it was.

But her desire to regain the trail of BleakWarrior was overwhelming to a point she couldn't resist. Whatever it was she felt for The Sisters was strong without being strong enough. The grip of BleakWarrior, however, was unrelenting.

But why? Why did she wish to destroy him so much?

She shook the questions from her head. Now was not the time or place. She would think about it in more detail when she was far away from wherever it was The Sisters of No Mercy wanted to take her.

In the meantime, The Sisters of No Mercy walked behind her with their heads bowed together, whispering.

"Sister, fuck, I think I'm in love with this girl almost as much as I'm in love with you."

"But not as much?"

"Not as fucking much at all."

"Well," said Little Sister, "I have to say that I think I feel the same way."

"That's it, then," said Big Sister. "We're in love."

"Love, Sister, is what we were fucking born for."

20. BleakWarrior Switches to Automanic

By mid-afternoon, BleakWarrior had entered the City of Antiquities in pursuit of the mystery girl of the Girnan Howe, wending his way through crowds of pedlars, revellers and harmless drunks, only to find that he himself was being followed.

He continued without exhibiting alarm or any such signs of urgency that would betray his knowledge of being pursued; and, by degrees of cunning, he managed to assess the person who was following him: a girl of negligible appearance, with blonde hair falling over her head like a demolished haystack. Her shoulders were hunched as if she suffered from some kind of chronic shyness; and, whoever she was, she seemed nervous, even terrified, and it occurred to BleakWarrior that perhaps she was a liner human that, for some bizarre reason, was seeking his help—for such was the sense of weakness she demonstrated in the way she moved.

In spite of this, there was evidence to suggest she was not of a linear extraction. She radiated a kind of over-anxious and tremulous alertness to her surroundings, like a cat avoiding fire crackers at a winter carnival. She also seemed to suffer a myriad of distractions that gave the impression of an insanity derived from concentrating too much on the presence of things that weren't really there. It seemed to BleakWarrior that to expose oneself to such a constancy of interferences, while continuing to attempt to follow someone, was a severely outlandish mode of behaviour—indicative, perhaps, of a Demi-Thurganic turn of mind.

He had gathered all this while crossing a street full of human-carried litters being transported by frantic local hirelings seeking to exploit the tourists for the sake of earning a decent crust. The litters presented enough of a hazard for BleakWarrior to swing his head from right to left as he crossed, as if to seek safe passage from one side of the street to the other without being hit (which, in fact, he was). But he was also taking the opportunity to throw enough glances at the person following him to make an assessment of her general character. Whoever she was, she had about as much in slyness as a hatchling fallen from its nest, while the same could not be said for BleakWarrior.

When he reached the other side of the street, he double-backed the way he had come, pretending to be lost in unfamiliar urban terrain, but with a lack of concern that suggested movement without purpose, in the manner of a visitor seeking local enjoyments.

This impression, too, allowed him to take stock of the girl who was following him; and, this time, the extent of her agitation was confirmed by the fact that she had stopped at a liquor rack to purchase a bottle of Sopid's Immaculate Deepest Condolences.

Clearly in need of a hard-hitting beverage to soothe her rattled nerves, she opened it and drank. The look on her face was a reminder of the fact that the liquor had been aptly named.

The manner in which she demolished the bottle of Sopid's IDC further convinced BleakWarrior that there was something decidedly non-linear about her. And it was at this point that he began to wonder if she might have been the mystery girl whose traces he'd followed through the ID network and beyond.

But, no, it didn't seem plausible. The Shepherd's

description was clear with its pronouncements of a formidable woman with a calm and violent nature, who had brutalised him on the moor with the nonchalance of a seasoned psychopath. The same could not be said for this baggage of broken nerves that jittered after him like a moth after a distant flame.

Nevertheless, BleakWarrior decided he was going to have to prevent her from doing whatever it was she was trying to do by possibly abducting and killing her.

With this in mind, he watched for her to cross the street and resume her pursuit of him. Her avoidance of the rushing litters was like watching a rabbit picking its way through a pack of wild dogs. He slid into the entrance of a costume specialist and waited for her to recover his trail (which, by now, she'd lost). She seemed distraught by the fact she'd lost sight of him, and launched herself into the melee of pedestrians like a leaping frog.

BleakWarrior emerged and snatched her by the arm as she blundered passed him, drew her into the doorway. Then he levelled the Dirk against the back of her neck and said, "If you move, I'll sever your spinal cord."

Her response was to shake like a leaf in the grip of a hurricane.

"Who are you?" demanded BleakWarrior.

"Automanic," she answered.

"Are you following me?"

"Yes."

"Why?"

"Because I want to kill you."

"Want to or will?"

"Want to," she sobbed, now verging on tears and adding, "But I probably won't."

"No," said BleakWarrior, "you won't."

Automanic struggled to maintain her posture, evidently growing weak at the knees.

"I'm sorry," she said, straining to prevent a convulsion.

"Sorry?"

"Yes."

"Why?"

"Because . . . I can't help it. It's what we do."

BleakWarrior pressed the edge of the Dirk against her neck.

"Is it?" he said.

"Yes," she whispered.

"If that is the case," said BleakWarrior, "you will have no objection to me killing you."

"Please." Her body tensed so much that her shaking gave way to a state of near paralysis.

BleakWarrior allowed the Dirk to relax a little.

"You do not wish to die?" he said.

"No." Her reply was little more than a squeak.

"Well then," said BleakWarrior, now lowering the Dirk and concealing it quickly, "if that is the case, why don't we go for a draught of ale instead?"

Automanic looked up at him through blurred eyes, and nodded.

BleakWarrior took her to a place called the Receptor's Intellectual Terminus, a tavern done up in the style of the Epoch of Learning, which was not unlike the Brain Exchange for its emphasis on mental stimuli (here supplied by music, dancers, theatre groups, live painting exhibitions, comedians, orators, folklorists and puppeteers). BleakWarrior avoided the hub of the tavern's activity and requested a private booth where drinks and chatter may occur without interruption. The booth would also present opportunities for BleakWarrior to kill the girl, if that became necessary. She was probably unaware of the fact that she'd just been abducted; and, indeed, as Lodolo said, *The best abductions are those in which the victim is unaware of their victimhood.*

When their drinks arrived, BleakWarrior waited for the waitress to depart and said, "How is it that you came to recognise me for what I am, to the point that you should follow me outright—albeit, badly?"

"The Lenses," she said, taking a deep breath before going on. "I . . . I keep dossiers, with details of everything I see and hear and learn about our species."

"Dossiers?" BleakWarrior frowned.

"Yes," she said. "I collect strange facts, pieces of hearsay from local tales. I study books and civic records. I plunder the folk memories of linear humans. I question Free Traders of Interest for evidence of peculiar events and extreme cases of criminality. I follow people. I have compiled my dossiers meticulously over the years, and studied them in great detail, so that all the information contained in them is as clear to me as my own memories. I'm sort of like a walking encyclopaedia of our people, BleakWarrior. See? I even know your name. I suppose that we all have our uses, and this one happens to be mine."

"It is an interesting use," said BleakWarrior.

"Thank you," said Automanic, and lowered her head. "I knew it right away, when I saw you enter the city gates—what you were, who you were, what you were capable of." And then her face brightened when she said, "I'm really good at perceiving things."

BleakWarrior looked at her with only a mild hint of scorn. "You look to me as if you perceive too much of anything," he said.

She turned away and blushed, betraying that element of chronic shyness that BleakWarrior had detected upon first seeing her.

"So you followed me," he said, letting a moment pass and leering over his foaming glass like a vulture over a piece of carrion, "in order to have me killed."

"What's wrong with that?" said Automanic, suddenly defensive.

"Nothing."

"I didn't say I would actually do it."

"Or could."

"I could if I tried."

"Trying," said BleakWarrior, "is never the same as doing."

Automanic pouted and swigged from her glass.

"Tell me," said BleakWarrior, "how many of our number have you killed?"

"More than you think."

"My impression is that you haven't killed any."

Automanic rolled her eyes in the manner of a teenager under the scrutiny of an accusation.

"One," she muttered, and turned away. Then she turned back again and, not looking up: "And she was asleep. And maybe even dead already."

"You were right, then," said BleakWarrior.

"About what?"

"About killing more than I thought."

Automanic sighed and said, "I need to kill more. It's the only thing that brings me relief."

"From what?"

"From myself."

BleakWarrior looked at her through the glare of the Lenses. He could see the effect it had on her. She was terrified of the imperceptible sentiment that lay underneath.

"There is something very wrong with you," he observed.

"Yes," she said, "there is."

"And what is it?"

"I'm scared."

"Of what?"

"Of everything."

"Everything?" BleakWarrior was incredulous.

"I'm a victim of my vulnerability to terror—mostly of myself—and am very capable of making myself go mad with anxiety, which is the reason, specifically, why I'm terrified of myself and am very capable of making myself go mad with anxiety."

"That's an interesting dilemma," said BleakWarrior.

"It's a fucking mess," said Automanic. "My head, I mean." She leaned forward and said, "The fact is, my lack of control over my own thought processes is a kind of vicious circle without the curves—more like a circle of vicious angles. Which is why I need someone to help me."

"To help you what?"

"Kill people."

"Kill people?"

"Like I said," said Automanic, "it's the only thing that brings me relief beyond the temporary measures of drugs and alcohol which, in the end, make me worse."

BleakWarrior hardened the Lenses on her like packs of ice.

"What about your dossiers?" he said.

Automanic hunched her shoulders in an overly precious kind of way.

"It's a useful distraction," she said. "Actually, it's more of an obsession. Or maybe it's a symptom—not a distraction at all."

"A symptom of what?"

"Of my anxiety. Which is a symptom of my need to kill people."

"So killing is a cure for you?" BleakWarrior inclined his head in doubt.

Automanic looked away and bit her lip. Looked back again.

"Maybe," she said, "or maybe not. Sometimes I think it isn't possible."

"What isn't possible?"

"For me to be cured. And the thought that it isn't possible terrifies me to the point that I actually believe it isn't possible. And the fear of believing it isn't possible fills me with a fear of doing harm to myself that's eventually going to be used to harm others."

BleakWarrior frowned.

"That doesn't make sense," he said.

"Fear makes me dangerous." Automanic held up her head as if in pride.

"But . . ."

"Unless they harm me first."

"But . . ."

"Which makes me believe that they really will harm me first."

"Who?"

"The thought of which makes me more dangerous than I already am." She smiled and added, "Hopefully. "

"I'm not sure I—"

"I've got potential," blurted Automanic.

"Having potential is not the same as using it," said BleakWarrior.

"Exactly."

Automanic leaned over the table and took BleakWarrior's hands in her own. He flinched at the sudden warmth of her grasp.

"Will you help me?" she said, looking like an abandoned puppy. "Will you help me kill people?"

BleakWarrior lowered his voice to a whisper:

"Be thankful I don't help myself to killing you."

Which Automanic understood as meaning, Yes.

Which it wasn't.

BleakWarrior leaned back and drained the frothy pulp of whatever it was that lay in the bottom of his glass. Automanic withdrew her hands and did the same. They drank and talked some more about nothing. At some point, BleakWarrior regarded Automanic through the spooky glare of the Lenses and saw that it made her stiffen with discomfort, which stiffened him with discomfort of a different kind, given that her vulnerability had a definite sexual attraction to it.

"I understand fear," he said, lifting the hideous brew to his lips but drinking it anyway, "and that fear is rather a fear of fear than a fear of something in itself."

"Does that make a difference?" Automanic slurred. She was drunk already. "The fact that you're afraid in the first place makes whatever you're afraid of kind of irrelevant."

"Then it is better to fear nothing."

"Pah." She waved a hand. "If you fear nothing it's liable to kill you."

"Time is an illusion that is revealed to us when it must end," said BleakWarrior. "It is not the duration of life that counts, but its intensity."

"Not if I do nothing," said Automanic. "Not if I do nothing and just live and do nothing so that there's nothing for me to be afraid of."

"The world requires of us action rather than abstinence. It is better to partake of this with an attitude of carelessness rather than concern."

"But," said Automanic, mulling over her words in an attempt to choose them carefully, "it is not that I am in the grip of fear so much as a sense of repugnance for the mental state it requires me to enter." She sat back, satisfied, and almost fell off her chair.

"The trick is to care less about life and regard it with an ironic scorn that is more proportionate to life than caring," said BleakWarrior.

"Is that what you do?"

BleakWarrior stared.

"No," he said, and drank a fulsome draught of his ghastly brew. "It is in my nature to suffer."

"To suffer what?"

"To suffer the need to suffer."

"But how can you suffer the need to suffer?"

"I believe that my need arises from my suffering which arises from my need to suffer."

"But that's crazy."

"I am mad."

"So am I."

"No, you're not. You're anxious."

"But my anxiety makes me suffer."
"Suffering is not madness."
"But my suffering is real."
"Your suffering is a consequence of your fear."
"Which is a consequence of my personality."
"Which lacks nothing that cannot be overcome."
"Whereas yours does?"
"Fear can be overcome. Need cannot."
"Why?"
"Because need needs."
"But need stops needing when it's satisfied."
"Therein lies the madness," said BleakWarrior.
"How?"
"Because madness is a need that cannot be quenched."
Automanic's face fell into a frown.
"But I have a need that cannot be quenched," she said. "That's why I need a doctor, to quench it for me."
"A doctor?"
"Psychiatric therapy." Automanic smiled. "I require a physician for my head."
"There are better things for you than doctors," said BleakWarrior.
"Like what?"
BleakWarrior studied her for a long moment and said, "Do you have a Weapon?"
Automanic frowned.
"The Shard of Glass," she said.
"The Shard of Glass?"
"Yes."
"But . . ."
"But what?"
"But when you injure someone you're just as likely to injure yourself."
"Apt, isn't it?"
"Yes," said BleakWarrior, washing over her with an amber stare. "It is apt."

Automanic held out a hand and opened it to reveal a single scar across her palm.

"These are the kinds of trophies I collect," she said.

"They are impressive trophies."

"I would rather not collect any."

"But you forget," said BleakWarrior, "that your trophies are a legacy of your success."

"And my success is equal to my pain. It's a fitting metaphor for my stupid situation."

"We are not in the business of living our lives as allegories," said BleakWarrior. "Our pain is literal."

"And what about our successes?"

"Our successes are metaphors."

"For what?"

"For the literal pain that underlies them."

Automanic looked somewhat glazed.

"There is one thing that bothers me," she said, chewing her lip.

"What?"

"You don't care if I live or die, do you?"

BleakWarrior stared through the Warped Lenses.

"I don't care if anyone lives or dies," he said.

"Not even you?"

"It is by not caring that I survive."

"But I thought you said you didn't not care about life. I thought you said you suffered."

"Perhaps it is because I don't care about life that I suffer."

For the first time, Automanic held her gaze with the Lenses rather than glanced.

"Well," she sighed, "that's me fucked, isn't it? The reason I'm scared is because I care so much about life that I'm terrified of losing it, so I probably will."

"Unless you change your ways," said BleakWarrior.

Automanic shook her head and, savouring the irony, smiled as if with an arrow pressed against her throat.

"You talk a lot of sense for someone who's meant to be

mad," she said, cupping her cheek in her hand and eyeing him unsteadily. "Makes me wonder what those are for." She pointed at the Lenses.

"My Lenses are filters for the world that make it normal for me."

"Normal?" She restrained a laugh.

"What?"

"Nothing." She shook her head. "It's just that, how can you be mad if you've never known what it's like to be sane?"

BleakWarrior looked blank.

"What do you mean?" he said.

"I'll be damned if I know," said Automanic, "but it sounds to me like your state of mind is relative to your suffering, not relative to you. That's what suffering does to us, BleakWarrior."

"My suffering is a condition of my madness which is normal to me."

"Exactly," said Automanic. "In which case, you emerged from your pre-existence as perfectly sane—" She leaned over the table and whispered—"and still are."

Later, when they were both drunk and arguing about how bad she'd been at following BleakWarrior, Automanic said, "You got me at a bad time. Things have been heating up around here, mad boy, and I've been, like, much more on edge than I normally am anyway." She leaned over the table, her chin almost touching the table top. "I might have messed it up with you," she said, slurring as if her tongue had turned into a slug, "but not with these other bastards, I can tell you."

She leaned back, a look on her face of satisfaction mixed with impertinence.

BleakWarrior grew rigid with interest. He fixed the Lenses on her like limpets onto rocks.

"Other bastards?" he said.

Automanic shrugged.

"There's probably about a half a dozen of them," she said. "Pretty mean looking violent types. Just like you."

"Like me?"

"Just. Like. You." She jabbed her finger at him and let her head drop. Then she swung her head up again and said, "But, see, I'm waiting for my chance to take them out, one by one, once all the shit starts to hit the fan. I've been watching them. I know where they eat, I know where they sleep. I know who's been following who, and who hasn't been following who. It's like some kind of game, and I'm like the games master. The only thing is, I need to kill them, and that's where I stop being the games master and start to become the master of chickens. But you—" She looked up at BleakWarrior, struggling to keep her head straight—"you can help me. I know you can."

"Describe them to me."

"Well, let's see. There's one of them I know by name, who's been here a while. He's called Liver Dye and he, like, needs to cut out the livers of women to rub into his feet. I don't know why. And then there are these two girls who might be sisters. And then there are these sort of spindly types dressed in costumes from a really stupid era called The Hiding. And, so, you can help me kill them, and we can make a plan. I'm not really so stupid, you know. Being scared doesn't make me stupid. I've had a few ideas already."

BleakWarrior leaned over the table and said, "I will help you to kill them, if that's what you wish. But, before I do, know this—that they must fall before my questions before they fall before our blades."

Automanic's head sprang up as if she had sat on the point of a dagger.

"Questions? What do you mean, questions? That's not really part of the plan."

"I am looking for something," said BleakWarrior. "I need answers to questions that I must ask them."

"I don't really think they do question and answer

sessions, BleakWarrior. They only do killing sessions—of that I'm sure. And they all look pretty good at it, too."

BleakWarrior's face fell cold, formidable.

"They will die beneath our blades," he said, "but only after I have interrogated them, if and when this proves possible."

And the manner in which he said it filled Automanic with an ice cold sensation, as if she'd been lowered into a cold lake head first. But, because she was drunk, she was feeling reckless enough to not care.

"What the fuck are you looking for that you would ask these crazy fuckers questions?

"I prefer to keep it to myself."

Automanic tightened her lips and said, curtly:

"You haven't asked me." She turned away and turned back again. "I suppose I'm not good enough for your silly questions, is that it?"

She folded her arms and slammed her back against the bench.

BleakWarrior's mouth fell open.

"I had not thought to ask," he said, but did not add, "because I doubt you'll know the answer."

"It's OK," Automanic sniffed. "I'm not much use for anything anyway, as I'm sure you're aware."

BleakWarrior ignored her and said, "I am looking for a place, and the place is called the Talking Well. If you have seen or heard of such a place, I would like to know."

Automanic frowned.

"Why?" she said.

"Because I wish to go there."

"Go there?" Automanic looked surprised. "That might be difficult."

Now BleakWarrior frowned and said, "Why?"

"Because the Talking Well doesn't exist."

BleakWarrior turned the colour of ash.

"You've heard of it?"

"I've heard of something, but I don't know if it's what you're looking for."

"Tell me what you know."

The veins on BleakWarrior's arms and forehead stood out as if they contained more lava than blood. They stood out even more as Automanic said, "'Come the day and come tomorrow, drink ye from this common cup of water from the Talking Well, that sings of joy and speaks of sorrow.'"

BleakWarrior stared as if he'd seen a vision of unaccountable worth. He stared so hard that his eyes might have burned holes through the Lenses to reveal the world as it was, with his madness restored to its fullest pitch; and yet the words that were spoken by Automanic had told him nothing.

"What is the meaning of this?" he hissed, with such vehemence that it caused Automanic to cower away from him.

"It's a riddle put to rhyme by the poet, Manto," she said, quickly.

"A riddle?"

"A riddle that expresses the true nature of love—that to partake of the cup of love is to experience both its joy and sorrow."

"Sorrow?" BleakWarrior's face displayed a range of contortions, each one a measure of wonder or pain, his face creased with a thousand positions of strained curiosity. "Sorrow?"

"If you have ever loved," said Automanic, quietly, "you will know what that means."

BleakWarrior felt the image of Achlana Promff leap into his head like an appearance of real flesh. He felt her love for him sear through his veins like a venom.

"Yes," he said, hardly aware of what he was saying, "I have drunk of the Talking Well. I know what it means."

Automanic cast her eyes downward. Her body swayed with the impact of her drunkenness. But she was otherwise upright and capable of making sense.

"Where did you hear this?" said BleakWarrior.

"It's a riddle put to rhyme, commonly known to linear scholars in the continental north—like a lot of Manto's poems. He's considered one of the three great masters of the classical period." Automanic tried to sound soothing. She didn't know why, except for the fact that BleakWarrior's reaction seemed to warrant such a response on her part. "So, you see," she said, "I don't think it's a place. Not a real place anyway."

"No," said BleakWarrior, "it's a state of mind."

Then it came to him with the force of a gale, the enigma of having undertaken a quest which he had already concluded without having arrived at a point of satisfactory completion. He had found the Talking Well. He had already leapt into its depths, had immersed himself, and had drank of its dire waters.

Might he drink of them again?

But it was all too vague.

"Surely," he rallied, "there must be a point of inspiration which Manto has used to inform his poetic riddle," he said aloud, meaning it more to himself than Automanic. "A real point in space and time, where rests a Talking Well of actual proportions."

"It's possible," said Automanic. "And it throws up an interesting question as regards this search of yours."

BleakWarrior focused the Lenses on her.

"Go on," he said.

Automanic took a deep breath and said, "If Manto did use a real Talking Well as a source of inspiration for his riddle, he might know where it is."

BleakWarrior's face blackened considerably.

"Do not mock me, Girl of the Shard who has killed no one. Manto is dead and has been so for centuries."

"I know he's dead—of course he is—but his work lives on. Manto left behind him many volumes of poems, philosophical treatise, essays on politics and history, scientific accounts, and . . . travelogues." She paused to let the implication settle in. “Manto was an explorer, BleakWarrior. He travelled far and wide and, in the end, he wrote about it in a series of journals.”

BleakWarrior’s eyes burned through the Lenses, almost causing them to ignite.

“I can help you, BleakWarrior,” whispered Automanic. “I know his works. I know where they are.”

“I can find his works in any library in any city of the known world,” said BleakWarrior.

Automanic shook her head.

“The journals were never published. They still exist, but they’re not available for public scrutiny.”

“Where are they?”

Automanic allowed herself a smile.

“You’re not going to tell me,” said BleakWarrior.

“Not until after you’ve helped me kill my victims,” said Automanic. “Then I’ll tell you where they are and who keeps them. But, before that, I need to get some blood on my hands.”

And the Lenses burned so brightly that it was a wonder she didn’t turn to ash.

Prior to leaving the Intellectual Terminus, BleakWarrior went to the bar to gather what he called “supplies,” which he then placed within the security pouches of his sealskin coat.

As they stepped outside, Automanic’s drunkenness began to subside in a manner proportionate to her rising adrenalin.

She said, “Let’s go and get the one who seeks the livers first. I don’t like him at all. And he lives pretty close to my own apartments in the District of the High Revels.”

BleakWarrior nodded. The District of the High Revels was an area of some affluence that hosted some of the city’s most venerated commotions.

“I have apartments in five different cities of the

continental mainland," Automanic was saying, "and a villa on the Isle of Smir. I've built up quite an empire, actually. Like I said, I'm clever. I've studied at some of the world's most prestigious linear institutions."

"I am very impressed by your accomplishments," said BleakWarrior, "but it makes me wonder if you are not better suited to such pursuits than you are to the toils of war."

She stopped and lay a hand on his arm. BleakWarrior stopped also. Her nerves seemed unusually steady when she said, "Let me spell it out for you, BleakWarrior. I need to kill someone. I need to kill someone very badly. I need to kill someone so badly that, if I don't, this whole thing is going to kill me. That's the bottom line of it, BleakWarrior, and, believe you me, I've reached it already."

She turned and walked on.

BleakWarrior cocked his head and looked after her, raising his eyebrows in subdued wonder, before striding after her towards the District of the High Revels.

21. The Sisters of No Mercy Get None

"It's them," hissed 4 from the bar on the other side of the street. "And look, they've got someone with them!"

46 compressed his lips under the "O" of his mask. 17 rubbed the underside of his mask as if it were a chin, which it wasn't.

"Another girl," he mused. "This makes it better if we want to guddle them."

"I prefer them when they're dead so they can't scratch my eyes," said 4.

"But," said 17, "you're wearing a mask."

4 considered.

"But they can poke their fingers through the slits," he said. "They've got skinny, bony fingers like crabs' legs." He poked his own fingers into the slits of his eyes to prove the point.

"Brothers," said 46, "before we turn our thoughts to secondary pleasures, let us think of the pleasures that come first. We can be near to certain that these women are not linear; and, so, they must die for the furtherance of our Father's cause."

"Let's go and get them now," hissed 4 from behind his mask.

"No," said 46.

"But, why?" said 4, like a child who'd been refused a treat.

"We must bide our time," said 46. "We have them within our sights. Let us not forget that two of these hussies succeeded in cropping the remover of livers. They are strong for all their female lack of worth, and we must destroy them with careful measures of stealth and strategy."

"Stealth and strategy?" 4 was incredulous.

"It is better, Brother, to catch birds in a net instead of lancing them from afar. To kill these cunning bitches requires a cunning after their own kind. Then," he said, laying a hand on 4's shoulder, "you may guddle them for all as takes your fancy—alive or dead."

The gravitational allure of the maelstrom is irresistible for those who are drawn to its brink. The currents rotate to an insubstantial whirl of froth that detracts from the darkness that lies within its concentric doom.

There are certain attractions to keeling over against its void. The thrill of knowing the end of life is never the same as not knowing that life has ended.

The City of Antiquities was caught in a convergence of mighty tides that, by and by, when brought together, must do what meeting tides do—

Implode.

—Anonymous, Attendances to Mayhem

The Sisters of No Mercy led the girl whose name they didn't know up the spacious stairwell of Liver Dye's tenement block.

They froze on the stair when they saw that the door of his apartments was leaning slightly ajar.

"There's someone inside." Big Sister mouthed the words rather than spoke them and, slowly and silently, drew the Short Sword.

Little Sister's face grew black. She slowly and silently drew the Long Sword. The girl whose name they didn't know drew a pair of metallic objects from pockets in the sides of her trousers: skewers.

They crept up to the door and listened.

Nothing.

Little Sister shoved it slowly open with the tip of her toe. The three of them craned their necks around the edge of the door to see what they could see inside.

They saw the wreckage of furniture and streaks of blood across the expensive Smirnian rug that covered most of the floor. The bed, as yet, was hidden from view. Little Sister made a motion with her head and the three of them, swift as lizards, slipped inside the apartment. They held their Weapons in readiness to defend or strike—but there was nothing to defend or strike against.

"Check the other rooms," said Little Sister, retaining the Long Sword in an upright position and taking careful steps towards the bed.

"Fuck," she whispered.

And she was right.

Liver Dye was still bound up in the knot-work that, in some places, had been untied or cut or twisted out of shape. A foot protruded from his mouth, its toes crammed between his teeth as if to fit a shoe it would never fit. The other foot lay on the sheets beside it, cut raggedly across the ankle. The bottom of Liver Dye's legs were also ragged with gore and mangled so much you could hardly call them stumps.

Big Sister returned from her search of the adjoining rooms.

"Nothing," she said, and looked at the corpse of Liver Dye. "Well," she said, "looks like he's been cut down to size."

"Damn right," said Little Sister, who now began to study his body like a butcher sizing up a slab of meat.

"Sister," said Big Sister, "what is it? The fucker's very dead already."

Little Sister positioned the Long Sword in preparation for an incision.

"He's not been dead for long, so I reckon we need to get his liver into the alchemical container as quick as possible. It might get damaged by the loss of blood or the sudden drop in body temperature. It might be damaged already, so it might not do whatever it is we hope it'll do for the resurrection of Middle Sister."

"Oh fuck," said Big Sister.

And she held the corpse steady as Little Sister opened it up across the belly and chest. Little Sister scooped out a few coils of this and that with the flat of her blade and said, "I think I see it."

She lay the Long Sword aside and wrapped her hands around a vital organ that was resplendent with a lush rubbery wetness and supremely ruddy hue. Big Sister came beside her with the container at the ready, and Little Sister dropped it inside and sealed the lid.

"We can think about cutting it up later," she said. "The main thing is, we got it preserved. Now we need to get the fuck out of here."

"I'm in agreement with that. Let's go, girl." Big Sister turned to look for the girl whose name they didn't know. "Where the fuck is she?"

Little Sister, holding the container in her hands, looked around the room.

"Girl," she cried. "Girl, come on. We've got to go."

Big Sister made a quick search of the outlying rooms.

The girl whose name they didn't know wasn't there.

She checked the veranda.

The girl whose name they didn't know wasn't there either.

Lastly, they checked the stairwell thinking that maybe

she'd waited outside because the sight of so much flesh and blood had proven too much for her.

The stairwell was empty.

"Sister," said Big Sister, "I've got an awful feeling that we've been dumped."

"Very dumped," Little Sister agreed.

"There's no way I can accept that," said Big Sister with mounting panic. "There's something about that girl that I really need—something I crave about her."

"That's right, Sister, and I know what it is."

"What?"

"Her pussy."

"No, Sister, it's more than that."

"No, it's not," said Little Sister. "It's her pussy, and I need it like I need a fix."

Big Sister looked aghast.

"Fuck me, Sister, you're right," she said. "It's her pussy juice."

"It's an elixir."

"An addictive elixir."

"A very addictive elixir."

"And I need more of it."

"So do I, Sister," said Little Sister, fixing her teeth into a grimace, "so do I."

Welter of Impermanence decided to retrace her footsteps back to the hardware store and, from there, to get herself out of the City and onto the open road.

It was with some regret that she'd left her newfound friends behind her. But she was on a mission for gratification upon which she had focussed all her efforts, and she wasn't going to let it go until she'd gotten it done. Then, maybe, she would seek out The Sisters and either receive their forgiveness or fight them to the death, and that would be the end of it, one way or another.

It was sad to leave them but that's how it was. She felt utterly compelled to resume her search for BleakWarrior—was unable to stop herself. There was something about him—something that extended a magnetic force over her personality and drew her in—as if his underlying madness had swept her up in its existential entanglements, its sensory rifts and its intellectual juxtapositions. She wondered for a fleeting moment whether she truly wished to destroy him or whether there was something else that motivated her in this senseless pursuit of him. She had committed herself to finding him with an abandonment of her senses which had mired her in confusion and the weltering depths of her unfathomable desire. The gravitational demands of her feelings were pulling her in different directions. And now she felt as if she no longer knew what she was doing or why she wanted to do it. She only knew she must go on.

Or die trying.

The streets began to empty of revellers as Welter of Impermanence entered the Normal Quarter with its banal facades of rectangular shops that leaned in upon themselves in static rows of unattractive neatness. She turned a corner into a lane that led into another lane that led into another lane where the hardware store was situated.

And that's where the Sons of Brawl stood loitering in the shadows in wait for her.

And that's where they smacked her on the forehead with a pipe that knocked her senseless to the ground like a drunk who'd lost her footing on a crooked road.

And that's where she was manhandled on the cobbles under a burst of light that consumed her vision with a whiteness that was quickly turning black.

Welter of Impermanence felt herself slip into the vacuum of unconsciousness. There was a thought in her head that she wouldn't recall when, later, she woke up—a thought about The Sisters:

They're sucking the juices out of me like creatures with

nothing more on their minds than the juices they're sucking the life out of me.

"What the fuck do we do," said Big Sister. She was frantic.

"Cool it, Sister, and look."

Little Sister then proceeded to do something that looked incredibly stupid. She stuck her tongue out between her lips and moved it around like she was licking something that wasn't there.

"I noticed this before," she said, "when we were walking back to Liver Dye's from the hardware store. I had a fucking weird sensation like there was something in the air I thought I could taste. And then I realised there was. And then I realised *what* it was."

"What, Sister, what? What the fuck are you saying?"

"Her, Sister. The girl. I can fucking taste her, Sister. She leaves a trace of herself in the air that I can taste." She stuck out her tongue, drew it back in, swirled it around her mouth. "I can fucking taste her now, Sister. I can fucking taste her now."

Tentatively, in a sort of manic kind of way, Big Sister unrolled her tongue from her lips and started to lick.

"Oh fuck, yes," she said, "you're right." She licked some more. "It's not even a scent."

"No fucking way," said Little Sister. "It's a taste. A definite taste. Like if I do this—" She threw back her head and sniffed—"absolutely fucking nothing. But if I do this—" She stuck out her tongue and licked—"I can taste her sure as I can taste my own blood if I bite my lip."

Big Sister nodded and nodded some more.

"Do you think we can . . ."

"Follow it?"

Big Sister nodded.

"Well, Sister, I'm no fucking expert. In anything. But I'm

so fucking desperately in need of lapping her saps that I think we maybe fucking can. Or, let me put it this way." She looked Big Sister straight in the eye and said, "Do we have a choice?"

Big Sister blinked, once.

"No, Sister," she said. "No, Sister, we don't."

"There," said Automanic, when they had sat themselves on the stools of a table outside a bar on the other side of the road from Liver Dye's apartments. "That's where he lives. For now." She sipped her drink—a cocktail full of absurdly multi-coloured liquids—and said, "He tends to shift from place to place to cover his tracks. He's sneaky that way. That's his balcony up there on the third floor. The one with the shutters open."

BleakWarrior said nothing and stared.

Automanic sipped her drink a few times in quick succession, then said, "What do you think?"

BleakWarrior shifted slightly, as if he'd only just become aware of her presence.

"Thinking is for thinkers," he said. "We will finish our drinks in consideration of our aspirations, then go to the—"

Automanic had laid a hand on his shoulder and gripped like a crab.

"Look," she hissed. "those dark haired girls over there. It's them."

"Them?"

"The mad sisters. They just came out of the stairwell to Liver Dye's apartments. *They must have been there!*"

BleakWarrior's eyes beneath the Lenses narrowed like slits.

"What in the name of the shattering mirrors of truth is going on?" said Automanic.

BleakWarrior took a deep breath and said, "It would appear that the dark-haired sisters have taken action against the remover of livers. I suggest an adjustment to our plan. While I investigate the apartment to see what has become of Liver Dye, keep your eyes on the sisters until I return, which I will do with utmost haste. If all is as I suppose it will be, we will follow the sisters and seek to arrange their downfall when an opportune moment presents itself."

Automanic gave a series of sharp little nods and squeaked:

"OK."

And when BleakWarrior returned with news of the remover of livers discovered abed with a foot in his mouth and his innards strewn all over the bed sheets like scraps from a butcher's, they hurried after the dark-haired sisters just as it seemed they would almost lose sight of them.

46, 17 and 4 dragged the girl through the empty streets of the Normal Quarter with deliberate roughness. Occasionally, they were seen by a citizen who was out on the street performing a duty. They would glower at the citizen to ward them off, then drag the girl with additional roughness just because they wanted to.

They took the girl through the outskirts of the City of Antiquities to a building in a quiet area that was hexagonal-shaped and currently closed. It was currently closed because during the day it was always open. The Sons of Brawl cut a hole in the wire of the fence that surrounded the building and dragged the girl through it and kicked her a few times because they thought she was showing signs of recovering consciousness. They used the heels of their ridiculous boots to stamp on her head, but not enough to cause her to slip into a coma or die. They had done this kind of thing so many times before that they knew exactly how to kick a person in the head to produce whatever effect of injury or death they desired or thought was necessary.

They dragged the girl across the grass to the big brown door of the building that had a sign above it that said, “Aquarium.”

This is where they were going to hide themselves tonight. And this is where they were going to rouse the girl to give her a grilling to find out as much as they could about the other girls the girl was with, so they could think about how to capture them and make them die by stamping on their heads with the heels of their ridiculous boots.

But not too quickly.

From the preservations of the shadows an ember glows, tightly knit with light, glowering from its crust of gloom, unseen in the cusp of its meagre warmth.

It throbs for the softness of flesh, which is vulnerable to the deterioration of applied heat. It runs deep with a desire to remain warped within the parameters of its scorn.

Burning Hot Coals smoulders in the blackness of his cosmic matter. He directs himself over the outlying movements of relative bodies he wishes to draw within his megalithic spheres of influence. He is convinced that he will absorb them into the gravitational fulcrum of his wrath.

And, when he does, such bodies will disintegrate like stars on the fringes of black holes, to be returned to the enigma of their essential nothingness, and swallowed out of existence, forever.

The Sisters of No Mercy followed the taste of the girl whose name they didn’t know through the sweat and swill of hundreds of people who were enjoying themselves in the City of Antiquities.

But the sweat and swill of hundreds of people had no

effect on the lingering taste of the girl whose name they didn't know whose trail, it seemed, was leading them through the same streets of the Normal Quarter from which they had come earlier.

Little Sister put her tongue back into her mouth and said, "It seems to be leading us through the same streets of the Normal Quarter from which we came earlier."

Big Sister made a noise like she agreed.

But when they turned a corner into a lane that led into another lane that led into another lane where the hardware store was situated, they began to detect an alteration in the prevailing essence of the taste.

Big Sister stuck her tongue back in her mouth and said, "What the fuck is that?"

Little Sister licked the air and said, "There's something missing from the abiding flavour. It's as if—"

"It's as if there's something fucking wrong with the girl that wasn't wrong before."

Little Sister nodded.

The Sisters of No Mercy stepped up the pace. With their tongues hanging out over their lips, they looked like dogs without jowls that slavered the way dogs would if they didn't have them. Similarly, their eyes were full of the mindless thrill of their unsatisfied craving. They had begun to feel remarkably uptight, as if they were lacking some kind of essential protein in their bloodstream that, after a while, was starting to have an effect on their brains.

Their anxiety quickened when the trail of the taste started to deviate away from the lane where the hardware store was situated.

"What the fuck is going on?" said Big Sister at one point, but they didn't stop to consider the fact—and, in fact, carried on until the trail led them through the outskirts of the City to a building in a quiet area that was hexagonal-shaped and currently closed.

Here, the taste grew stronger.

"She's in there," said Little Sister, drawing the Long Sword.

"Damn right she is," said Big Sister, drawing the Short Sword.

"We've got to go in and get her," said Little Sister.

"Going in to get her, Sister, is what we were fucking born for."

BleakWarrior and Automanic watched from the shadows of a neighbouring street as the dark-haired sisters drew their swords and entered a large hexagonal building with a broken-in door and a sign hung over its lintel that read "Aquarium."

"What shall we do now?" said Automanic, all too eagerly.

"I wonder if it is better to wait," said BleakWarrior.

Automanic was silently for a moment, then:

"Wait for what?"

BleakWarrior took a deep breath and said, "The dark-haired sisters are about to enter into a conflict situation, which is confirmed by their actions of drawing their swords. Whatever is afoot—and I suspect your spindly types with the costumes may have something to do with it—if we were to enter the fray at this stage, there are good reasons to believe that we would die. If, however, we bide our time, we can expect the respective parties to seriously damage or weaken each other. That will make it far easier for us—meaning *you*—to pick off the remainder."

"Oh," said Automanic, slightly piqued by the fact that she hadn't thought of this herself.

BleakWarrior, in the meantime, plucked two bottles of Ramford's Delectable Motions from his sealskin coat, a beer imported from the Isle of Smir that contained, among other things, a mixture of spices that helped to unloosen the knots of nervous dispositions on occasions like this one.

"When we have finished drinking our Delectable Motions," said BleakWarrior, handing one to Automanic, "then we go in."

And BleakWarrior swigged from the bottle and relished the cool draught as it entered his system and, in contrast to its actual temperature, spread warmth throughout his body, soothed his nerves. Then he held it up and squinted at it, careful to note the amount he had drank. Timing was everything in such cases as these; but it could only be gauged by instinct or, as he preferred, by the length of time it took to drink a bottle of beer.

"Hey!" Automanic whispered suddenly, drawing herself into the wall and prompting BleakWarrior to do the same with an outstretched arm across his chest. "Who in the name of the great plagues is this guy?"

BleakWarrior peered through the crispy darkness of the oncoming night and saw a hunched and filthy-looking figure enter the grounds of the Aquarium, now making his way towards the breached entrance, pausing to take stock of what lay beyond it before shifting inside. The figure was carrying a sack over its back that seemed to be issuing some kind of trail of smoke or a heavy fume.

"Have you ever seen this one before now?"

"Never," said Automanic, her face hardening perhaps with the indignation at having failed to extend a total surveillance of the City's area. "Do you think he's one of us?"

BleakWarrior fixed the Lenses on the filthy figure and focussed hard.

"Yes," he said, "he's one of us. Of that we can be sure."

The Bastard Sons of Brawl had used an iron bar to lever open the big brown door of the Aquarium: it had given way easily and without a sound. They'd shoved the girl through the door and stepped inside. They'd kicked her three, four, five times around the ribs. The girl had wheezed. 4 had kicked her in the face to shut her up. Then they'd closed the door behind them and stood still while the girl lay on the floor on her back, panting through bloodied lips. 4 had then kicked her in the face again to shut her up. 17 cuffed him on the head and warned him, "Don't overdo it."

4 looked sullen. It was clear that if he'd been left to his own devices he would overdo it to the widest possible margin of kicking her till the floor ran wet with her blood and brains.

In the meantime, there were three corridors leading from the foyer of the Aquarium that ran in completely different directions from each other.

"The middle one," said 46, even though he had no idea why or where it would lead them to.

It led them along a passage that was awash with a watery luminescence arising from electric valves positioned behind or within the long dark walls. The light was filtered through strategic gaps that filled the gloom with static ripples that somehow made the gloom seem gloomier than it already was.

"Where's the fish?" said 4, nosing the darkness as if trying to impersonate one.

"Up ahead," said 17, instructively. "Look."

17 pointed to where parts of the long dark walls gave way to long glass panels that contained haggard-looking displays of aquatic scenes with rocks and weeds and pokey spaces where creatures lurked without being visible to the naked eye. The Sons of Brawl hurried up the corridor to scrutinize the murk behind the long glass panels. The watery blackness was vaguely a-swirl with minute scintillations of silt—and that was all. They grunted in disappointment, then smeared the girl's bloody mouth over the glass as if to attract a creature from its rocky nook, but nothing came.

On the walls beside the panels were notices declaring the inhabitants of each tank: "grimlups," "fluberts," "speckled glems," "corpolusses," "mangle fish," and so on. 17 looked at the notices and said, "These stupid little fish have names without faces. We, on the other hand, have faces without names. This is why I like wearing a mask, because I don't have to put a face to the name I don't have anyway."

Pleased with his remark, 17 pressed on and was delighted to find that the corridor widened into a more spacious viewing chamber with broader panels and bigger tanks. The scarce visibility was alleviated by an effusive radiance that wallowed from some hidden source. The tanks were aglow with uncommon varieties of mollusc and fish that went about their business like figments of some over-spilled imagination.

"Up here," cried 17, and his Brothers, dragging the body of the girl behind them, hurried to catch him up.

The Sons of Brawl *oohed* and *aahed* in glee at the exhibition of basic life forms. They dumped the girl on the floor and, while she huddled and shook, they studied each creature with eyes pressed hard against their eye-slits. The fish were mostly slow and laborious with disc-shaped bodies, drifting over a clutch of rocks like deflated balloons. One or two had the look of wrinkled penises, while another had the look of a fat head that had accidentally grown a tail. All of them wore the same expression of failing to make sense of their lack of intelligence—speaking of which:

"I want to see them eat each other," said 4, bouncing up and down like a monkey tied to the end of a stick.

"Brother," said 46, looking up at a sign hanging over the entrance of a corridor leading off of the viewing chamber, "I think you might have given me an idea."

"An idea?" 17 followed his Brother's gaze up to the sign and started to nod. "Yes," he said, "I think I understand you, Brother."

"What's that?" said 4, looking up at the sign with no idea what it said because he couldn't read.

"Stingletips," announced 46.

"Stingle what?" said 4.

"Come," said 46. "Take the girl. I'll show you."

The Bastard Sons of Brawl proceeded along the corridor that led them into the most important feature of the Aquarium, known as the Stingletip Sanctuary, where a footbridge spanned a large round pool that shimmered under the inapt palatial magnificence of a broad silver dome.

The Sons of Brawl walked out onto the footbridge dragging the girl behind them. Below them, in the water, shadowy creatures moved back and forth with unhurried swiftness, like shadows possessed of the efficacy of substance. Occasionally, something lean and black would break the surface of the water like a subconscious terror barging into the realm of sleep.

"Rouse the girl," said 46.

4 grabbed her under the arms and lifted her head so 17 could slap her briskly across the face until her eyes fluttered open. 17 slapped her harder until her eyes grew wide, and wider still as she started to realise the full extent of what was happening to her. Welter of Impermanence stared up at them in deference to their masks, sensing her vulnerability to their unlimited cruelty. The Bastards began to shake her violently and assail her with questions:

"Who are the women you were with?"

"What are their names?"

"What are their Weapons?"

"What are their strengths?"

"What are their weaknesses?"

"What are they doing in the City of Antiquities?"

"What are they going to do next?"

"What are you doing with them?

"What is your name?

"Are you one of them?"

"Are you one of us?"

"Are you one of anybody we should know?"

"Do you wish to live?"

"Do you wish to die?"

"Do you wish us to introduce you to our friends?"

"The stingletips?"

The last was a signal for them to hoist her over the rail of the bridge and dangle her arm and a leg above the pool like the drooping branches of a tree. She looked down at the dark shapes, unsure of what they were but knowing they were bad.

Then one of them broke the surface and made a lunge for her arm. Tentacles thin as wire shot up from its mouth. It could barely reach her hand but caught hold of it for long enough to rake its tiny spikes across her skin—and, where it touched, her skin was flayed as if by a thousand burning hot needles.

Welter of Impermanence screamed and begged them, "No," which caused the Bastards to cackle in satisfaction of their interrogation techniques. They pulled her back over the railings and slapped her hard across the head while badgering her with further questions:

"Who are the women you were with?"

"What are their names?"

"What are they doing here?"

"What are they going to do next?"

"Are you a member of a cabal?"

"Are you a member of a coterie?"

"Are you a member of a linear cartel?"

"What will we do with you if you don't tell us?"

"Did you like the feel of the stingletips?"

"Shall we throw you into the water naked?"

"How would you like that?"

"A bitch like you would probably like it, eh?"

"How long do you think you'd last in there?"

"Five minutes?"

"Ten?"

"Half an hour?"

They grabbed her by the arms and lowered her over the bridge so that her feet were nearly touching the surface of the pool. The stingletips gathered and launched their tentacles against her boots. Her boots were shorn away within seconds. The Bastards left her feet exposed for some moments to allow for a light flaying. Then they hauled her back onto the bridge and let her fall in a shivering, sobbing heap. Blood and slavers hung from her lips. Strings of ruined skin hung around her feet like rotten parchment.

The Bastard Sons of Brawl continued their interrogation, slapping her around the head, punching her stomach and groping her groin.

"Who are the women you were with?"

"What are their names?"

"What are they doing here?"

"Where are they going next?"

"Oh," a voice said suddenly, echoing through the dome like a series of chimes, "I think I can tell you where we're going next."

And another voice said, "Right. Fucking. Here."

Little Sister stepped out of the corridor onto the bridge. Big Sister stepped out of the other corridor onto the other side of the bridge. The Sons of Brawl wore a look on their faces like the ghosts of their mothers had appeared before them from beyond the graves they'd never given them.

And a little peal of quiet, manic laughter lifted up to the roof of the dome like mercury from a tap—the girl whose name they didn't know—caught in the drastic switch of one emotion to another, and lost in the mad thrill of her relief that verged on hysteria.

Which, as a matter of fact, is exactly what it was.

The Sisters of No Mercy charged simultaneously from either side of the bridge. There was an additional fervour to their fierceness. They were not so much wild as demented beyond the limits of their questionable sanity. As a consequence, the Long Sword and Short Sword blasted aside the shoddy weaponry of the Bastard Sons of Brawl and began to delve.

46 was far too slow to withstand the speed of the onslaught. He was good when it came to planning a strategy, but useless when it came to recuperating the sudden loss of a manufactured advantage. He was hewn down like an old log, cut across the chest by the Long Sword, then slashed at the neck as he fell to his knees from the initial strike.

17 was extremely capable with his piece of pipe and was managing well until the girl whose name they didn't know grabbed his ankle from the floor and sank her teeth into the tendon connecting his heel to his leg. 17 looked down at her in surprise and, when he looked up, saw the Short Sword flash across his face, and that was all.

4 was like a stoat—cunning and vicious and highly evasive with the twisting motions of his body. He was giving Little Sister severe problems with his double-headed hand axe (which he'd stolen from a linear mercenary whose throat he'd cut after an argument regarding the scarceness of his facial hair). He swung it well in response to Big Sister's manic swipes. He dodged her with success and succeeded in applying some reasonably hard-hitting counterattacks. Then he twirled on his feet in order to convey a momentous hit, but the heel of one of his boots snapped off under the pressure of his misaligned body weight.

4 collapsed against the railings of the bridge in an ungainly sprawl that made him look like a cat thrown out of a top floor window. Before he could regain his poise, the girl whose name they didn't know was standing before him like an external manifestation of his worst nightmare. She reached a hand between his legs and gripped his crotch, then rammed a forearm against the underside of his chin. Then she heaved him up and, using her knee for extra leverage, turned him over the railing of the bridge and hurled him into the water below.

The Sisters of No Mercy and the girl whose name they didn't know watched keenly as 4 began to thrash against the accumulation of sinewy black shapes. He tried to pronounce his terror by opening his mouth in order to scream. But water rushed into his throat and staunched his lungs, and he choked and rasped in the manner of a degraded circus animal. The stingletips wrapped him from head to toe in threadlike tentacles. His skin was shorn from his body like a withered fleece that had never grown to the fullness of wool. An effluvia of blood spread in the water like a storm on the horizon. The stingletips rose to a greater frenzy and, soon, were thrashing through layers of flesh as if it were foam.

The Sisters of No Mercy withdrew from the railing and took the girl whose name they didn't know into the warm clutch of their bosoms. They undressed her, gently, and tended to each bruise with soothing kisses, licked each wound with hot, distended tongues. The girl whose name they didn't know succumbed to their attentions with complete abandonment. Her pain was dissolved by the lushness of their touch. Her muscles were loosened. Her loins grew warm and summoned wetness.

Soon, the contact of lips and tongues upon her skin became more intense and erotically brazen. They sank to the floor of the footbridge and made love while 4 was threshed to pieces beneath their deliciously intertwining bodies.

The Sisters of No Mercy allowed their tongues to delve deeper and with an urgency which the girl whose name they didn't know accommodated with the inevitability of her willingness to let it happen.

Afterwards, The Sisters of No Mercy experienced a sense of revival that restored them to their routine levels of excessive composure. They had ceased to shake like blades of grass in the grip of a vexatious wind. They were defused of their anxious bluster. They felt an immensity of peace settle over them like a goodly source of heat in the darkness of a cave.

Normalised, The Sisters of No Mercy and the girl whose

name they didn't know left the bridge with expressions of blank satisfaction on their faces and a calm radiance of after-sex that shone in their eyes like burning hot coals.

And Burning Hot Coals sprang from the darkness of the corridor as they approached from the bridge, appearing like an existential rot in the exuberance of gloom.

"With complements from my brother," he rasped.

And he slammed a burning hot coal (which he was holding in the palm of his hand) into the eye of Big Sister. Big Sister's eyeball was dissolved in a sodden hiss. Liquid blurted from her eye socket like the splash of a stone in a pot of honey. She fell backwards onto the curve of the bridge, gasping in shock with an undertone of stilted whining. It was the sound that someone makes when they know that something bad has happened without knowing what it was and why.

Little Sister and the girl whose name they didn't know were too startled to react quickly as Burning Hot Coals started to swing his heavy soot-stained sack of burning hot coals at their faces and heads. The girl whose name they didn't know took a sound hit across the cheek and reeled to one side. Little Sister didn't quite know what she was doing, but she threw herself at Burning Hot Coals and started to grapple with him at close quarters.

It was probably the worst fight she'd ever been in. The two of them went stumbling, clawing and rolling into the darkness like a single entity fighting with itself to gain control of two opposing but equally pernicious urges. Burning Hot Coals was trying to get a hand inside his sack whilst shoving his other hand into Little Sister's face, digging his black and broken nails into her facial orifices and attempting to prise them. She, for her part, struggled to a get a grip of the sensitive parts of his body and rip into them with all the force she could possibly muster. This, however, was made difficult by the fact that he was attired in thick layers of heavy sackcloth that hung on him in baggy reels of hardened grime.

And, so, they remained for some minutes in the amalgam

of their rage, unable to commit themselves to causing damage, except in the sense of sapping each other's strength to a point where they barely had any. They grunted and panted and pushed and pulled and tore and squeezed to little more effect than to prolong their equal grip of each other.

It lasted for some time until, finally, the sack of burning hot coals spilled its contents onto the floor and Burning Hot Coals, perhaps inspired, made a frantic grab for one of its glowing lumps. Little Sister allowed him to make the grab, sensing a potential countermove. All at once, she heaved him towards the spilled coals and tried to push his face into the rancour of their heat. Burning Hot Coals responded in kind and, using his legs, managed to roll himself on top of Little Sister then twist her head towards the outermost spillage of the coals. Little Sister felt locks of her hair begin to singe and a burning presence against her ear. She held fast but, without a doubt, Burning Hot Coals was causing her to weaken.

There was a moment when she felt her neck and head begin to bend against the coals with an appalling lack of stamina. Her ear was becoming thoroughly scorched by the nearness of the embers. A searing pain spread like a stain across her scalp. She roared through gritted teeth and struggled to breathe as Burning Hot Coals ratcheted his full weight against her.

Little Sister had to admit that her situation was looking uncertain. But Big Sister wasn't going to let it get any worse than it already was now.

Big Sister's broken nose was swollen and, worse than that, she was missing an eye that had been taken out by a fucking lump of burning hot coal. The nose would heal all right, and perhaps require the attentions of a good surgeon; but the eye was fucking history.

As she lay in shock, Big Sister began to absorb the full implications of what had happened. She felt a leap of panic in her breast when she realised, clearly, that she had lost an eye which would never be recovered as anything more than a happy memory. In spite of this, Big Sister made a decision to postpone her panic until such a time as she was able to endure it with appropriate amounts of strong alcohol. In the meantime, she rose to her feet and drew the Short Sword from its sheath, which still ran wet with the blood of a Bastard Son of Brawl. She had to angle her head in order to discern the grappling shapes of Little Sister and the filthy fucker who lay across her like a man attempting rape. But once she got them in the sights of her remaining eye, she walked, quite calmly, towards them and, taking her time to get a good aim, drew her sword slowly and surely across the lower back of Burning Hot Coals.

Big Sister's intention was to sever his spinal chord and immobilise him in a way that wasn't fatal; and it seemed to do the trick. Burning Hot Coals made a noise like he'd received a fright from the appearance of a deadly spider. He strained his body against the sensation of cold steel in his back, but it didn't last long. He stiffened then sagged like a stuffed toy, as if his bones had suddenly turned into feeble stalks. Little Sister was able to throw him off and roll away from the flaring debris of the spilled coals. And, when she did, she looked up at Big Sister who looked down at her with her remaining eye, with liquid dripping from her hollowed socket like resin from a knot of wood.

"I've got to say," said Little Sister, "I love you more than I always have but more than ever."

Big Sister's lips formed a weak smile. She was very pale and swaying on her feet. Finally, she collapsed in a faint of sheer exhaustion due to the supreme effort of saving Little Sister from the filthy fucker who'd taken out her eye.

Little Sister rushed to the aid of Big Sister and sought immediately to attend to her conditions of multiple injury. She searched for the girl whose name they didn't know to plead for assistance.

And it struck her like a slab against her head—the girl whose name they didn't know was gone.

Burning Hot Coals was still alive by the time that Little Sister had revived Big Sister and, to her relief, found that Big Sister was coping well with the effects of her wounds.

"Sister, fuck, he's taken out my eye with a burning hot coal. I'm going to have to wear a patch."

"I think it'll suit you just fine," said Little Sister, stroking Big Sister's hair and attempting a smile.

"Damn right it will. A patch is going to suit me if it's the last fucking thing I do."

"It won't be," said Little Sister. "We've got quite a lot of things to do." She held up the alchemical container containing the liver of Liver Dye. "Beginning with this."

Big Sister's remaining eye widened with excitement.

"Sister," she said, "I'm with you. But," she added, aware that something wasn't right, something that, so far, had remained unsaid, "where's the girl?"

Little Sister lowered her eyes.

"She's done it again," she sighed. "Dumped us. We're going to have to get a hold of her taste and chase after her all over again."

Big Sister looked sour.

"What is it with her, Sister?" she said. "If she's so appalled by us, why doesn't she try and kill us? Why does she have to keep accepting us then running away?"

"I don't know," said Little Sister. "But maybe she likes us. Or maybe she's scared. Or maybe she's confused."

"Not *that* confused, Sister."

"Why not?" said Little Sister. "Maybe she's never been in love before."

"Or maybe she isn't in love at all. Maybe she's poisoned us."

"Poisoned?"

"With pussy juice. Who knows what it'll do to us if we don't renew our fix."

"Stop it, Sister," said Little Sister. "You're making me feel like I need my fix already."

"I think I do."

"No, you don't," said Little Sister. "It takes longer than that."

"But—"

"Listen, Sister," said Little Sister, using her serious voice she sometimes used when she had to say something that Big Sister wasn't going to like. "I think we're going to have to grasp the fucking nettle and abandon this darling little bitch of ours. She's becoming a distraction and, don't forget, we're on a mission to save our Middle Sister, Sister."

"But, Sister, if we don't get our fix, how do we know we're not going to die?"

"Die?"

"Die of our withdrawal symptoms."

"Well," said Little Sister, "that's a chance we're going to have to take. I mean, we don't even know if the pussy juice is a poison or whether it's just a really fucking powerful elixir."

"But if we die, Sister, Middle Sister dies, and then we'll all be dead, and there'll be no one to fill us up with reanimation feeds to get us back to the world of the living."

"Wait a minute." Little Sister's eyes widened like beacons on a dark shore.

"Wait a minute for what?"

"We're missing the point, Sister. We're completely missing the fucking point."

"What point?"

"The only one that matters."

"Do we have one?"

"Middle Sister, Sister, is the whole point of why we're here, right?"

"Right."

"And just look at us. We're fucking wrecks."

"I'm not sure what you're getting at, Sister."

"It's like this . . . The girl whose name we don't know has

infected us with the poison of our addiction to her and, like all addictions to substances of unknown worth, it's fucking with us, and fucking with us bad. So, think about it, Sister."

"I'm trying, Sister, I'm trying. But I think I need some help."

"It's right in front of our, uh, tongues, Sister. The taste, the allure, the effect of her biochemical properties—it's massive, right?"

"It's fucking huge."

"So, shouldn't this mean that we can use it as a reanimation feed for our Middle Sister, Sister? I mean, look at the effect it's having on us!"

"But the effect is good."

"Not when we're not under the effect of it, Sister. I mean, the effect is fucking awful when we're not under the effect of it. It's causing us major fucking harm. That's what addictive substances do. So what effect do you think it'll have on our dear departed Sister, Sister?"

"Ah," said Big Sister, "now that really is a point well made."

"I know."

"I mean, the girl's pussy would be like a fucking well of reanimation fluid flowing without end from the depths of its source."

"I know."

"And Middle Sister could be revived, and then we could all be addicted to her without having to worry about losing her, right?"

"Right."

"So she could to stay with us forever."

"Forever."

"Like a slave."

"Yeah. Sort of. Maybe. I don't know. But what we've got to do is get this girl to love us without being confused so that she stays with us without dumping us so we never have to chase after the darling little bitch again."

"OK," said Big Sister, "let's go get her, then."

"No. It's got to wait," said Little Sister. "Right now, we've got some serious scientific business to attend to—the science of revenge." Little Sister held up the alchemical container. "Let's get to work on this nearly dead fucker over here before he dies first."

Burning Hot Coals lay on his back staring up at them with eyes darting around his head which he couldn't move on account of his paralysis.

"I would like to commend you on the skill of your incision," said Little Sister to Big Sister.

"Thanks," said Big Sister. "It was my pleasure."

"And it was my pain that you prevented." Little Sister glared down at Burning Hot Coals. "Which is not to say that I didn't fucking feel any."

Little Sister began to unseal the alchemical container.

"Wait," said Big Sister. "First things first."

Big Sister picked up a lump of smouldering coal from the debris of coals that had spilled from the sack and blew on it until its heat was restored to a full burning. Then she kneeled beside Burning Hot Coals and positioned the coal exactly over the top his eye and pushed it hard against his eyeball until it burst with a wet pop of mixed fluids. There was nothing Burning Hot Coals could do to resist the assault, except scream. But his screams were more like the hoarse vocal chafes of an extinct bird.

Big Sister leaned close to his face and said, "Even while I'm sure you'll be deriving a sense of satisfaction from having removed my fucking eye, let's agree that you are, in hindsight, now questioning the wisdom of your actions."

She leaned back and said, "Let's do it, Sister."

Little Sister gave a single nod and opened the alchemical container with a careful series of manipulations using her blade. She cut and removed a small piece of Liver Dye's liver, clamped a hand around Burning Hot Coals's chin and opened his mouth. She inserted the piece of liver into his throat beside his tonsils. Then she worked his jaw until he was compelled to swallow the piece of liver through his automatic need to force it down in order to avoid choking.

Little Sister and Big Sister dragged him back onto the bridge of the Stingletip Sanctuary where there was plenty of light to assess the results of their experiment; nor were they disappointed by what they saw.

They stood over Burning Hot Coals with their arms folded across their chests and their faces full of the expectations of students undergoing their first exposure to live dissections. By gradual stages, Burning Hot Coals' general appearance began to assume a darker complexion than before. Then his skin began to turn to a more definite purple hue as if his body had become inflamed without becoming inflated. It seemed, in fact, as if the swelling was internal and that his body was undergoing a tremendous pressure of bloating that pressed on the inside rather than out. Blood began to seep from his pours. His remaining eye became intensely bloodshot until it also began to bleed. The bleeding became more intense as the minutes passed and it was clear, by his relentless croaking, that Burning Hot Coals was experiencing a hideous discomfort that extended beyond mere pain.

It took a sufficiently long time for Burning Hot Coals to bleed to death, if bleeding to death is what it was. By the time he was dead, his skin was the colour of black grapes, while his clothes had become a soaking burl of unprecedented blood-loss.

"Well," said Little Sister, "that was interesting."

"Very interesting," Big Sister agreed.

"But not *that* interesting."

"Not really fucking interesting at all."

"Still, it provides us with another subtle means of killing people, if the need arises."

“That’s exactly what I was thinking.”

“And it’s a really wonderful addition to our collection of feeds for Middle Sister.”

“That’s exactly what I was thinking, too.”

“But,” said Little Sister, “we really need to get moving so we can catch up with this girl of ours.”

“I totally agree,” said Big Sister, “except that we’re forgetting something.”

“What?” Little Sister frowned.

Big Sister held a finger up to her hollowed socket.

“I need to get a patch for my missing fucking eye.”

22.
A Death Match Made in Heaven

Newly enlivened and becalmed by the effects of the Delectable Motions, BleakWarrior and Automanic had entered the Aquarium. They paused and listened and, upon hearing a series of distant screams, opted for a corridor that led away from the left of the foyer.

They proceeded through darkness, the screams accompanied by underlying shouts of battle, howls of pain and exclamations of savage ridicule. Sometimes, the screams seemed further away, then closer, then further away again as they crept through the interior of the Aquarium.

BleakWarrior strained his ears through the gloom as they walked. The noise of the screams were, for now, somewhat distant. But then . . . something closer.

BleakWarrior stopped and raised a hand. Automanic walked directly into the back of him and bounced off as if hitting a brick wall.

"Wait here," BleakWarrior commanded; and he slowly waded into the darkness as if through a pond of uncertain depth.

Whatever he had heard—which he believed to be the soft tread of footsteps—had diminished into silence. He continued down the corridor, however, his eyes adjusting to the gloom, which made him feel less vulnerable to whatever it was that lay out there.

And something fleeting moved beside him, falling from the outer walls like a shadow—reaching around his shoulder and pinning him hard against the neck with an implement of excessive sharpness—a needle or a skewer.

"If you move, I'll kill you."

The voice was like a cool draft of air through an unventilated mineshaft. BleakWarrior said nothing.

But, then, something in him stirred as he felt his attacker's breath against him. He inhaled the fullness of her exhalations, drank deeply of her sweats, beheld her secretions and scents in his mind's eye. He approved of them with a strange longing that stirred in him a passion he had known before now—the same which he'd experienced from the euphoric waft of the mystery girl in the maze of IDs who had led him unto the blasted heath of the Girnan Howe.

"If you only knew," she said, "how committed I've been to killing you."

BleakWarrior's face tightened.

"The things we do for death," he remarked without humour.

"No," she said, and stepped away from him, releasing her grip.

BleakWarrior turned and looked on her with indications of surprise. He saw her battered face, her bloodied nose, the cuts across her cheek that would become rough contours as time went on. Something inside him smouldered with a growing warmth and brightness. The Lenses gave off an amber glow as if the eyes beneath them were conspiring to explode.

Trembling, she said, "Not for death, BleakWarrior. I . . . I don't know what I . . . I thought I wanted to . . . but now I see that . . . I don't know what it is but I'm . . ."

Her arms fell to her sides. The skewer fell from her fingers and landed on the floor with a flurry of tinkling.

BleakWarrior hardened the Lenses on her like concrete.

He drew the Dirk.

The Dirk came wanting.

Welter of Impermanence had undergone a transformation which hadn't fully come to light . . . until now.

She had been driven by the force of an obsession that she had understood in terms of a will to do violence against a foe who, by degrees of random interjections of circumstance, had eluded her grasp—the effect of which was to make her murderous with her fury and staunch with a need to perform savage injunctions against him.

And now, at the moment of her triumph (if that's what it was), she was filled with a sense of emptiness that revealed the nature of her hatred for what it was—a superficial accumulation of dire emotions that, in themselves, were meaningless and, ultimately, without foundation.

And then, as she held the skewer in readiness against the neck of BleakWarrior, this sense of hatred broke up into little pieces of failed emotion, revealing a sudden lack of urgency that fell away from her like a shell. A hatchling of realisation emerged from inside the shell with an eagerness to taste the exorbitant range of pleasures and sensations that a new life brings.

It had never been hatred. It had never been a will to do violence against him. Her obsession was one of a drastic need to discover herself *through* him.

She had, in other words, been driven beyond the desire for violence and, in its aftermath, had discovered a need for something she had hitherto believed impossible.

Love.

And as she looked upon his straining body, upon the contorted features of a face screwed up with a thousand mental tortures he could not resolve, she found herself raising a hand to touch his cheek, to feel its blazing warmth against her palm, and to raise her lips to lay upon his. They had come together as if by a magnetic impulse that had transcended both of them; and now it was time for them to merge . . .

It was a reflexive measure which he withheld, though the Dirk was willing itself to the task of embedding itself in her chest, which presented itself with a defenceless vulnerability which, in other circumstances, would have been quite welcome.

BleakWarrior, however, resisted the Dirk's command upon his person—perhaps for the first time ever. His body was swaying slightly, as if imbibed with a hard liquor.

The mystery girl had rested a hand upon his cheek and had raised her lips with an aim to kiss him. BleakWarrior stared at her, his eyes like smelts. There was something in her manner, something in the way she appealed to him, her presence sinking into him in ways he couldn't fathom. It was as if she had always been inside of him and, now that he was with her, she appeared in front of him as an outward revelation of what was always already there.

BleakWarrior lowered the Dirk. The girl stared, her eyes searching out of darkness, gleaming with the wetness of tears.

BleakWarrior reciprocated, unable to resist. And, in the instance of their lips connecting like two desperately lonely creatures confined to a subterranean blackness, he felt a sense of mental transportation that came as naturally to him as his visionary apprehension of his days with the Bard.

It was a sense of mental transportation that brought with it a further sense of reconstruction within a quasi-physical dimension (again, like his recollections of the Bard, but stronger), within which he and the girl were together in a wild land of glowing hillocks and shallow glens—a land that filled him with a sense of stark recognition, yet in such a way as seemed different from his initial, primal remembrance of the scene.

They wound their way through the concourses of the glens, accompanied as much by their mutual joy of each other as they were by the sun that beat down on them with relentless warmth.

BleakWarrior's eyes seemed oversensitive to the expulsions of light that bathed the landscape in the golden glow. And then it dawned on him that the Warped Lenses had been removed, that they no longer covered his eyes, that he was free to see as others saw. No monsters, beasts or manifestations of maddening beauty accosted his vision as he looked upon the outlying scene. Beside him, the girl gazed up at him, a smile on her face that flushed her cheeks with a stunning radiance—a sight more beautiful than anything he had ever laid eyes upon. Yet no harm came to him as a consequence of his visual apprehension of her—no vagaries of mental stupor triggered by the bliss of her appearance. She was as she was—beautiful, radiant, full of smiles—and that was all.

It appeared, then, that the insanity of love had rendered him sane, and that his emotional juxtapositions had been resolved by the presence of the mystery girl, who was no longer a mystery to him but totally clear and full of meaning.

BleakWarrior moved in a semblance of serenity and a calm enjoyment of their time together. The lushness of the moss beneath their feet wove a natural path through the beds of heather that rose up the slopes in purple thatches. As they walked on, he had no idea where they were going, but it seemed as if they were being led through the shallow glens by an instinctive awareness of where they were going and how to get there.

After a period of time, that felt as if no time had passed at all, they emerged from the end of the shallow glens into a small and slightly elevated piece of pastureland. A herd of cattle with bells around their necks chewed lazily on the grass, casting unruffled stares in their direction. At the centre of the pastureland was a structure of ancient bricks, ruggedly arranged in a small circle. As they walked towards it, a sound came from within its interior—the sound of an echoing voice through liquefied air.

BleakWarrior knew at once that they had reached the Talking Well. He felt no surprise but only a sense of expectation that had been duly fulfilled. They stood before the Talking Well, arm in arm, as if undergoing a marriage ceremony; and, as they gazed into its glittering depths, the sound of the watery voice rose up at them, with words like ripples in a void that said,

With such measures of silence
We are taken within reach of sound,
Where silence speaks without words
Until the meanings are formed
That only excited hearts will hear.
The music of the heart
Is anchored in joy and sorrow
So that the heart is pulled in two directions;
Whereupon, in being bound to nothing
It is also, always, nowhere bound.

BleakWarrior and the girl, with arms around each other's waists, stepped onto the rim of the Talking Well and prepared to jump in . . .

Who calls the eagle from its roost? Who calls the shard of lightning from the thundercloud?

As surely as the dam must burst under the weight of a gushing enthusiasm, the wall of fear in Automanic gave way to an underlying desire to save a friend by slaying the enemy who threatened to bring him down.

As Welter of Impermanence raised her hand to stroke the burning cheek of BleakWarrior, Automanic saw it through the gloom as a hand raised in belligerence. As Welter of Impermanence pressed her face against the face of BleakWarrior, Automanic saw it as a motion intended to do him harm.

She rushed forward, swung her arm wide and, side on, plunged the Shard of Glass into the jugular of Welter of Impermanence: the vein exploded and was instantly severed beyond all hope of either repair or any temporary stifling.

Welter made a surprised sound like a whimpering dog as she went down, her hands clawing at her wound, her fingers running red with blood, like rapids gushing through struts of rock in a canyon floor, her gleaming eyes wide with the laser brightness of her shock.

BleakWarrior followed her collapse with the Lenses that were illuminated profusely with a measure of confusion. He issued a sound that seemed like the groan of a man reliving old nightmares. He searched for an explanation and . . . Automanic stood staring at him, open-mouthed and unable to comprehend his obvious distress. BleakWarrior fixed the Lenses on her and, with his voice like that of a broken creature, he rasped:

"What manner of action is this against a no-longer foe who stayed her hand against me? What manner of cruel blunder against the rekindler of my heart's flame? She vanquished my courses of madness by the command of her kiss. She led me through the shallow glens to the abatement of my sorrow. And you, hapless Metaphobe, have lain her low with fullest assurances of her life's evacuation!"

Automanic made slight motions with her head of a stark refusal to comprehend.

"But she was going to—"

BleakWarrior's fist collided with her forehead and sent her spinning into the darkness like a scarecrow struck by a cannonball.

Silence followed: she did not rise.

BleakWarrior returned the Lenses to the figure of the mystery girl on the floor, her eyes wide with lifeless wonder, her blood pooling around her head and upper body like a discarded shawl.

They had come together like bodies in space destined for an astral conjunction. None of it made sense, but nothing ever did. Meta-Warriors were drawn to each other like moths to their mutual flame, to perish in each other's heat, whether or not they wanted it to happen.

He looked down on the mystery girl and considered the sudden power of her allure that rested in him with an immovable weight of her dreadful loss, which he knew would grow much heavier as time went on.

Tears from beneath the Lenses wetted his cheeks. But his state of bewildered mourning came to an abrupt conclusion when the sound of hurried steps, accompanied by a fearsome blether, echoed through the gloom towards him . . .

The Sisters of No Mercy emerged from the watery darkness of the corridor leading from the building's interior. Like a pair of half-drowned cats, they jumped to a standstill and drew their swords upon seeing BleakWarrior. Big Sister, holding a hand over her eye to stem the leaking blood, said, "What the fuck is this, Sister?"

"Fuck me," said Little Sister, "it looks like some kind of bedraggled fucking flying insect?"

"A bedraggled fucking flying insect, indeed, Sister. I mean look at those fucking eyes. What in the name of a thousand flying insects are *those?*"

"What the fuck indeed, Sister. And what the—"

Little Sister's words were suddenly transformed into a guttural, choking stream of sobs: "Oh fuck. Oh no. Oh fuck, Sister, no. Oh fuck, Sister, look."

And Big Sister looked. And Big Sister saw a corpse on the floor. And Big Sister saw the mass of blood that was pooling around the head and upper body of the girl whose name they didn't know. She saw her pale face emerge from the black liquid overspill like a perfect mask. She saw the wound in her neck, a broad gash beyond repair—and the vanquished life of the one they loved, beyond recovery.

There were a few moments of something that felt like more than shock. It was as if the world had been switched off, as if time had stalled, as if a dial had been turned that drained the world of its last reserves of energy.

It did not last.

BleakWarrior realised that he was still holding the Dirk in his hand.

It looked bad.

He issued an immediate disclaimer:

"Stay yourselves, demented wenches. I am not responsible for her demise."

"Demented fucking what? Did you hear that, Sister?"

"Hearing, Sister, is what I was fucking born for."

"And—let me get this straight—did he just call us *wenches?*"

"That's what it sounded like to me, Sister—*wenches.*"

"So, not only has he extinguished the fucking centre of our universe, he's also called us fucking *wenches.*"

"That's how it seems to me, Sister."

"Then if that's the case, Sister," said Big Sister, now looking BleakWarrior straight in the Lenses with her one good eye, "this flying fucking insect's got to fucking die—*right fucking now!*"

The devastation felt by The Sisters of No Mercy had an object upon which it could vent itself. The name of that object was *The Flying Fucking Insect Who's Got To Fucking Die—Right Fucking Now!* And the sense of devastation that sank into the very souls of The Sisters of No Mercy was instantly capable of re-emerging as its near neighbour, the cutting edge of extreme rage.

BleakWarrior, meanwhile, had felt a stirring in his blood like a form of music that, instead of following an arrangement of sounds, followed an arrangement of chaotic impulses, which also engendered a powerful glow of transfixed emotions which could only mean one thing.

Madness.

BleakWarrior's desire to destroy his enemies sprang to the surface like an underground spring in the aftermath of a heavy rainfall. It would not subside; nor would it recede from the brick wall of his better judgement. The rational application of arguments piled like sandbags against the rising floodwaters began to over-saturate with the bitter implications of his fury.

"I have spoken the truth," said BleakWarrior, holding the Dirk before him like a firebrand. "You may choose to believe it and turn away . . . or else, *you die.*"

The response of the Sisters was to fall upon him like banshees haunting a battlefield over which they had attained a status of unassailable domination. Yet, their contorted faces were strangely beautiful in the half-light of the corridor. There was something deeply sad about them—something tragic, as if the loss of the mystery girl had somehow melted the inner core of their entire being—just as it had for BleakWarrior. As he fended off their assault, BleakWarrior realised he was putting himself at a serious disadvantage. He was starting to feel sorry for them—and the fury he had summoned was starting to subside as a result—the very thing it couldn't do, it shouldn't do and never had.

The matter was a strange and difficult one which wasn't helped when, as he rebutted the wild swings of the banshees with the staunchness of the Dirk, the little banshee adroitly slipped her hand under his guard and lay a hold of his testicles.

There were circumstances in which BleakWarrior would have welcomed a rough manhandling of his sack of pearls.

This wasn't one of them.

He managed to dislodge the fierce grip of the little banshee, but only after the pain of his trauma had spread across his loins like the routing of a root vegetable. It wasn't enough to double him up. But it was enough to off-set his posture and set him off-balance like a man walking a tight rope. The taller banshee took advantage of this. She feigned a downward slash, then twirled her sword and slashed at him sideways instead.

It was an excellent move. The only problem was: due to her missing eye, her judgment of short distances was completely off-kilter. She missed BleakWarrior altogether and sent her short sword fizzing towards her banshee companion. The little banshee gave a short cry of astonishment before throwing herself backwards out of range of the sword swipe. In doing so, she landed with force against the stone wall, cracking her head against it and falling down in a heap, like a bird flying into a clear glass window.

The little banshee's head struck the ground for good measure as she rolled into the pooling blood of the mystery girl, where her own head came to rest and made a generous contribution of blood all of its own.

The taller banshee gave a howl of combined emotions all of which coincided with torment. BleakWarrior was in a state of some hesitancy as she repeated the manoeuvre she'd attempted before, this time making it work to greater effect. Her sword impacted against BleakWarrior's rib cage and, for a brief moment, embedded itself in his flesh, raking the bone, until the taller banshee heaved it out and strove to cleave his flesh anew.

This time, BleakWarrior dodged the oncoming blade. But, sidestepping into the pooling blood around the mystery girl's head and body, he slipped and fell with a complete loss of control of his limbs that left him totally exposed to the taller banshee's imminent death strike.

BleakWarrior was down, unlikely to rise. Yet the sense of joy he had known from his visit to the Talking Well filled him with a lack of instinct for protecting himself; he merely awaited the blow (and wanted it) without raising an arm in his defence. The taller banshee's sword was poised to fall. But, then, she seemed to hesitate, her single eye registering some form of unpleasant surprise. Then she made a wheezing sound like a burst bladder pipe. Absurdly, she lowered the sword and let it drop at her feet. She stiffened, keeled forward and, with a violent unchecked slam, fell on the floor beside BleakWarrior, where he saw at once the Shard of Glass sticking out of her back and, above that, Automanic standing with her hand outstretched, a gash in her palm dripping gouts of blood over the newly slain bodies below.

When she had roused him from his stupor (of whatever it was she wasn't sure), Automanic led BleakWarrior from the Aquarium. He was weak and breathless and reeling as if on the deck of a merchantman on a stormy sea. The wound in his side ran very deep. His sealskin coat was saturated and dripping profusely.

In the City of Antiquities, there were plenty of physicians who were used to attending victims of injuries sustained through drunken behaviour and the impromptu hooliganism of historical fads re-enacted too keenly. But news of the unprecedented slaughter at the Aquarium, whenever it spread, would cast BleakWarrior and Automanic under too strong a glare of suspicion for having acted as principal agents in its murderous outcome. Therefore, while the city remained in darkness, she would take him back to her apartment to attend to him herself, thereafter attending to her own wound, which had left her feeling dizzy with its blood loss (not to mention the concussion sustained from BleakWarrior's blow against her forehead).

Automanic had approached the night with an enthusiasm that had made it seem like a childhood dream come true. But the brutality of what had come to pass had made her more frightened than she had ever been in her entire life. It was, however, a genuine fear—a fear of something real instead of imagined; and, because of this, she felt enthralled.

It is true that the initial shock of killing the scrawny girl had made her think that she hadn't actually wanted to do it. There was a void beneath the delirious heights of the frenzy required for killing someone—a void within which the victim, rather than the assailant, was thrown. And to open that void for someone else was to know at once that, one day, that void would be opened up for you.

Terror, then, had been the first of her reactions. But it was quickly overcome by the excitement of the act of wiping out another life form. It was as if, by taking another life, it became your own. It made you stronger. It revitalised you. And this is how it had been for her: killing had substituted her tendency towards panic with a rock solid inner core of strength that had prepared her for further violence, while arming her with a foreknowledge of what it entailed.

Automanic now knew she had discovered the confidence to go on and develop her skills as a killer to be used against other such foes as she'd encountered this evening. Under such circumstances, perhaps BleakWarrior might agree to form a partnership with her, so that they might tackle their foes together as a team, hunt them down and wipe them out, wage a campaign of stark brutality against fellow assassins who, if left unchecked, would wage the same against them.

Yes, she thought, the plan had merit. And she could use her knowledge of the whereabouts of Manto's unpublished works as a means of brokering a deal with BleakWarrior that, in time, would allow them to form a redoubtable bond of friendship—perhaps something more. What began as a partnership born of necessity might become a—

BleakWarror's body careered away from her and crashed onto the gravel of the perimeter around the Aquarium. He rolled over onto his back with a breathless groan, his limbs spread-eagling on all sides of him.

"Get up. Get up!" cried Automanic.

And she fell to her knees and bent over him, slapping him on the face and shaking him, commanding him to regain his feet and make the journey back to her rooms. She grasped at his fallen body, hauled him up off the ground by the lapels, throwing his arm around her shoulder and bearing his weight.

Yes, she thought, she had grown much stronger, no longer inclined to panic and weep like a baby bird that had fallen from its nest. Her muscles were taut, her thighs full of leverage. The veins in her sinewy arms pumped like rivers in spate. For the first time in her life, she felt power surging through her; and it felt sublime.

Even so, it was a struggle to shoulder BleakWarrior through the streets, and there were moments when he appeared to pass out altogether and fall into bouts of delirium, sometimes muttering gibberish about the scrawny girl, or some such thing. But she was physically empowered and, to this extent, was able to half-carry, half-haul BleakWarrior through the streets. There were plenty of late night revellers and debauched specimens staggering and capering about the city centre with drunken abandon, which ensured that BleakWarrior and Automanic, lolloping from side to side as they walked, were able to blend in quite seamlessly. They proceeded unmolested; and when, at last, she succeeded in bringing him back to her rooms, she lay him on the bed, tore off his sodden wet clothes, and hastened to fetch whatever she could to hasten his revival.

When she returned with towels to stanch his wound, BleakWarrior called out in desperate tones for something to slake his thirst. Realising how weak he was, perhaps even nearing death, she hurried and returned again with a beaker of water which she angled into his mouth and began to pour in. BleakWarrior's reaction was to cough and splutter and spit the stuff out over the bed sheets.

He seemed to convulse, then straightened himself out and, rising shakily onto his arms, he said, "For the love of all that hurts, woman. Bring me a bottle of Delectable Motions and put an end to my suffering, once and for all."

Later, about the break of day, Automanic woke up on the bed she had shared with BleakWarrior. She had fallen asleep beside him while nursing his wound, having collapsed with exhaustion in the aftermath of the night's excitement. The sun had risen and was slicing through gaps in the shutters with hard-edged sleeves of light. Automanic reached out a hand in search of BleakWarrior's warmth (or his deathly lack of it), but felt only cold air and emptiness beside her.

She sat up sharply, saw the indent in the pillow where his head had been. She saw the bloodstains marking the sheets, the empty bottle of Delectable Motions on the mattress beside her, like a neglected trophy.

Automanic drew her hand about her neck, suddenly feeling vulnerable. She searched the empty room with her startled eyes, now coming to terms with what was already obvious to her.

BleakWarrior was gone.

Epilogue: You Can't Keep a Bad Girl Down

A flickering of interconnecting brain cells that produced a thought:

"I am going to die."

Then a further flicker of interconnecting brain cells that produced a further thought:

"Dying is what I was fucking born for."

And then, as the sparks in the brain fell one upon the other in quick succession, a train of thought evolved that came to the conclusion that:

"I'm not fucking dead yet."

Then there came a reaction of movement—a twitch. And then there came a reaction of further movements—a series of twitches. And then there came the flicker of an eyelid opening up and an eye beneath it that saw only darkness.

Little Sister was caught in a limbo between the darkness of the corridor that filled her vision and the brightness of death that filled her head space. Both were appealing in their own way, and Little Sister felt herself being pulled in two directions simultaneously.

In mental terms, Little Sister was clinging to a skitter of rocks on a shoreline being buffeted by the weight of an ocean. She clawed and clung at the slippery incline, seeking purchase on limpets of hope and the seaweed of her determination. At the same time, the waning currents urged her to submit to the eternal motions, which was tempting, given the extent of her weakness, and the ballooning pain of her multi-fractured head.

In time, the wetness and the pungency of the salty aroma began to arouse her to a state of semi-consciousness. Not yet dead, she had lain with her head in the spillage of the girl whose name they didn't know's bodily evacuations, the smell of which had entered her nostrils and triggered her brain like smelling salts. She regained awareness after a kind, relying more on instinct than the direction of her half-formed thoughts. She tilted her head, which swung easily to one side, and extended her tongue towards the floor. The tip of it touched the surface of the spillage and sent shockwaves through her brain like a treatment for psychological disorders.

Little Sister responded with a sense of desperate thirst that compounded her need to angle her head further into the spillage so she could lap at it with a growing fervour and an increasing computation of what she was doing and why she needed to do it.

As soon as she had accrued a small mouthful, she swallowed hard, then lay there in the hub of the bloodletting, feeling exhausted after the effort that lapping the blood had required of her.

Little Sister knew that, if she shut her eyes and allowed herself to drift into a slumber, she would die. But then her dizziness began to subside. The fuel of the blood had lit a small flame at the back of her head, like a small fire at the back of a cavern. The flame grew into a definite glow that began to spread its warmth through her fingers and toes, her arms and legs, her belly and her facial features.

Little Sister, shaking inexorably, and hanging on to the threads of life, crawled over the floor like a phantom defeated by an exorcism. She was little more than a movement in the shadows, a desperate heaving and dragging of nails, a slow and painful mustering of departed strength, now miraculously revived to the barest minimum of her animated properties.

Somehow, only half-aware of what she was doing, she managed to lift herself on top of the girl whose name they didn't know until she and the girl were aligned, face to face; then she pressed her mouth over the wound in the girl's neck and supped on it for all her worth. The process was slow, and she vomited half as much of the liquid as she'd taken in; but the blood was running warm enough to facilitate her tentative hope of further revival.

With enough strength in her to confirm a definite

resurgence, she swung her body over the girl whose name they didn't know, revolving it so that, in time, her battered head was in alignment with the girl's crotch.

Traces of the aroma of her lingering love juice reached Little Sister's nostrils and planted sparkles in her brain that turned her trains of thought into shooting stars. She tore at the binding of the girl's pantaloons, already loosened from her ordeal with the Bastards. She clawed at it with barely functioning fingers, gnawed at it with her teeth. When it snapped free, she hauled the pantaloons down (there were no undergarments to contend with). A dense thatch of pubic hair sprang loose; thighs were bared; the bottom half of her belly was exposed. The girl's body temperature had plummeted so much that her skin was as cold and hard as marble. But a trace of warmth emanated from between her thighs and a smattering of dampness that warmed the air like a mirage over a glacier.

Little Sister pulled apart the pale thighs to allow enough room to gain access to the source of her definite revival. She paused for a moment . . .

What about Big Sister? What had become of her?

Little Sister raised her head, looked around, and saw Big Sister lying face down with blood on her back, in a position of total death.

Tears might have started (and maybe later); but with her mind now picking up speed, Little Sister wondered if it was possible to fill up her mouth with the elixir of the girl, crawl over to the corpse of Big Sister and deposit the elixir into her mouth to see if it induced a revival on her part also.

"Wondering what the fuck is possible," said Little Sister, breathing hard over the exposed pussy of the girl whose name they didn't know, "is *not* what I was fucking born for."

And she flexed her tongue in preparation for the work required of her, mustered her reserves against the onset of death, and licked her way to a re-entry into life's rich pageant, where further appointments with death were as likely as she believed them necessary.

Acknowledgements

For their invaluable help and inspiration, my deepest thanks to Anna Tambour, Scott Nicolay, Edward Morris, Joe Pulver, John Klima, Neil Williamson, Kirsten Bishop, Liz Williams, Chris Butler, Jacey Bedford, Cherith Baldry, Kari Sperring, Stuart Falconer, Sue Thomason, Ruth Nestvold, Martin Šust, Roman Tilcer, and to my excellent friends, Froogie, Nomi, T, Brother Col, Crombo, Fabrizio Luzzatti, Paolo Poidomani and Ivan Perfetti.

Special thanks to Tessa Kum, whose guidance and insights helped me turn the chaos into its better neighbour: organised chaos, and to my wonderful editor, Geoff Hyatt, whose guidance and insights finally allowed the order to prevail.

It is unlikely that this novel would have seen the light of day if it hadn't been for the part played by Ann and Jeff VanderMeer. They took the risks so I'd get the rewards and, for this, I am eternally grateful.

About the Author

Alistair Rennie has published dark fantasy and horror fiction, essays, and poetry in *The New Weird anthology, Weird Tales magazine, Fabulous Whitby, Electric Velocipede, Mythic Delirium, Pevnost, Schlock Magazine, Horror Without Victims, Weird Fiction Review*, and *Shadowed Realms*.

He was born and grew up in the North of Scotland, lived for ten years in Italy, and now lives in Edinburgh in the South of Scotland. He holds a first class Honours Degree in Literature from the University of Aberdeen and a PhD in Literature from the University of Edinburgh. He is a time-served Painter and Decorator and a veteran climber of numerous hills and mountains in the Western Highlands, the Cairngorms, and the Italian Dolomites.

Rennie is also a member of the dark arcane music project MONGALIECH.

Made in the USA
Middletown, DE
21 September 2024